ALL SIGNS POINT TO YES

ERIC SMITH

G. HARON DAVIS

ADRIANNE WHITE

CAM MONTGOMERY

TEHLOR KAY MEJIA

BYRON GRAVES

KIANA NGUYI

LILY ANDERSON

ALEXANDRA VILLASANTE

ROSELLE LIM

KARUNA RIAZI

ALL SIGNS POINT TO YES

inkyard
PRESS

EDITED BY
G. HARON DAVIS, CAM MONTGOMERY, AND ADRIANNE WHITE

Recycling programs
for this product may
not exist in your area.

ISBN-13: 978-1-335-41862-3

All Signs Point to Yes

CONTENTS

To those who have been called too much and not enough—
may you always find yourself among the stars.

ARIES

Venus in Aries

* *Extremely direct, assertive, and at times seemingly selfish*
* *Adventurous, energetic, and daring*
* *Flirtatious and playful*
* *Very fond of spontaneity*
* *Loves the thrill of the chase—but might get bored with the catch*

ruler and killer
g. haron davis

The first time Chi killed for Coronet Álava was mostly accidental but thrilling nonetheless. The only spell she'd learned from her mother, gods rest her soul, should've protected the man from harm. Something must have gone wrong, the wrong word uttered at the wrong time or some other elementary-level mistake, because he looked up at Chi with lifeless eyes, widened in surprise, as she siphoned his essence from his arm.

"Forgive me," she said once she finished collecting his blood. She closed the top on the glass jar and set it aside. His dead-eyed stare set her skin crawling. She used her two forefingers to shut his eyelids. "May the gods have mercy."

The task was sustenance, and perhaps she'd thought too

small, but there seemed nothing better to sustain those like the Coronet than fresh blood. She'd read once that they liked type O negative. It took her nearly a week to find someone with that rarity, someone her mother would have referred to as *unmissable*. Had she known that she would fail at protecting his soul from death, she would've put him out of his misery to begin with. But regrets didn't serve anyone, and she couldn't waste time dwelling on a life lost if it meant her own life would be so dramatically improved because of it.

The jars clanked in her satchel as she moved along the road back toward the castle. Her grip tightened on the strap as a chill passed through her; each noise seemed like it would give her away at any second, would alert a patroller to her presence and they'd see all the blood and she'd be immediately arrested and killed. But no one looked her way. No one cared at all, and for that she was grateful. Sometimes it paid to be so nondescript, so unremarkable.

It took twenty minutes to walk back to Vela, and in that time, uncertainty settled into Chi's bones. Was her hunch in assuming the Coronet would want blood correct? Had she taken a life callously and without cause? Would this somehow disqualify her from winning the Coronet's hand? She shook her head quickly as if that might banish her racing thoughts, and once she reached the castle gates, she stopped to admire her temporary home.

Eddows Castle loomed over Vela, high on a hilltop and surrounded by a thick forest of aggressive-looking trees. Growing up, Chi had listened to stories about what went on in the castle, how people would venture in but never return, the screaming that echoed through the canyon below. She'd been in and around the castle for hours and hadn't heard anything but couldn't deny that the place felt...alive.

Hungry.

She squared her shoulders and nodded at the guards at the gate, who let her through after scanning the participant identification card around her neck. Her hands clutched the strap of her bag even tighter as she funneled all her anxiety into that grip. *Never let them see on the outside how you feel on the inside*, her mother always said. Right now, Chi couldn't afford to let anyone know she was terrified.

Two other participants were already waiting in the front courtyard of the castle when Chi approached, and she silently swore. Hopefully, being first didn't hold much weight in this competition. And besides, she was still early; from her estimates, there had been at least a hundred people left after the first round of dismissals, all with varying motives and interest levels, listening to the Coronet's abettor Erze drone on about the competition, the rules, the prize.

The Coronet would be reaching their seventeenth year on Saturday, and as tradition dictated, they would need to have a betrothed in place for a year-long engagement and marriage ceremony to come on the occasion of their eighteenth birthday. Normally, or at least for the short duration of Chi's lifetime, royals had their betrothed already, and an engagement celebration would simply be a formality. But the Coronet hadn't had any suitors. They had hardly shown any interest in the typical royal courtship traditions. They hadn't shown interest in much of anything beyond maintaining their garden.

Chi eyed the black roses to her left and smiled a bit. The Coronet had an extensive assortment of dark flowers, plants with beauty and lethality, trees whose twisted branches looked haunted. The whole courtyard exuded a sickly-sweet scent that seemed designed to draw in unsuspecting victims. It was beautiful, but not everyone felt that way. And judging by the faces of other suitors waiting in the courtyard, these people didn't understand the Coronet the way Chi did.

She'd followed the Coronet's life closely, ever since her mother had mentioned one day when Chi was small that she and the Coronet shared a birthday. Chi wasn't much concerned with celebrating her own birthday, but it fascinated her to have a connection, no matter how superficial, to a royal. She watched the Coronet grow up as she herself did. She spent night after night lying on her straw pallet, beside her mother and some stray animals, wondering what it would be like to be sleeping in a real bed like the Coronet surely was. She knew every fleeting obsession, every milestone. She knew she belonged there.

None of the competitors present in the garden seemed the type to pique the Coronet's interest, and she felt grateful for that, too. Across from her, a portly, dark fellow with fancy shoes and crisply creased pants sat swatting and scowling on a bench near the hemlock. Some gold-horned butterflies had taken a liking to something about him, probably some tacky fragrance he'd no doubt bathed in. Chi lowered her head to hide her smile when a butterfly landed right on the man's glistening bald head. He was almost certainly not competition.

After nearly an hour of waiting, a horn startled Chi. She clung to her bag, then relaxed once it registered that this wasn't a siren signaling a raid or dragon attack; the guards were simply announcing the deadline for returning to the castle. The gates began to shut, and a young woman in the distance started to run forward, shouting. None of the guards acknowledged her cries, and two drew their guns as she clung to the iron bars to plead her case.

"Please remember," Erze's voice boomed from seemingly nowhere, "we enact certain rules and restrictions for a reason. Punctuality is extremely important to the Coronet, and if you cannot adhere to that one simple requirement, then you have no business being here."

Chi peered over her shoulder shyly to watch the commotion at the gate. She felt for the woman on one level; to be so close and fail must have been heartbreaking. But that was life, and that meant one less person between her and the Coronet.

"We began the process with nearly seven hundred of you," Erze said. Their hands were clasped in front of them, a large black sunhat covering their face. Only their blood-red lips were visible as they spoke. "Now less than a quarter of you remain. The number you were assigned at the start of the day indicates the order in which you will submit your offering of sustenance for the Coronet. When your number is spoken, you will come forward and give your offering to the curators. The Coronet and all relevant persons will inspect each and every offering. When the trial reconvenes in the morning, only twenty-five of you will remain. We wish to waste neither the Coronet's time nor yours. If you are eliminated, you will be removed from the premises immediately. If we find there has been fraud, or cheating, or any other kind of deception, you will be removed from the Kingdom."

Chi shuddered involuntarily. Her mother had been removed from the Kingdom three years prior, taken to the edges of town and given an unceremoniously grim execution under suspicion of witchcraft. An accurate suspicion but devastating nonetheless. Witchcraft had been outlawed in Vela for centuries, dating back to the Great Rebellion, when hundreds of witches attempted to overthrow Coron Sonor IV. The manifesto left behind claimed they needed to dethrone him based on his refusal to afford witches the same freedoms as other beings, like the fae or lycanthropes. But Chi's mother often said the real reason was that the witches wanted to rule, exhausted by centuries of Aponmhir rule and subsequent oppression. Witches once had the upper hand, and they wished to have it again.

The rebellious witches failed, and they were hanged.

Chi knew the stories of her lineage. She knew that several of her ancestors took part in the Rebellion, a point of pride her mother would speak of with reverence. She also knew only a small fragment of that power lived within her. Still, fear took hold at the thought of someone learning she had murdered a man with a spell—a poorly-cast spell, at that. And if someone found out, she'd be removed—worse, she would never get her chance with the Coronet.

A guard yelled her number—613—and snapped Chi out of her spiral of negativity. She straightened her spine and held her chin high despite the snickers and whispering of other contestants. She was among the youngest there, from the looks of the others, and probably the poorest as well. But her mother had taught her that shame belonged only to the shameful, and her existence was to be celebrated, not hidden away.

The jars clanked as she set them on the offering table. The curator stared at them, then at Chi. Rather than admit to nerves, Chi simply smiled. The curator rolled his eyes and motioned for the jars to be collected, and the next number was called. Chi exhaled in relief: so far, so good. Her gaze lifted to the castle as she turned to walk away, and for a second, she swore she saw curtains move in one of the windows.

* ◊ *

With all offerings amassed beneath a white tent, it was time for the contestants to be escorted to their temporary living quarters. The apartments sat hundreds of yards away from the main castle, hunched in the shadow of the woods surrounding the property. Chi hesitated entering; she'd been desperate for a proper place to sleep for years but thought for a moment she'd rather go back to Squatter's Field than this place. A white X on the doorframe made her shiver.

Protection from becoming a meal. Or worse.

A guard read off Chi's number and pointed her toward a room on the second floor, and Chi felt a small bit of relief upon walking through the open door. She hadn't been paired with a man, thank the gods. Men made her nervous, especially the thought of sleeping in the same room as a male stranger. But her new roommate was a girl who looked only a touch older than Chi herself.

The girl stood on the other side of the room fiddling with the sheets on the bed as if they hadn't been made up to her standards. Her dark violet hair rested in tight French braids on the sides of her head, and her mouth was turned down in deep concentration. She was stunning, a kind of beautiful that Chi hadn't seen apart from the Coronet.

Chi immediately felt doomed to lose this competition.

"Hello," Chi called out. The girl by the bed paused and looked up, and Chi gasped a small bit. "Oh."

She hadn't intended to sound rude, but she also hadn't been expecting the girl to have white eyes. She'd heard once, many years ago, that that was a sign of the Marked. Those who'd fallen out of favor with the gods. Those who used magic in wicked ways and thus were stricken with unseeing eyes. A foolish take, and certainly not one Chi believed, but for just a second...

For just a second, Chi forgot that of the two of them, *she* was the one with wicked magic.

"If you're going to pity me, don't," the girl said in a voice like velvet sliding along skin. Chi shivered. "I get enough of that every day."

"I don't pity you," Chi said. "I was startled. Not that your appearance is startling, I just—"

"I'm Alberta." Chi sighed, grateful for the interruption keeping her from further making a fool of herself. When she stepped forward to shake Alberta's outstretched hand, she noticed how much softer Alberta's dark brown skin was. Not a worker, it seemed. "Call me Bertie."

Bertie, a few hairs shorter than Chi, returned to fussing over her bedding, and Chi wondered if she ought to give her own name. Names were sacred, she'd been taught. Names had power.

"In polite society," Bertie said while fluffing a pillow, "someone introducing themselves means you do the same."

"I'm not acquainted with polite society." Chi paused. "Ana."

"Nice to meet you, Ana. Turn out the light."

Chi did as instructed, then moved toward the second bed and pressed a hand to it. It had been so long since she'd slept in a proper bed, and even then, no bed she'd ever been on was even remotely as cushy as this one.

The pull of a good night's rest spoke to her more fervently than a bath or making polite conversation with her temporary roommate. She set her bag down and carefully lowered herself to a seat, bouncing a bit. She couldn't keep herself from smiling. A quick rest of her eyes, she told herself as she shifted to press her head against the pillow, and then she'd get up to bathe. Just a few seconds.

She awoke with a start. Something sharp scraped against the window nearest her bed, slow and deliberate. It sent a shiver through her, and she shifted to see if Bertie heard this as well.

The scraping tapered off, but Chi didn't have relief for long. She listened to the window slowly open, and the night air chilled her only slightly more than these noises. She closed her eyes again and hoped to appear asleep. It seemed like a possibility to keep safe, or at the very least to not see whatever was about to happen.

"Girl." The breeze carried a familiar voice into the room, a whisper that wrapped around Chi and made her eyes spring open again.

It was the Coronet.

At her window.

On the second floor.

"Girl," the Coronet whispered again with more insistence. Rather than continue to feign sleep, Chi rolled over to look toward the window.

The Coronet appeared, visible from the waist up, hands rested against the windowsill. Their dark brown curls flowed around their shoulders as if underwater. Their eyes reflected an unsettlingly intriguing silvery violet. And the moonlight above added a mischievous glint to their smile. Their sharp, dangerous smile.

Chi wanted nothing more in that moment than to touch those teeth.

"You used magic," the Coronet commented. It had no weight of accusation or anger—simply a statement of fact.

"I—"

"Don't worry," the Coronet said. "No one noticed. No one was looking for it. I, however," the Coronet leaned closer, and Chi found herself leaning in along with them, "I find myself fascinated by the old tales. The witches. Like you."

"I'm not a witch," Chi said. Her voice shook as much as her hands did, but at least she could fiddle with her skirt to occupy her hands.

The Coronet smiled wider. A chuckle roiled from deep within them that Chi could swear gently shook her bed. She glanced to her roommate again, but Bertie hadn't so much as rolled over. She wondered how anyone could sleep through all the noise.

"She can't hear me," the Coronet said. "Because I don't want her to. Don't be frightened. Invite me inside."

Chi gulped. She had read, many years ago in an old tome of her great-grandmother's, that Aponmhir had powers. That they differed across variants, but some traits were universal among them. That they had powers of persuasion, could read minds, some even—

"I can hear you," the Coronet said in something of a song. "Your thoughts. They're very loud. Let me in? I'll tell you all about what I can and can't do."

It happened with such swiftness that Chi couldn't quite recall even agreeing or saying the words *Come in*, but she suddenly found herself face-to-face with the Coronet. Eye to eye. Very nearly nose to nose. The Coronet made themself comfortable in Chi's bed, and the two of them lay face to face. Chi's hand came to rest against the Coronet's curvy hip, and she marveled at the silky fabric of their skirts. She felt a bit like a mouse in a trap, the way the Coronet watched her. She didn't dare move.

"I've never met a witch so young," the Coronet said. "But I suspect you've never met an Aponmhir." Before Chi could respond, the Coronet reached long, slim fingers out and caressed her cheek. "You're very pretty, little witch," they muttered. "I've decided to help you win."

Chi's heart thumped harder against her ribs as the Coronet's fingers grazed down her neck. "Why?" she asked in a whisper.

"You intrigue me," the Coronet said. "Call me Álava."

The Coronet—Álava—moved even closer to Chi, and she felt their cold breath against her lips and desperately wanted to breathe it in. She shivered as Álava moved their hand to her waist and gasped as she felt her skirt being slowly shifted up her legs.

"The competition in the morning," Álava said, and their lips grazed Chi's, "will be a test of logic. You'll be given a scenario to work through. It's very boring. I cannot choose someone who knows nothing about what it might take to run a nation."

In the last few months, Chi had found herself letting her mind drift to thoughts of Álava, to the way the Coronet's lips would feel against hers, to lying wrapped up in each other and simply listening to one another breathing. She'd had so many fantasies of a moment like this that she momentarily considered she'd drifted off to sleep unknowingly. The Coronet's icy fingertips against her thigh made her shiver enough to know this wasn't another dream.

"Wait," Chi said quietly. "I don't… I'm not…"

She'd only spoken of her discomfort with being touched beneath her clothes once, with an older boy who worked the stables of a farm near her old home. He hadn't taken her very seriously, laughing at the idea, and Chi vowed not to say anything to anyone else. But Álava would never laugh at her.

Álava smiled and pressed another soft kiss to Chi's lips. "Understood," they said quietly as they smoothed Chi's skirts back down. "You're a fascinating specimen."

"So are you," Chi said. Álava laughed, a quick hard breath against Chi that made Chi smile. "The protection marking doesn't work on you."

"Those are fake," Álava said, scoffing. They began to twirl one of Chi's curls around their pinky. "None of those so-called protections work. They're simply a placebo."

"But I still had to invite you in."

"I respect consent." Álava paused, then cupped a hand to Chi's cheek. "You should rest. I'll be in the room with you for the next trial. Watch me for cues."

Chi nodded, and Álava crawled closer. They straddled Chi momentarily, staring down at her as if they considered making her a meal. Instead, they leaned closer and kissed Chi again before continuing on their way to the window. When Chi gathered her wits to look out, Álava was gone, and Chi was solidly, wildly in love.

The heavy velvet drapes of the conference room allowed not one ray of light in. Chi could hardly believe it was nearly eight in the morning; with only a few strategically-placed candles, including one directly in front of her, it seemed like midnight or later. It felt like a séance would begin any second.

Instead of a planchette, Erze, sitting directly to Chi's left, slid a notebook and pen toward her.

"You may take notes," Erze said. This time, their face was covered with a lacy black veil. Chi couldn't recall ever seeing Erze's face, and her mind wandered to all the possible reasons for that. "I'll not repeat myself. Your goal is to present a reasonable resolution to the dilemma I present to you. You may ask three questions before giving your response. Upon completion, we will dismiss you to discuss your response. If your resolution is deemed unacceptable, you will be escorted off of the premises immediately. Do you understand?"

Chi understood that she couldn't let that happen. She understood that she had to relax and breathe and try to think like a royal and not like an obsessive sixteen-year-old orphan. Her gaze shifted to Álava, at the far end of the table directly in front of her, nearly buried by all of the puffy black fabric of their outfit. Álava smiled and gave a slight nod, and Chi gave her own affirmation.

The scenario went completely over Chi's head. She knew

nothing of land disputes or official treaties. It bored her to no end, and she had to keep pinching the palm of her hand to keep herself from drifting into daydreams. She did her best to focus on the scenario laid out to her, and when Erze stopped talking, she looked to Álava.

A dull pain started behind her left eye. She squinted some and rubbed at her eye, then shuddered as a chill went through her.

The Coronet was in her head. Clear as a ringing bell. She could hear them plainly, and yet Álava wasn't saying a word from the other side of the table.

"I… Well, a revision of the treaty would be necessary," Chi said with none of her own certainty but plenty of Álava's. "It would be best to hold a meeting, then agree to new terms. If that didn't work, the matter might need to be escalated. But likely it wouldn't come to that."

The air thinned, and the pain dulled as soon as she stopped talking. Álava's smile in the candlelight seemed soft, but still a bit terrifying. Chi didn't know how to feel about how much that element of potential danger excited her.

She jumped as Erze stood suddenly, their chair scraping against the floor. "Thank you, 613. You may go," they said.

Chi stood slowly, still not entirely sure if she'd done the right thing. She made her way toward the door, toward Álava, and felt her heart speed up as she approached. Even better, Álava stood once Chi was close enough. Chi stopped, and Álava extended a hand to her.

"Nice to meet you, 613," Álava said. Their handshake was brief, but it sent Chi's head spinning to touch Álava again.

And then, she noticed the note pushed into her hand.

Rather than draw attention to it, she bowed to Álava and made her exit into the hall. She smiled briefly at the people waiting, then hurried to find a private spot to open her note.

side courtyard 8

Chi's heart leapt once again, and she glanced to a large clock patterned like the moon on a wall. Not long until 8 now. She considered the possibility of dying of anticipation before she could see Álava again.

The time zipped by, much to her delight, as she spent it trying to find something nicer than her own clothing to wear. Thankfully, she'd discovered extra outfits in her closet upon waking that morning. She picked out a royal-blue velvet gown with a tight-fitting bodice and wide flowing skirt. The shoes she'd been given felt too stiff, too unlike her, so she stuck with her own boots, grateful that the dress was long enough that Álava probably wouldn't notice how shabby they were.

The side courtyard was surrounded by a thicket of trees and a tall shrub fence. The fountain in the center had a statue of a woman that looked remarkably like Álava—same rounded face and high cheekbones, same Rubenesque build, same perfect nose. This was the Coronet's great-grandmother, Davila, said to have fended off a whole army on her own and settled the area for her family. She was celebrated annually, and the town felt a shared sense of joy when Álava had been born on Davila's birthday.

Chi turned away from the fountain and found herself lip-to-lip with Álava. She startled momentarily, completely unaware that Álava had even approached, but then relaxed into the Coronet's hold on her cheeks. She hadn't kissed very many people before, to be sure, but she was certain that kissing Álava was as good as it got. A quick graze of Álava's fangs against her lower lip sent a thrill through her that she knew she could never admit.

"I want you to show me," Álava said gently before giving Chi's lips a small lick.

"Show you what?" Chi could hardly breathe to get the words out.

"Show me how you did it. Show me your magic."

"I told you, I—"

"You're not good at it, according to you," Álava said. "But you used it, and I want to see how. Please?"

They walked off the castle grounds right through the front gate, with the guards seemingly not even seeing them. Chi wondered if Álava had something to do with that, and when she looked to the Coronet, she found them looking back at her with a mischievous smirk.

Twenty minutes of silence later, they made it to the Bottoms, a less savory section of the town that Chi was sure Álava had never been in before. Nobody important ever came to, or out of, the Bottoms. And nobody would care if someone went missing.

She took a deep breath as Álava clutched her hand. It felt more intimate, more real, than all the kissing they'd done just moments before leaving the courtyard. Their fingers intertwined, and Álava swung their arms a bit as they looked around.

"Everything here looks ancient," they commented. "And dirty."

"Because everything here *is* ancient and dirty," Chi said. She stopped walking and stared ahead.

Not fifty feet in front of them, a tall man stumbled his way along behind a rather irritated-looking woman. He shoved her every few steps, which made her continually stop and yell at him. Wrist-grabbing, more shoving, more yelling. It tightened Chi's chest.

"I could show you with him," Chi said. "He seems like—"

"An asshole," Álava interrupted. She whistled loudly, and the man turned to them. This gave the woman a chance to hurry off, away from his harassment. Álava used her free hand to motion the man closer.

He stumbled his way closer, the scent of rum hitting Chi before she could even see this man's eye color. She turned her head away in the hopes of sparing her nostrils.

"What's your name?" Álava asked. Chi couldn't understand the man's answer, but it didn't matter.

She closed her eyes and concentrated the way her mother often had, and the world faded away. It felt like fainting but without falling over, the way her senses tunneled and her hearing faded into the quiet thump of her own heartbeat in her ears. Until it wasn't just her heartbeat. She could hear his.

His blood type wasn't O, but she figured Álava didn't actually care about that this time. This was purely a demonstration of what Chi was capable of.

When she opened her eyes, the stark shock of all her senses coming back at once nearly knocked her over. She steadied herself against Álava and felt warmth run through her when the Coronet put an arm around her waist.

"Follow me," Álava was saying as Chi came around fully.

She let herself be pulled along, nearly side by side with the drunk man as Álava took the lead. They wound up in an alley that reeked of piss and worse, and Chi felt her stomach churn. Álava let her hand go and walked closer to the man, leaning in, almost kissing him. Chi felt even sicker at that. But instead of a kiss, Álava whispered something, and the man froze. Like Bertie had frozen, like the guards earlier. Álava turned to her.

"Do you drain them first?" Álava asked. "Or do they die first and then you take their blood?"

"Technically," Chi said as she moved closer to the man. She hated his booze stink so much. "They aren't meant to die. I did something wrong before."

"Do it again."

Chi looked to Álava with some suspicion at that. She wasn't in the habit of murdering people, to be certain. But she also wasn't prepared to lose Álava's attention.

Touching this man made her shudder, but she pressed her hand to his forehead, covered in grease and sweat and soot, and muttered an incantation to herself. The man shook, loud gurgling rising from his stomach. Foam slid from his mouth. He dropped to the ground in seconds, still convulsing. Eventually, he grew still again, and Álava knelt down beside him. They tapped his cheek a couple of times, then laughed quietly.

"You're more powerful than you realize," they said, looking up to Chi. "Or more than you're ready to admit."

"Your people had my mother murdered for her abilities," Chi said with a bitterness she didn't realize was within her.

Álava stood again, and Chi took a step back to avoid whatever wrath was likely coming. But instead of anger, a hand, gentle and soft, went to Chi's neck, and Álava pulled her into a kiss. She could almost taste the apology on their tongue.

"I can help you get her back," Álava whispered, "if you stay with me. Say you'll stay?"

"I'll stay," Chi nodded.

She hoped that Álava meant forever.

She was shaken from a dream in a way that felt almost violent, yet without a single physical touch. Another trumpet trilled, and she sat up with a frown. She'd fallen asleep with her street clothes on, still on top of the covers, no scarf on her head. The last of those irritated her the most; now her hair would be an unruly, frizzy mess for the final trial.

The final trial. The horns. Of course.

She looked out of the window to try to estimate the time, and as the trumpet sounded again, she hurried her way toward the bathroom for a quick washup. After drying herself, she opened the wardrobe, then stared at the dress bag with the *Final* label affixed to it. She hadn't peeked into it because she'd thought it would somehow jinx things, but now came the time to put on whatever was awaiting her.

With a deep breath, she unzipped the garment bag. It took a moment to wiggle her way into her dress, but she managed without running into the hall to ask for some help. Bertie was nowhere to be seen, and Chi felt a twinge of sadness. Still, she couldn't deny that the overwhelming reaction was relief that she hadn't also been sent home.

She ran through the courtyard to the arena, dress skirts

balled up in her fists, and made it just in time for Erze to reach the microphone on stage. Even without seeing their eyes thanks to another massive floppy-brimmed hat, Chi knew Erze was glaring at her, and she looked toward the stands rather than possibly incur their wrath.

Standing in the center of an empty arena felt unnerving. The dirt floor beneath her boots bore dark stains that could only be interpreted as decades of blood seeped in. Only a handful of guards near the exits, Erze on the stage, and the round man from the courtyard yesterday several paces ahead of her. Thousands of empty seats stretched up beyond Chi's view, seemingly straight up to the sky. Not that the sky was visible— like so much of the rest of the castle grounds, the arena featured a covering to block out the sun, leaving the interior appropriately shady enough to keep any Aponmhir within safe. Chi started to wonder if the stands weren't as empty as it seemed, if the idea that Aponmhir could turn themselves invisible had any truth to it.

Erze cleared their throat, and their voice echoed through the mostly empty arena.

"Congratulations," Erze said as they gripped the microphone stand. "Despite one of you nearly arriving late…" A pointed pause set Chi on edge. "You have exhibited a worthy assortment of traits befitting the future spouse of a Coronet. However, one trial still stands before you receive the title of Coronet Consort, and it is arguably the most important. This is a test of honor, of loyalty, and of strength.

"As you can see, we stand here within Eddows Arena, a well-trodden field in which the most notable warriors worldwide have come to showcase their prowess for the entertainment and lauding of our leaders for centuries. And this afternoon, *you* will join their ranks. A duel, by request of the Coronet Álava, for their hand. Number 18, Polymbus Fasse."

The man from the courtyard stepped forward. His bald head glistened with sweat that he attempted to dab away with his necktie. Fear in his eyes penetrated Chi and bloomed along her spine. A duel against a man who was at least three times her weight and twice her height—the odds had not been quite so stacked against Chi since she was orphaned upon her mother's death.

"And number 613, Chiana Houghton."

Chi kept her jaw set firmly to not outwardly reveal that fear swirling inside of her. She listened as Erze went through the history of this ceremony, the pomp and circumstance, the final trials of previous Coronets. Her focus started to drift around fifteen minutes into the speech but snapped back upon noticing one of the guards approach her.

The guard clutched the hilt of a sword in both hands as his rigid march led him ever closer to Chi. He extended his arms and held the sword straight out in his open palms. Chi hesitated. Polymbus already seemed comfortable with his sword, swinging and thrusting and blocking an invisible opponent. But Chi had never so much as seen an actual takouba in person, let alone handled one herself.

She had read plenty about this sword as used by fighters within the arena, but she wasn't prepared for how heavy it was. It didn't escape her that the guard laughed quietly at her nearly dropping it when she took it from his hands. She ran her thumb over the hilt engraving, a serpent wrapped around a rabbit. She considered, for just a moment, that she was the rabbit.

"Participants, please make your way to your designated position," Erze was saying as Chi studied the hilt.

Polymbus shuffled his way over to the left starting line, and Chi moved to the right, turning away from Polymbus to wait for the start of their duel. She toed the line and noted it was simply white chalk. If she wanted, she could erase it and move to wherever she wanted. The guard that had presented Chi with her takouba snapped to bring her back to attention. Any second now, Chi would be stabbed to death. She felt it in the air, in the way the guard seemed to look at her with pity. She would be killed, and she'd never have Álava.

Losing immediately became a non-option.

A strip of lights ahead of her switched from a deep blue to white, signaling the start of a match. She knew to keep a hand behind her back, but trying to control the sword with just one hand seemed impossible. But not for Polymbus. Not for this giant man coming directly at her, pushing his sword close enough to her face that she could see the nicks of the blacksmith's hammer on the blade.

She shifted out of the way and managed to bring her sword up to block. In swinging it, she scraped her blade against Polymbus's face. He growled something in a language Chi didn't know, and his fear seemed to give way to rage. Honor went out the window; he shoved her down and hoisted his sword to the sky, then brought it slamming down with both hands. Her sword clattered as she tossed it while falling, and before she could reach for it again, she had to roll out of the way. Polymbus stabbed into the dirt so deeply his blade stuck in the ground.

Something had hold of Chi's skirts. She struggled, grunting as she attempted to free herself. Polymbus had her pinned with his sword, and he bore down on it to make it harder to stand. He'd started fighting dirty, and she had no trouble following suit. With another loud grunt, she slammed her boots against his chest as hard as she could. He flew backward with a yell, and she ripped her skirts free and scrambled to grab her takouba.

"You stupid little—"

She couldn't hear what he called her, her own screams overpowering his voice. Pain exploded through her side, and she hit the ground again. Another kick landed against her spine. The world went white, and Chi tried to swallow back the vomit welling up within her. She retched a couple of times, clawing at the ground to try and regain her wits. Another kick, this time hard enough to spin her around. Polymbus brought his sword down again, and she felt too tired to move out of the way.

Why wasn't someone stopping this? Why had the rules become unimportant? Erze had said this was a matter of honor, and nothing about the way Polymbus came at her was honorable. He was aiming to kill. And Chi couldn't let that happen.

She screamed, deep and primal and louder than she'd ever done in her whole life, and everything froze.

Polymbus hovered above her, face twisted and snarling, her dirty boot prints on his formerly pristine shirt. Spit from his mouth hung in the air but didn't fall onto her. He didn't seem to even be breathing. She pushed herself as best she could out of the way of his sword and tried to stand. Her ribs burned. She swore and looked to a guard, only to find him frozen as well. Everyone in the arena, aside from herself, stood statue-still.

Chi took a few deep breaths to fight through her pain and process what was happening. She'd stopped—what? Time? Life? Whatever she'd done had at least bought her some time before dying. She spit again and winced. Her blood spattered against the dirt. This man would certainly kill her the second he unfroze. She couldn't die, not like this. She had to win. For Álava.

She grabbed her sword and positioned herself in front of Polymbus. Lifting her takouba, she took on a stance that would let her at least have a fighting chance of winning. Her head spun, and one eye started to swell closed, but she felt at least a little more capable this way. And when she screamed again, Polymbus stabbed the ground rather than piercing right through her heart.

"Hey!" She waited for him to look up before giving a wry smile. "You lose."

Slicing through flesh felt easy, in a way. Natural. More intimate than killing with magic. She thought briefly, as she watched him slump to the ground, that maybe that was what Aponmhir felt with their kills. She jabbed her blade into his chest and leaned against it to drive it deeper. The competition no longer mattered; all Chi considered was making her mother proud and the promise Álava had made of bringing her back.

A bright white light surrounded her as soon as she entertained that thought. The others faded away—Erze, Polymbus, the guards. The only thing left was the blinding light in her eyes. And then, there was Álava.

Álava, stepping into the light, a vision in a silver gown that looked almost like liquid, the way it flowed down their body. The knowing smile that stopped Chi's heart. The train of their gown that trailed right through all of the blood surrounding Polymbus's lifeless body.

They were barely a breath apart once Álava reached her, and Chi held her sword tightly to her chest as if it might protect her from whatever the Coronet had planned.

"This look suits you," Álava said quietly. "All the anger, all the blood…"

The spotlight turned off as the lights rose again, and Erze stood just off in the distance. This time, they had no hat. This time, Chi could see them staring directly at her. Staring, motionless, with bright white eyes.

Chi frowned, looking around in confusion. "What…"

"I have a confession." Álava reached and brushed their fingertips against Chi's cheeks. "I chose you a long time ago. I wanted to make sure I was right. And… I was."

"You set this all up?"

"I set this all up," Álava repeated. "To see how far you'd go for me. And apparently, the answer is quite far. I knew it would be you. I knew you had more power in you than you realized. And I knew you'd be perfect to shake things up around here. With me. Together."

"Together…" Chi smiled some. "So I win?"

"You win," Álava nodded. They leaned forward and kissed Chi softly. "Now, let's bring your mother back."

*   *   *   *   *

TAURUS

Venus in Taurus
* Comforted by routine and reliability
* Romantic and affectionate
* Grounded and practical
* Enjoys a slower-paced kind of love
* Potentially possessive and overindulgent

The Taste of a Kiss
Roselle Lim

Appetizer

No matter what anyone says, I, Lauren Chiang, fell in love with Korean fried chicken first.

I mean, yes, falling in love with a person was what everyone expected, but, really, can a kiss compare with perfect crispy chicken skin? How it separates from the juicy dark meat underneath to bubble and fry into a potato chip crunch. And the spice! Spicy enough to numb and tingle your lips, but not phet mak-mak (Thai-level spicy).

Find a delicious guy-shaped equivalent, then—maybe—I'd change my mind.

My favorite Korean restaurant left Toronto four years ago.

Cravings drove my desperate hunt for decent fried chicken as I stalked every restaurant and food truck around the GTA. The lure of good food was all the motivation I needed to get my driver's license a year and a half ago.

It was a rare quiet Saturday afternoon. I had finished my physics and chem lab homework when my phone buzzed with a text from my bestie, Aaron.

Korean fried chicken food truck at MLS. U coming?

I grabbed my Moleskine journal off the nightstand and crammed it into my half-empty Kanken backpack. I always left room for any food I might bring home.

"If you're going out, sneak out the patio doors. Mom wants to talk to you about university." Jess, my older sister, leaned against the open doorway.

Her slightly wavy hair fell half an inch below her jawline. Being at home didn't deter her from applying heavy, winged eyeliner this morning. She was as gorgeous as she was smart. The rare combo would have made any sibling jealous. Her unfailing kindness and generosity wouldn't let me stay green for long.

She sauntered into my room. "She's dead set on Queen's or Waterloo."

The two choices were Mom's and Dad's alma maters. They emerged with master's degrees in electrical engineering and economics, respectively. Jess followed in the family tradition of overachievement: pre-med at McGill. She came home once a month to do laundry and to eat as much home cooking as possible before having to revert to a ramen-and-Pepsi diet.

I rummaged through my closet for my favorite cropped black cardigan. "What's the point? I don't know what I want to be."

"Then, pick something that earns enough to support your food addictions." Jess plopped down on my bed and squeezed a nearby fuzzy teal pillow. "Your followers are growing."

As soon as I got my first phone, I'd started blogging from every restaurant and from every food truck I visited. Photos cross-posted to Instagram, Twitter, and even Facebook for the boomers. Jess drove me to all the early reviews and bought the food. It became our thing. I grinned whenever I caught her commenting on my posts.

Everything would be so much easier if *food blogger* was a viable career, but there aren't any university courses on Best Insta Filters for Street Food.

"But you need more content," she continued, rolling over. "Where are you going?"

"Aaron texted me about a new Korean fried chicken food truck."

She threw the pillow at me. "You serious? Get going! This is what you've been waiting for. I'll distract Mom. Take transit. It's faster than driving."

I gave her a quick hug and crept down the stairs.

Mel Lastman Square was busy. The autumn sunshine streamed through papery leaves of red and gold. Colorful food trucks lined the streets, bringing with them the aromas of roti, okonomiyaki, Nashville barbecue, sopes, and Penang curries.

No sign of the new Korean food truck.

I power-walked the perimeter and texted Aaron about his

rumor. While I waited for a response, I spotted that the oko-nomiyaki truck was now offering Osaka-style. I lined up and peeked ahead to see if the presentation had changed. The newest iteration was decorated with a filigree of light sauce and ephemeral bonito shavings. In contrast, the original Hiroshima-style on the menu sported a cluster of chopped spring onion.

I sent a photo to my sister. She demanded I bring food home.

My head swiveled with each passing plate. If my unicorn food truck was here, then someone would be carrying some evidence. Sure, I'd love to get the first scoop—it was the easiest kind of fast content. I'd only had three ever, and they were a product of pure luck.

What I lacked in scoops, I made up in gorgeous food-porn pics and insightful write-ups—food writing became my brand. Maybe Mom and Dad would accept a creative writing pro-gram, if that was even the right way to go.

"Hey!" Aaron called from three trucks down and sprinted toward me.

Aaron Prabhakaran had two loves in his life: the Toronto Raptors and great food. Wearing his black-and-gold cham-pionship cap and a puffy jacket, there was no question he was probably wearing a matching jersey underneath.

"Number 7 or 23?" I asked.

"Steady Freddy," he replied, indicating the latter. Tall, ath-letic, and good-looking. Varsity point guard. And my best friend since grade one. I already noticed four people check-ing him out. High cheekbones, full lips, and thick, naturally-sculpted brows along with a heartbreaker smile facilitated without the help of orthodontics. Aaron's charm was even more devastating when he spoke. His was a deep voice with a low register, and yes, he killed karaoke nights.

"Any sign of the truck?" he asked.

"Nope. Did you see any fried chicken around?"

He shook his head. "But the guy on TikTok swore it would be here."

"What's the name of the truck?"

"Chikin," he said with the highest amount of smugness.

I grabbed his arm to steady myself.

Chikin.

I'd been stalking the Insta account of this truck, *praying* they'd come to Toronto. Based on the West Coast, they had never driven out here, not even for something big like the Canadian National Exhibition—the biggest equivalent to a county fair that our city had to offer.

"Why didn't you tell me this in the first place?" I punched his arm. "They didn't say anything about traveling or leaving Vancouver."

"Because G is G. He isn't going to tell you where he's going to be. Can't blame him. It drums up hype. Besides, I wasn't sure if this was legit or an idiotic hoax."

I stepped up to the counter and placed my order. Aaron declined. His attention drifted to ogling attractive people walking by.

"No more Corinne, huh?" I tucked my wallet away.

His full lips flattened into a hard line. "You aren't allowed to comment. You're allergic to dating."

"But—"

"Yeah, no. When you get yourself a boyfriend, then maybe."

My family and my life left no room for a boyfriend. My job was to get good grades and have enough extracurriculars for the university applications, so I did. Steady, solid, no surprises.

Except that lately, I'd started thinking, was that really all there was to life?

I remember watching *No Reservations* with my parents as a child. Bourdain's travels were inspirational, and I declared—at nine years old—that I had found my dream job. Travel, learn, and eat. My parents gently corrected me. Bourdain started as a chef first, they said. I replied that I had no interest in cooking. I wanted to do what I saw on the show.

They laughed. Mom patted my head. "Work and play are two different things. Work puts food on the table."

When my order came up, I handed the okonomiyaki to Aaron.

"You know the drill."

He tipped the plate to find the right angle.

"The sauce looks better on the lower left. Let me rotate." His big, beefy hands adjusted the savory pancake. Even though I teased him often about their size, he had no problems helping his Nani-ma with her embroidery work or pulling his moves with the ball on the court.

I took a burst of different shots using varying angles and made sure they were decent before depositing the pancake into a flat, plastic container. After I tucked the container into my backpack, I rolled my shoulders to straighten one of the straps. Then I smelled it—cheong-gochu, combined with the unmistakable aroma of chicken fat and rice bran oil. Dakgangjeong.

"I smell Korean fried chicken! Do you see it?"

"It has to be nearby." He scanned the crowd. "There!" He pointed to a couple sitting on a bench to the north of us holding a container of golden drumsticks.

I took off, chasing a moment more than a decade old.

Entrée

When I started kindergarten, Jess told me that I had one job. "Make a friend. You just need one to start."

I took her advice to heart. I made exactly one friend.

Kindergarten was a jungle of noise and zipping chaos—kids eating things not meant to be eaten, shoving things into places not meant to be shoved, and various body fluids smeared over all the shareable items. By lunchtime, I eyed everyone as the enemy.

I chose a seat away from the others. My lunch was a ham and cheese sandwich on white, two grape-juice boxes, and a packet of Goldfish crackers. Nothing I wanted to keep and, judging by my classmates' boxes, nothing they'd trade for.

An Asian boy, the quiet one whose cubby was next to mine, sat alone. He shifted in his seat, eyes darting to and fro, trying to catch anyone's attention. The other kids were oblivious. After a while, he gave up and brought out his square thermos and cutlery. His lunch smelled so good. I couldn't resist, and despite myself, I packed up my meal and took the seat beside him.

He smiled a lopsided, toothy grin.

Fried chicken on a bed of white rice with a side of kimchi.

I held my head over the thermos. The crisp of the chicken made me drool.

"You want to share?" he asked.

"I'll give you my extra juice box."

"No, thanks." He shook his drink bottle. "I don't want to drink too much or I'll have to pee."

I giggled.

He handed me a drumette. My fingertips ran across the crispy skin before I even took a bite. The crunch blasted my mind as the juiciness of the dark meat underneath filled my mouth. It had the perfect seasoning and spice. My little lips tingled from the heat.

"This is the best fried chicken," I declared with reverence.

"My mom made it." He held out his hand. "I'm Eugene."

I gripped his hand tight. "Lauren. I wanna be your friend."

Eugene Choi was my best friend for the next two years.

On the last day of senior kindergarten before we headed to grade one in the fall, he brought me a sticker from his collection and stuck it on the side of my plastic bento box, his small thumb rubbing down all the edges.

"Batman is now watching over your lunch and guarding it. No one will steal food from you now."

When his family moved to California that summer, I cried until I couldn't anymore. Losing a friend was like losing a part of yourself. Back then, I didn't have many parts to me, so losing one felt as crucial as losing a limb.

First grade brought me Aaron. I traded him some of Dad's beef lo mein noodles and he had the best biryani made by his Nani-ma. Best friends ever since.

Still, I missed Eugene and never forgot his mom's signature dish. All my years of searching, yet nothing ever came close.

I tried googling him. His common name made it impossible to find him. I dreamed that he was happy with his comic books, maybe pursuing a career in illustration. His drawings and paintings were the best in class. His horse actually looked like a proper one with the right amount of legs and heads.

I wondered if he shared his fried chicken with anyone else.

When I reached the couple with the plate, I controlled the urge to steal their food. Barely.

"Hi! Where did you get that?" I asked as politely as I could while sucking in lungfuls of cold air.

The woman pointed to the east. "New food truck. We were lucky. They pulled up beside us. It was swarmed by the time our food was ready."

"Thank you!" I screamed, running to one of the side streets.

"If you ran like this during PE, you could be on the track team." Aaron pulled up beside me in an easy jog. Damn his long legs. "I'll do you a solid and go ahead."

I saluted as he zoomed past.

Slowing down, I noticed a long line beside me. A hipster with a flat cap and groomed beard stood in front of me.

"Is this the line for the fried chicken?" I asked.

"Yep. Hope they'll have some left by the time we get there."

Crap. I texted Aaron. He was already jogging back by the time I had put my phone away.

"The line snakes around the corner and across the street." He joined me in line. "But, it's Chikin. I couldn't tell if G is there, though. The crowd is massive."

While we waited in line, he and I chatted about our univer-

sity applications and what our parents wanted. Aaron negoti-
ated to take something in engineering versus law or pre-med.
His parents wanted him in postgraduate studies. They were
willing to entertain his hoop dreams as long as it led to schol-
arships. His grades, especially in physics and math, were excellent, but mine were better. He joked that it was only his time
on the court that stopped him from beating my GPA. As if.

"Are you staying in Canada?" I asked.

He shrugged. "Don't know. Coach heard from a few scouts.
If we make nationals, there'll be more attention. I haven't told
my parents yet."

"I'm sure they'll be proud." I patted his arm. "I'll miss you
like crazy, of course."

"I'll miss you too. There's always texts, but stuff like this?
It won't be the same." He put away his phone and studied his
surroundings, drinking it in as if he was committing every
detail to memory. "What about you? Accounting at Waterloo, right?"

It was what I thought last week. I hadn't filled out the ap-
plication yet. "It's the best for me, isn't it? Something solid
and dependable."

Aaron looked at me with the full blast of those dark eyes
framed by long lashes. His serious expression—the one he re-
served for his Nani-ma and for me when he had something important to say. "For as long as I've known you, the only thing
you've been passionate about is food. Not accounting, or com-
puter science, or whatever you think will make your parents
happy. Maybe, just maybe, it's okay to be what you want to be."

Work and play are two different things.

"Instability isn't so scary, Jelly." He drew me close as I

leaned my head on his upper arm. "Sometimes, it's the only way to find out what our limits really are."

"Easy for you to say, Belly," I laughed.

We took our nicknames from the packets of jelly beans we had shared since second grade. Every pack we opened, we always picked out the two flavors—his, juicy pear, and mine, toasted marshmallow. Birthdays meant a supposed surprise random pack of new flavors to try.

"It's going to be okay. You'll figure it out."

I leaned back, shifting my weight between my feet. "They better not close before we get there. I want my damned fried chicken."

"Usually they'll let people in line know if they're going to be out."

Three people left the counter. We moved up a spot. Four groups of people were ahead of us, with five people being in the first group. They better not...

"You're killing those innocent people with your glare," Aaron whispered.

"I sweatergod if they get the last of the chicken, I'm gonna—"

A short Korean woman in her late forties jumped out from the back of the truck. She cupped her hand around her mouth. "Hey, folks! I'm so sorry, but we're out. I know you're disappointed, but check our social to find out where we'll be next!"

A sizable groan came from all of us in line. I wanted to sink into the pavement and weep.

"Hey, it'll be all right." Aaron nudged me. "I'll make sure to get the car if you don't have yours. We'll get your fried chicken. I promise."

I held out my pinky, and he locked his with mine.

Three days later, Chikin posted an update on their Insta with a pic of the most delicious fried chicken, naked without sauce—highlighting the bubbling, crispy texture of the skin having separated from the meat underneath and a side of pale baek kimchi contrasted against the protein:

Thank you for showing up in droves at Mel Lastman Square. We ran out in two hours!

We won't be in Toronto for long. Catch us on our last stop before we head out!

Pacific Mall parking lot. 8 PM. Will be there until we're out.

Hope to see you!

The text from Aaron came a minute later.

Already on my way. See you in 5.

Their announcements rarely gave anyone much of a heads-up. I told my parents where I was headed and, after proof of my completed physics homework, hopped into Aaron's blue Camry.

"Two dates in Toronto." I buckled my seat belt. "Are you kidding me?"

"I heard they're heading south toward NYC. Competing in a big-time Food Network show." Aaron adjusted the heat to compensate for the cool fall night.

If we couldn't get there on time or if the crowd was too

much, Chikin would move on without me. I *needed* to eat that chicken. I'd been waiting for this truck my whole life.

"I can't lose out on this. This is probably the closest I'll ever get to perfect."

"Yes, it's your Holy Grail. You had two crushes in your life. The kindergarten boyfriend and the chicken."

I laughed. "I was too young to have a crush at five."

"Hey, I was married twice in kindergarten! I proposed with Ring Pops both times."

"Polygamist."

At five, Eugene was cute and kind. He was a close friend. I remembered him as clearly in my head as though it was our first lunch together again. My feelings for him colored my memories into the rosiest shades of glass. He was what I wanted him to be.

But people could change.

Aaron turned north onto Kennedy Road. "Do you want my opinion?"

"Sure. You're better with this stuff."

"You're going to be disappointed. If you ever meet him again, he's not going to be what you hope or expect. He's a stranger at this point. Maybe if he hasn't forgotten about you, then you'd have a chance to begin again."

"Can't I just do what you do? Kiss the other person to know their soul?"

He choked, gasping for air. "Don't do that. Also, I'm driving."

I laughed and continued to rib him until we pulled into Pacific Mall's parking lot.

The giant glass complex housed shops arranged like a minia-ture city with the rows between stores named after streets. Aaron and I got our curry fish balls, bubble tea, and snack-shopping fix here. We would go more frequently if it wasn't for the parking. No matter the day, finding a spot was always a pain in the ass, but only sadists and masochists went on the weekend—Asian aunties and uncles using cars like swords and shields.

Chikin was parked at the northeast end. A line had already formed around it.

"Park faster!" I drummed my fingers along the edge of the door. "There's a spot two rows down. Let me out!" I snapped off my seat belt and ran to the empty spot. With arms spread, I hexed every moving car in the vicinity until Aaron pulled in.

In my eagerness to get to the truck, I yanked his arm before he was fully out of the car and took off for Chikin.

"I can run faster than you," he said while trying to pry my little fingers from his sleeve.

I released him.

He made it to the line two minutes before me. He wasn't even winded and not a hair out of place while I had a healthy flush across my cheeks. We had arrived in time. There would be no missing out tonight.

"I really hope this chicken is everything you imagine." He finished swiping through the messages on his phone. "It looks good and smells amazing. Think you'll be satisfied?"

Of course it would live up to the hype. Anything else was unimaginable. I'd been waiting so long. Satisfaction was guaranteed. Jess had once made a mock-up of a wedding pic of me and a fried chicken drumstick as the groom. I was both offended and flattered.

"There's no such thing as bad Korean fried chicken, only

whether it's merely good or amazing. Today will be transcendent. I can feel it."

I pulled up Jess's Photoshop artwork on my phone and showed him.

He doubled over, laughing. "I mean, it's accurate."

A young Korean guy walked up to us and cleared his throat. "Excuse me, are you @nomyumgirl?"

Something in his light brown eyes seemed familiar.

"Yes."

He smiled, the same lopsided grin I remembered, now all grown. Did he recognize me somehow? My blurry Insta profile pic had kept me pretty incognito.

"Can I talk to you in private for a minute?"

"Sure."

Aaron stepped between us. "Somewhere where I can see you both."

"Totally understand." He led me to a light post a few meters away.

As we walked into the light's illuminated circle, I blurted out, "Okay, I know this is super weird, but are you Eugene Choi who went to Terry Fox Public School for kindergarten?"

Silence.

Great. I freaked him out. I should stick with food. So much easier to understand.

"I'm sorry. That was weird." I rubbed the side of my neck. My short bob cut brushed against the top of my pinky finger.

"I go by G now," he replied.

G. The chef of Chikin. The universe had united the two things I liked the most.

"I figured you were in California or maybe heading to art school, but you're doing *this*!"

"We moved to Vancouver because of Dad's work about seven years ago. Finished my GED early to cook with my relatives in the food truck."

He looked at me the way Jess and Aaron described me ogling delicious food. I blushed. The heat from my cheeks traveled all over my body, right down to my chilled fingertips.

"You must be proud of how well the truck is doing. I've been following you." I paused, blushing harder when he grinned. "I mean, following Chikin all these years. I heard you're headed to New York?"

"Yeah, they're starting to film a new show. We found out we're contestants a few weeks ago." He paused but didn't stop staring. "I guess I have my own confession to make."

I wanted so badly to use my phone as a mirror to make sure nothing was off.

"I've been looking for you. When I found your Insta, I wasn't sure if it was you, but then I saw your Badtz-Maru lunch box and the faded sticker on the right side."

Batman—well, at least his head—still guarding my food. I couldn't prevent time from peeling away at its edges. The sticky glue left a silhouette behind even after many washings.

A woman, the same one who'd made the announcement last time, peeked out from the back end of the food truck. She waved him over.

"I gotta get back to work." He shoved his hands in his pockets. "If you can stick around for an hour, we can talk. I'll show you the truck."

The line was now twice as long.

He asked in a rush of breath, "Are you seeing anyone?"

"Oh, that's my best friend, Aaron. I'm single…and I'll be here."

G gave me a short wave and hurried back.

I walked back to where Aaron stood.

"How was your first fanboy experience?" he asked. "Sorry about the whole overprotective older brother thing, but you never know, right? You good?"

"Yeah, I appreciate it. First off, not a fanboy." I lowered my eyes. "That was G."

I rocked back and forth on my heels. It was all too much. Meeting my childhood friend in a parking lot, only to find out he's a chef, and a chef making Korean fried chicken I had been keeping tabs on for years!

"Damn. Younger than I expected. Does he know you?"

"Aaron, he was looking for me. G is Eugene." I sucked in two lungfuls of air. "I'm trying not to lose it."

Aaron placed his hands around my upper arms, steadying me. "Hey, hey, listen. This is a good thing! Breathe. Why don't we start small and just focus on eating fried chicken? Can you do that?"

I nodded.

He pulled me against him, with his arm around me. I hadn't realized how much I'd been vibrating with nerves.

Eugene—G—had been looking for me too. I had rehearsed what I wanted to say, yet all those words evaporated. They weren't the right ones for the moment. I didn't know what to say, and even if words could be replaced by emotions, I'd still be sorting through a messy pile without a clue.

For a while now, I had been questioning the passion-free, sensible path in front of me. Yet here G was, running his own food truck. There was nothing sensible about that. He had ambition, and he had taken risks, and he had accomplished something incredible. I was passionate about food, and there was nothing sensible about that either. Yet being sensible had left me indecisive and unhappy.

Existential crisis at seventeen.

Aaron nudged me. "You having an argument in your head again? You versus you?"

"Kind of."

"You're supposed to be focusing on the chicken." He walked up to the counter and ordered two platters. I pulled out my wallet, and he held up his hand. "I got this."

"You better let me get you boba afterward," I countered. "I told G I'd wait for them to run out. We'll have enough time to get one and get back."

"Deal."

G wasn't at the counter. I suppressed my disappointment.

"Hi, Lauren! I'm Ana, G's auntie." She was the same older woman we had seen the other day. "You're sticking around after, yes?"

"I am."

"Excellent. G's looking forward to it." She called over the next people in line.

We took our completed orders and headed for a nearby curb to sit and eat.

The fried chicken on my plate was everything I had hoped for and more, and yet I couldn't help but stare at the food truck and think of the chef inside.

The two very things I'd always wanted were connected, and somehow, for the first time in my life, the food didn't seem as important as the guy.

Was this what real love tasted like?

Dessert

Marie Antoinette's famous saying *Let them eat cake* was a lie. She never said it, and it had nothing to do with cake. If a lie had a taste, I'd imagine it to be like cake: sugary, addictive, and palatable.

I'd been lying to myself all this time because it was easier than admitting the truth: I didn't know what I wanted—in school, in life, or in love.

"Is it weird that meeting him changes the expectations I have of myself?" I confessed to Aaron between sips of classic milk tea boba.

"When I met Fred VanVleet, I came away thinking I'm not good enough. Took me a bit to pivot and turn it into motivation. Think of it like staring at the sun after being inside for too long—you squint cuz it's painful at first, but after, you bask in the warmth."

Aaron's encounter with his favorite basketball player had *changed* him. He couldn't stop gushing for months. Afterward, he hit up the gym more often and worked harder.

"I'm trying to transition from squinting to basking."

The noise from a shuttering grill of the food truck drew our attention.

Aaron got up and tossed our plates in a nearby garbage can. "Hit me up when you're done. I'm going to drop by my cousin's and hang out. We have an NBA 2K19 beef to hash out."

I reached over and hugged his middle. "Thanks."

"Make this Freddy moment count." He made a gesture of going the distance before heading to his car.

G popped out of the Chikin truck and walked toward me.

I shoved my free hand into my jacket pocket and met him halfway.

I tried not to gawk. He was gorgeous. All the excitement and questions I'd had earlier evaporated, leaving me awkward and fumbling with conversation openers that weren't good enough to get past my lips.

"Hi again," I said.

"It's chilly out. Do you want to talk inside the mall for a bit?" he asked.

"Sure."

We dodged around the late-evening traffic and made our way inside. "My parents took me to the arcade on the top floor, last time I was here. Is it still there?"

"Funtime Arcade? Yep. Want to go there first?"

"Sure. I'm dying to play some claw machines."

We walked down the main corridor toward the central escalators chatting about our families and what his goals were. The more he talked, the more I wanted him to keep talking.

"It's all about the food, huh? Is that why you never posted your pic?" I asked.

"Yeah. I need people to focus on the flavors and what I'm making, not what I look like or how old I am. That's just noise. What about you? You don't post many selfies."

I laughed. "People are interested in the food porn, not me."

"I'm interested in both."

The way he looked at me made me blush, again.

"So the claw game… How good are you?" I asked.

"We were in Tokyo last year, and I basically spent all my free time leveling up in the arcades. Eating and claw machines. That was my summer. It's all about reflexes and your hands. My baby sister was really happy with all the stuffies I won her. Mom and Dad thought it was important for me to remember to have fun."

"Too busy chasing the dream?"

"Too obsessed. I know what I want, and I go after it."

We ran into the arcade like we were six again.

G noticed a giant Cinnamoroll plushy that had caught my eye. He parked himself in front of the claw machine and got to work. The blinking candy lights came to life as the crane shifted, moving toward its target.

G's perfect dark brows scrunched as his fingers tapped on the buttons. "The trick is to get it at the right angle."

I walked to his side. There's a fine line between leaning in to get a better scent profile and keeping enough distance as not to interfere. He smelled great too. The aromas of the grill mixed with a fresh, subtle cologne.

Our reconnecting was magical, but it didn't provide a portal allowing us to make up for lost time.

Much like the fairy-tale princess, I had this one night.

Cinderella realized her joy was worth more than her stepmother's wrath.

Whose happiness was more important—my parents' or mine? Could I endure their anger or, worse, their disappointment?

In him, I saw someone whose ambition never wavered.

I swayed now—teetering on the edge of my decisions, wondering if where I'd been heading was really where I wanted to go. Back home to the comfortable spot near the fireplace, or toward the royal ball to dance the night away?

G maneuvered the crane over the fluffy white bunny and

pressed the final button. The claw grabbed a chunk of the head and pulled it into the big exit. I showered him with applause. He presented me with the prize by wiggling Cinnamoroll's massive ears.

"Thank you." I buried my face in the plush and squeezed. "This is so sweet."

"Lauren, I'm leaving for New York tomorrow afternoon." He lowered his head. "I wish I could stay, but…"

"I understand. You're pursuing your dream."

"After the show is done, I'm coming back. I missed you. Now that I found you, I'm tired of the what-ifs I've been thinking about." He paused, a bit flustered. "I'm sorry if that was weird and sudden."

I threw everything to the wind—all the caution, all the sense, all the supposed-tos.

Live in the moment.

Truly live.

Nothing else mattered.

I grabbed G's cheeks and pulled him down. He tasted like every craving I'd ever had. I knew what I wanted: the taste of his kiss.

Phet mak-mak.

＊　＊　＊　＊　＊

GEMINI

Venus in Gemini
* *Communicative, smart, and expressive*
* *Averse to settling down*
* *Playfully flirty*
* *Interested in variety*
* *Can be unpredictable and mercurial*

Doublespeak
Tehlor Kay Mejia

We were born within two hours of each other, which is why whispers of *¡Ay, las gemelas!* have followed us since we were old enough to understand them.

The truth, whatever I told myself as a wishful-thinking seven-year-old with a youngest-child complex, is that we weren't twins, no matter how many shared birthday parties and matching outfits have been forced on us over the years. We were cousins. Cousins who didn't look the slightest bit alike. Not even the kind of cousins you say are like sisters.

Well, not anymore, anyway.

It was a lot easier when we were little, before Gloriana Villanueva grew up to be everything my mother wished I was, and things were still ice-cream-sundae, hot-pink-Barbie-car easy between us. Back when we spent every summer together—my mama working from home with her hair in a sweaty topknot, Ana's bossing grown men around at the fruit-packing plant during her summers off from the neighboring school district.

Back when—despite the growing differences in our personalities—our own parents couldn't tell us apart when we answered the phone.

Our identical voices were fun back then, a novelty since no one would have mistaken us for each other in person. Ana had long blond hair with a subtle wave, and mine was black and thick as a horse's tail. Ana had hazel eyes more green than brown that everyone commented on, while mine were so dark you could barely tell iris from pupil. Her skin was sun-kissed and flawless, mine was anemic and freckled; the list of differences went on and on.

But when we called our neighborhood friends—or even our grandparents—to pretend to be each other, no one ever caught us. It was a secret, like a disguise we could only wear together that lent a little magic to the long, sticky California summers. A way for me to try on being petite and gilded and glamorous for a few minutes at a time, while my body seemed determined to grow into the opposite archetype.

But like most magic, this power was destructive in the wrong hands, and Ana's got more disastrous every summer.

At first, her pranks seemed mostly harmless—at least, to me. She called my sixth-grade archnemesis, Kenny Jensen— a boy so abhorrent I'd been given after-school clean up duty twice for fighting with him—and confessed my undying love to him, hanging up without confessing to the joke. She borrowed money, as me, from my older sister, Esme, and used it to buy cigarettes and a lighter from a boy at 7-Eleven who took flirting as a form of valid ID.

I wish I could say I saw these things leading to their inevitable conclusion, that I set the boundaries my health teacher was always lecturing us about having in our *emotional toolbox* and stopped Ana before her so-called jokes could get me in any real trouble.

But I didn't. And the week before eighth grade started, she and some friends from her neighborhood trashed a teacher's car in a school parking lot, slashing the tires, breaking the windows, spray painting whatever was left. Hot-pink. Like the Barbie car.

I remember she called me late that night, voice trembling with fear. She told me she was afraid someone had seen her. That her life would be over. I promised I wouldn't tell. That I'd help her. Protect her. Despite everything she'd done, Ana just inspired statements like these. You'd know if you met her.

"You'd do that for me, Jamie?" she asked in a voice I knew too well. One that knew the danger while sucking you in like quicksand. "You'd protect me?"

"Of course I would," I said without thinking, keeping Kenny and the Marlboro Blacks in a rattling box buried deep, deep down. "We're primas, aren't we?"

She'd sounded so genuinely grateful when she thanked me, hanging up before she could explain what I could do to help, anyway.

But two days later it was all too clear. According to the principal of the elementary school where the car had been damaged, he received a phone call from a blocked number around two in the morning the night of the incident. A phone call from me. Confessing to the whole thing.

Apparently, I had acted alone.

And Ana's phone went straight to voice mail over, and over, and over.

In the end, even though she didn't answer, never explained or apologized or thanked me, I took the blame. A hundred hours of community service and a note in my school file that would follow me all the way through college. My mom saw right through it despite my protestations, knowing it was Ana right away, though I kept my promise never to confirm it. She went for Tía Lucille like a feral dog, but her sister took Ana's side, and the family was torn in half like one of those photo strips after a bad breakup.

Ana's things disappeared from the dresser drawer I always had to clean out in June, and the forty minutes between our apartments in neighboring suburbs stretched until we might as well have lived in neighboring countries instead.

Tía Lucille mysteriously found a summer job closer to home the next break, and Ana was too old to need a babysitter anyway, so just like that, our summers—tinged with the wild, sometimes destructive magic of her escapades—dried up like a puddle after a flash rainstorm.

Two of the empty seasons passed, then three. I grew taller—much taller than I wanted or needed to grow. My hair got longer and refused to behave, wearing comb teeth and broken hair ties like badges of honor. My skin wouldn't tan like my mom's, and my freckles only got darker.

There were other things, too. The way all the friends I'd managed to cling to since first grade had started giggling and pairing off with floppy-haired boys with vacant smiles, while I pretended to do homework at the same coffee shop just for the smile the girl at the counter gave me every hour or so.

I couldn't tell my mom about Emily. I couldn't tell anyone. About her nose ring or her lavender hair or the tiny stick-and-poke tattoo on the inside of her wrist. A little crab. A soft-hearted Cancer, I imagined. Just the thing to soothe my restless Gemini soul with its missing non-twin.

Ana had never returned my voice mails. Eventually I stopped leaving them, sure I was never going to see her again, even though she lived in my head rent-free, like a shadow I couldn't banish, reminding me how beautiful and perfect and fun I would never be without her. I had protected her, and she had abandoned me. How had I been so easy to leave behind?

I knew I should hate her, but I didn't. I missed her. I missed who I felt like with her. Like a girl who could ask Emily out on a date. Like a girl who wouldn't be too afraid of her mom's reaction to even consider it. But Ana and I had never had any-thing in common besides our last names and our voices, I told myself. That strange coincidence that had bonded us those early years and made me the perfect scapegoat. Nothing more.

The thought devastated me then—little did I know how wrong I was, and how much more devastating the truth would be than the sad fantasy I had constructed.

It started, as it so often had, with a phone call. The kind my mom hurried into her room to take, closing the door be-hind her. It lasted hours. She hadn't sat on the phone that long since she and Tía Lucille had stopped talking.

But it couldn't be, I told myself. Not unless...

I fell asleep wondering and woke up to the news: Tía Lu-cille had, indeed, been the one on the phone. Ana was "in trouble," she said, and though she wouldn't specify, the implications were clear. In a family like ours, the words *in trouble* could only mean a few things.

Either Ana was pregnant, she had gotten into drugs, or she was gay.

Whatever the case, the question was on the table. Tía Lucille now believed everything mom had told her about seventh grade and the prank. She wanted Ana to come live with us. To benefit from my good reputation. To get on the straight and narrow, so to speak.

My mom left it up to me. She knew things were complicated between Ana and me after the prank. If I wanted to say no, she would accept it, no question. Family was family, but I was her daughter, and my happiness (not to mention my grades and my aforementioned stellar reputation) came first.

"I'll start clearing out my dresser drawers," I said, trying to look conflicted. The truth was, no decision had ever been easier. Sure, Ana had wronged me once, years ago. That didn't mean she was the same—or that things would *be* the same. This was my chance to find out what my sacrifice had meant to her, to see how she had changed…

To find out what kind of trouble she'd gotten herself into this time.

Ana arrived on a Friday afternoon, to give her the weekend to supposedly settle in before school started. When she came into my room—*our* room, now—I barely recognized her. She looked like she'd just breezed in from some ultracool photo shoot. She'd been pretty enough to make me feel insecure when we were kids, but now she was in another stratosphere.

"What's up, cuz?" she said, like it had been a few days since we'd seen each other and not three years. "Nice digs." Her hair was cut in some asymmetrical thing that would have been a disaster on most people but looked effortless on her. She had on electric-green eyeliner that made her skin glow and her eyes pop.

I tried to be cool, I really did, but the first thing out of my mouth was "What did you do?"

She smirked. An art form I had never mastered. "Kelsey Smith-Rider," she said, and it took me a long minute to realize what she meant.

"Wait," I said, feeling my face heat up, thinking of my last-year's revelation and my endless hours at the coffee shop trying to catch Emily's eye and every other way I really believed I'd grown into myself since she left me picking up trash in every school parking lot in town for her crimes. "You mean...you..."

"Kelsey's stepdad is the VP at my school," she said with a shrug, flopping down on my rainbow beanbag chair and blowing a bubble with her pink gum. "Let's just say he wasn't too pleased to find his little girl playing tonsil hockey with me and my D+ average. And Moms... Well, you know how she is with that Jesus stuff, but also I'm low-key sure the VP threatened her job, so here I am in prima boot camp learning to *study hard and keep my nose clean* like you."

I couldn't answer. There was nothing to say. How long had I spent comparing myself to this girl? To her perfect hair and pretty eyes and the way she could make a paper bag look like fashion? And now, after thirty seconds in my room, she had not only taken my secret identity but she was already better at it than me.

Tonsil hockey? I hadn't even played lingering-glance hockey yet, and suddenly my thoroughly G-rated interactions with the only girl I'd ever gotten butterflies for seemed laughably uncool.

"Did I totally freak you out?" Ana asked around her wad of gum, and her sparkling eyes said me being freaked out would be some kind of victory for her, so without thinking, I met her eyes as steadily as I could and said, "Oh, no, not at all. It's just wild how it runs in families."

And with that statement, I effectively came out for the very first time to the absolute last person I should have trusted with a secret.

"Shut up," Ana deadpanned. "Shut up! And my mom thinks you're so boring. Ha!" She bounced up, looking at me as if it would be visible, some kind of mark across my skin. "Yes," she said. "I can totally see it now! You have like, that studious, flat-chested, library-queer thing going on. I bet the girls totally go for it. Tell me everything. Who was your first girlfriend? Does your mom know? Do you have a girlfriend now? Can you intro me to some cool people around here? God, I thought this was going to be a total snoozefest."

She was talking so fast, asking so many questions, and I was frozen. Like a flat-chested, library-queer statue.

When I realized she had stopped pestering me with questions and was just staring wide-eyed, I laughed, a hoarse half chuckle. "Sorry," I said. "I'm just not… Like… You're the first person…"

"Ohhh," she said, cutting me off—though, to an outsider it would sound like I'd just interrupted myself. I'd forgotten how totally uncanny it was, the matching voices that had even aged the same. "I'm the first person in the family you've told?"

I nodded, accepting this much cooler-sounding explanation, relieved I didn't have to tell the whole truth. That she wasn't just the first person in the *family* I'd come out to but the first person. Period. That I'd never even said the words aloud. That I had a lurker account just to watch lesbian Tik-Toks. That I'd never even had the courage to like or comment as a ghost just in case.

"Don't worry, prima," she said, zipping her lips and then opening them again immediately. "Your secret's safe with me. I know what a drag it is to have to hide your queer friends and girlfriends from your family. Though, this will be so cool! To have an actual Ramírez we can introduce people to!"

She was looking at me, in that moment, like she'd never looked at me before. Like I was finally worthwhile in her eyes. An equal, and not some square tagalong she could use to cover up her worst misdeeds. Maybe that's why I said, "Honestly, it's great timing, you coming to stay. My girlfriend—" I cast about wildly for a suitable sounding name "—Trixie, she just had to move to, uh, Atlanta. So it's been a total drag around here lately."

"Oh nooo," Ana said, hopping off the beanbag and squishing next to me on my twin bed. "You're heartbroken! Are you guys doing the long-distance thing, or was it a clean break?"

"Clean break," I said hurriedly. "She wanted to do long distance, but I thought it would be too hard. It was a big fight, phone numbers deleted, wiped from each other's social medias, the works." I didn't know where any of this was coming from, but Ana was clearly buying it because she threw her arm around me.

"This totally explains your tragic, housebound, makeupless look! I should have known."

I barely had time to bristle at this before she leapt out of my bed and threw open my closet doors. "Come on. No more. I've been wondering *why* the universe would send me here, but now I see! I'm needed! Call your friends. We're getting dressed, and we're going out!"

It was so intoxicating, the way she began pushing hangers aside in my closet, tossing things out onto my bed, practically vibrating with excitement. For a moment, I pictured what it would be like to actually *be* the person she believed I was. Someone bookish but cool, ingratiated into my suburb's nonexistent queer community in a way that would allow us to go out, meet up, get over my fake heartbreak together.

I should have told the truth, right then. But I didn't.

"Ugh, it's such a bummer," I said, standing up and picking through the pile of clothes Ana was making for me. "But mine and Trixie's friends were sort of...you know...mutual. None of them are super pleased with me right now."

"That is so tragic!" Ana called out, still buried in my closet. "I hate how small most queer friend groups are. It's like, whoever talks shit first keeps all the friends, right?" She emerged with a skirt I'd worn as part of a costume in the eighth-grade production of *The Little Mermaid*. A teal thing with sparkly scales. It had been flowy when I was fourteen but would definitely be skintight and above the knee now.

I could feel my eyes bugging out. I was really more a skinny jeans, sweaters and sneakers kind of girl, but Ana had her *I won't take no for an answer* face on already, and it had only intensified since she'd last used it on me. I was powerless.

"Put this on," she said, digging into her own suitcase and tossing me a vintage Yeah Yeah Yeahs shirt with the sleeves cut off. "And this." She surveyed the three pairs of Vans by my door and magnanimously added, "Any of these will work. Dealer's choice."

The skirt was just as tight as I imagined, and her T-shirt showed the side of my pink lace bralette on both sides. I slipped into my black-and-white checkered slip-ons, the closest thing I had to a comfort blanket, while Ana changed into a hot-pink bodycon dress with her own ripped T-shirt over the top.

"Good!" she said approvingly. "Now for the hair."

"What about it?" I said, still scrambling for more details of my fake life, wondering where exactly she wanted us to go all dressed up at two o'clock in the afternoon. Hopefully not to confront my made-up friends who had taken my made-up ex-girlfriend's side in the breakup I invented, I thought, wondering how, in the last thirty minutes, that had become a sentence that made sense in my head.

"Two braids?" she scrunched up her nose. "I know I haven't seen you since seventh grade, but it wasn't a look even then."

My stomach dropped when she said the words *seventh grade*. I had gotten so caught up in my shock (and the avalanche of lies that had followed so quickly after) that we'd never even talked about what happened. Why we hadn't spoken in the time it had taken us both to become completely different people.

"Right," I said, freezing up, this whole thing suddenly seeming dumb and juvenile. "Seventh grade."

There was a silence, just a beat, and I wondered if she'd apologize—if this cool, fake life I'd created made me a person who deserved closure or an explanation. She was looking at me like she was seeing me for the first time, and I promised myself if she apologized I'd be honest. Maybe we'd laugh about it.

"Down," she said after a long moment. "Your hair. With dry shampoo to pump it up a little. You gotta stop hiding from your volume, prima. Big hair is in again."

I wish I could say I was disappointed that this opportunity to have an honest relationship had passed me by, but honestly, I was relieved. There was a reason people lied, I thought. It was because sometimes the truth was unbearable. And my truth? That my entire sexuality was based on internet lurking and the stutter-step my heart did when I saw Emily tuck her lavender hair behind her ear? That I was basically a shut-in with no friends?

What could be more unbearable than that?

I loosened my braids, tossing my hair as she attacked me with an industrial-sized bottle of volumizing dry shampoo. After a little eyeliner and plumping lip gloss, I barely recognized myself. I actually looked cool enough to be the person I'd pretended to be.

"All dressed up and nowhere to go," Ana lamented, completing her own look with a pair of purple Doc Martens.

But looking in the mirror, a little flushed with the approval I'd been chasing since I was five, I suddenly had my second worst idea of the day. "Why don't we go get a cup of coffee?"

* ◊ *

Devo's Coffee was almost completely deserted, just a few older women chatting in the window seat, and two boring guys on laptops trying to look like they were writing the Great American Novel when they were probably just "playing devil's advocate" in someone's YouTube comments.

Emily was behind the counter, rearranging some adorable pink-frosted cupcakes in the glass display case, wearing her hair in two long pigtails tied with ribbons. Her T-shirt wasn't one I'd seen before, pink and long-sleeved with two characters I didn't recognize kissing on the front.

They were both girls.

My heart skipped a beat.

She looked up as the bell rang, that smile I loved so much rivaling the sun outside for brightness. "Hey, Jamie! Looking good!" she said. "Drip coffee two sugars, right? And who's your...friend?"

My mouth went dry. Suddenly I couldn't even swallow, let alone speak. She thought I looked cute. She had girls kissing on her shirt. She wanted to know whether Ana and I were friends. It was too much. I thought I was smiling back, but I was sure my eyes were too wide.

"I, uh, we... It's..." It was no use. All the dry shampoo and purple eyeshadow in the world couldn't make me cool enough to handle this moment.

"I'm her cousin, Ana," Ana said smoothly, stepping forward and smiling as I pulled it together. "I got in trouble at home so my mom sent me here to soak up some good influence."

Emily laughed, and every cliché on earth about girls laughing and bells and wind chimes made sense all of a sudden. "A troublemaker, huh?" she asked. "Well, Jamie must be the best influence. I swear she does more homework than anyone I've ever met."

I stepped forward, finding my voice at last. "Yeah, well, the atmosphere here is really productive, what can I say?" I didn't bother to mention that I almost never got anything done here, and it was all her fault.

"We try," said Emily, winking. "Anyway, what can I get you ladies?"

"A cure for utter ennui?" Ana said, slumping against the counter. "I thought my town was boring. And Jamie here's just been through a terrible breakup, so we need a distraction posthaste."

"A breakup? Oh no!" Emily said, her eyes widening in sympathy. "I had no idea you had a boyfriend. I never saw him come in with you."

It was the outfit, I swear; it made me much bolder than anything should have.

"Girlfriend," I said, before I could change my mind. "Trixie. She moved to Atlanta." The lie came so much easier this time, but there was some truth in it too, of course. The truth about me, not the imaginary Trixie.

And there it was, that same look of appraisal I'd gotten from Ana but with infinitely more thrilling implications. A look that said there was more to me than met the eye, a spark of interest beyond anything I'd garnered as a solo, presumed-straight Devo's customer.

"Such a bummer," Emily said, her eyes still on mine, making my stomach do flip-flops. "It's so hard to find other queer

people in this area, and then they have to go and move somewhere cool."

"And what's worse?" Ana asked, drawing Emily's eyes onto
her. "The witch poisoned all her friends against her, so she's
weathering this terrible heartbreak alone." She said all this
in a faux-dramatic voice that almost sounded mocking. But
it wasn't. Right?

"You know what they say," Emily said, leaning across the
counter. "A rebound works wonders for any heartache. Anyone you're interested in?"

I was going to say something clever, I swore it to myself.
Something that sounded cool and aloof and flirtatious all at
once. Something that would open the door just a little further, even if I wasn't quite ready to rush into it yet.

But I was too slow for Ana, who had already leaned forward herself. "I asked the same thing, but apparently no one
here's caught our girl's eye so far. A shame, right?"

"A shame," Emily agreed, and was it my imagination, or
did her eyes flick once more to me before she smiled at Ana
again. "But I guess it's a shame we'll have to do something
about. You guys like scary movies?"

* ◊ *

Fourteen minutes after we arrived, movie night, the happy,
hopeful balloon I'd been carrying around in my chest for hours,
was a shredded lump of latex on the floor. Like, ceiling-fan
shredded. Helicopter-propeller shredded.

We walked into someone's backyard shed to find five or
six other girls settling in with popcorn and sodas. There was

a futon and several beanbags, and Emily was approaching with that heart-stopping smile, and I was stepping forward in my ridiculous outfit only to watch her embrace Ana, kissing her on both cheeks and turning to me like an afterthought.

"So glad you could make it!" she said, with a decidedly less enthusiastic, one-armed embrace. She lowered her voice conspiratorially and leaned in close, giving me goose bumps all over my arms even as my heart sank right through the soles of my sneakers and drifted toward the molten center of the earth. "Some of these girls are cute, right? Operation Heart Repair is a go!"

I smiled, somewhat weakly, spared the indignity of coming up with a response by the fact that Emily had already turned back to Ana, her eyes practically doing the anime sparkle effect as she led her over to the snack table.

Introductions were made, and terrible as I was with names, I remembered them by things like *Septum Piercing*, *Blue Streak*, *Undercut*, and *Unicorn Shirt*. When it came time to settle in for the movie, Emily gestured me to a beanbag and didn't look at all upset when Ana joined her on the futon. I couldn't even look at Unicorn Shirt beside me, I only had eyes for my crush, who was currently drinking out of the same glass Coke bottle as my cousin.

I'm pretty sure none of us remember what movie was playing.

In the three weeks that followed, every second of my life was torture.

I told myself I'd barely known Emily. That she'd been more

of a fantasy than a reality, and that I shouldn't begrudge people happiness if they could find it in this mixed-up world.

But as Ana lay on my bed, giggling into her phone as she
FaceTimed with Emily for the fourth consecutive hour, my
hands shook too badly to hold my pencil, and I quit my pre-
calculus homework early for the first time in my life.

It went on for hours every day. The calls. The texts. The
endless gushing.

I learned things I'd always wanted to know about Emily
from the source I least wanted to learn them from. That she
was seventeen. Had been homeschooled. That the characters on her shirt were from a video game called *Fire Emblem*
that Ana now played endlessly on her Nintendo Switch. That
she'd never really had to come out to her parents, who had
just known and had been supportive like so many other liberal
Anglo white parents were.

I learned that her favorite color was turquoise, her favorite band was Beach Bunny, and that if she could live anywhere she'd live in a cabin in the Irish countryside raising
tiny, woolly sheep and riding a pony with saddle baskets to
the market.

While Ana told blatant untruths about her own home-
schooling, obsession with *Fire Emblem*, and goals to live off
the land, I tried to remember every reason to hate her besides my totally pathetic crush on a girl I had never spoken
to alone for more than two minutes.

It wasn't hard to find reasons.

But if Ana noticed the chilly silence that filled the room
as I remembered the hundred hours of trash duty on a loop,

she was too twitterpated (her word) to notice. Or too self-centered, or uncaring, or just downright awful…

I stopped going to Devo's entirely. Ana went every day after school and never asked why I didn't join her. Further proof of her total lack of concern for me. The only good part about it was that I no longer had to fake my heartbreak.

It wasn't about Emily, I told myself. Not really. It was about Ana, showing up and pretending to care when she was just going to steal the life I had just been trying to grow into for myself.

I'd be lying if I said I didn't think some uncharitable things during those weeks, about calling Emily from Ana's phone and picking a fight, but as fate would have it the first time I spoke to Emily as Ana, it was my cousin's idea.

She'd come in from the apartment-complex porch where she took her more private calls, the phone muted, the camera paused. She looked—there was no other word for it—bored.

"She always wants to talk about our feelings for like, *hours*," she said, and I thought again of the little crab on her wrist. "At first it was cute, but lately, ugh."

"Sounds rough," I said in my least sympathetic voice.

"Did Trixie do this kind of thing to you?" Ana asked, while Emily's voice continued faintly on through the phone speaker, spilling her deepest thoughts and feelings to no one.

"All the time," I said. "But some of us don't mind talking about our feelings."

There was a long pause. I thought maybe, for once, Ana might have noticed I was upset. That she was going to ask about it. That we could finally clear the air.

"Hold on," she said instead, looking at me intently for the

first time since she'd arrived here and turned everything up-
side down for the worse. "You actually *like* this feelings junk?"

"Live for it," I said, even though I had no idea. How could
I, when I'd never had a real girlfriend—or even a real friend
who knew enough about me to truly share anything? Ana had
come in like a whirlwind and stolen my best chance.

"Okay, I know this is gonna sound crazy, but...what if you
do it for me?"

"What?" I asked, startled out of my perpetual, unnoticed
chill. "What do you mean, do it for you?"

"You know, I'll go out and do the dates and the kissing
and the actual *fun* stuff, and when I get bored you can tag in
on the feelings talk."

I should have said no. I know I should have. It wasn't right.
But I told myself it was for Emily. That she shouldn't have to
deal with Ana's indifference to her. And for my cousin who,
despite her several *major* shortcomings, was family.

So I held my hand out for the phone, and I put it to my ear
as Ana stuffed her fist into her mouth to giggle, and when
Emily said "Ana, are you still there?" I closed my eyes for a
brief moment, unmuted the phone, and said, "Sorry, my aunt
was listening at the door so I had to mute real quick. What
were you saying?"

Emily paused for a brief second, just long enough that I
wondered if she'd noticed the change. If she would be the
first ever person to tell us apart. "No problem. Is your aunt
as strict as your mom was?"

"Nah," I said, heart sinking just a little, shifting into my
Ana persona as effortlessly as if it were three years ago and I
was calling Tía Lu to check in while Ana was out running

around the neighborhood riding Bobby Davis's new bike. "But let's not talk about her. I want to talk about you some more."

Emily giggled, and it was adorable, but it wasn't for me, so of course it was sad, too.

"What were you saying before I was so rudely interrupted?" I asked, aware of how many questions I'd always wanted to ask her, aware of Ana beside me giggling, aware that this was a huge joke to her and too serious to me, and that poor Emily had no idea.

I'd wanted her to figure it out. I didn't even realize how much I'd wanted it.

"I was saying that I've always wanted to be in a relationship where both people felt completely free to communicate honestly. Like, I really think even the toughest topics can be handled with grace and totally open communication."

"Couldn't agree more," I said before I could check myself, to really take in the hypocrisy of what I was about to say. "Total honesty is how we know whether or not we're meant to be together, right? People pretend too much, and then they end up with the wrong people because of it."

"Yes," Emily breathed. "That's exactly what I was going to say."

"You never get happily ever after on a lie," I told her, and unfortunately, I believed it.

My days became a blur of squirming guilt mixed with anticipation. My nights were spent mostly talking to Emily at great length, realizing how utterly right we were for each other and how wrong she was for Ana...

I had been pretending for weeks. Sometimes I forgot who

I was supposed to be. She never said Ana's name as we shared everything late into every night. I relied on these moments. I loved them. I was starting to love her.

And she still had no idea who I was.

Wedged against the railing of our little porch one night, I looked at the stars and listened to her breathe.

"Still there?" she asked.

"Always."

"Tell me something true," she said. "A secret."

My adoring upward gaze turned accusatory. *Are you messing with me?* I wanted to ask whoever was holding court up there. *Like, seriously, are you?*

The silence stretched. Ana would have made something up or claimed to have no secrets.

But I wasn't Ana. And this was my chance, I knew. To confess. To see if this was real enough to survive.

"I do have a secret," I said, heart fluttering hummingbird-fast at the base of my throat. "Something I've never told anyone."

She waited. She didn't push. God, I loved this girl.

"It's actually...about us." Was I really going to do this?

"Okay."

I took a deep breath. "Well..." Just then, Ana's shadow fell across the blinds. My hummingbird heart turned to stone. Sinking, sinking. I had thought of Emily, and of me, but I had never thought of Ana. What she would say. How she would feel.

If I did this to her, how was I any better than she had been?

"Oh, man, looks like secret time's gonna have to wait.

My m—tía's home, and she'll kill me for being on the phone this late."

"Oh." It was a deflated little sound. "Sure, of course. Talk tomorrow."

"Yeah," I said, but I didn't mean it. I was hanging up my rent-a-voice business for good.

The next day, I saw her for the first time since we'd begun. Emily. Walking down the street in front of the library, head-phones in, hair gleaming in the sun. She had a contented smile on her face. I wondered, before she saw me, if she was thinking of me.

Of Ana, I corrected myself, and then we locked eyes.

To my humiliation, my eyes prickled with tears. I had never wanted anything more than this girl. How could she ever want *me* when she had Ana? Experienced, fun, and *cool* in a way I wasn't. In a way I would never be.

"I gotta go," I said abruptly, cutting her off as she rambled about some new scone they had at Devo's. "Sorry."

I ran all the way home, where I waited in my room for hours. Pacing. I had to tell Ana now. Not just that I was quit-ting but that I had feelings for Emily, too. That I'd been lying to her. To both of them.

But afternoon turned into night before Ana appeared in the doorway, thunderstruck. "She dumped me," she said without preamble. Changing everything. "She just…dumped me. No one dumps me."

My heart sped up to a cool three thousand beats per minute.

"Did she say anything to you?" Ana demanded. "Was there any sign this was coming? You would have told me, right?"

"I would have," I said automatically, but in my mind I was racing back, trying to pinpoint anything that could have led to this. There was nothing. When she'd asked for a secret I'd felt something in the air. Something big. But it had felt like a good something.

"Such bullshit," Ana said, shaking her head and dropping her purse on the floor. "But whatever, I guess we're both single now, right? Let's go have some fun." She laughed in a way that made me sure she had never been heartbroken. That she might not have a heart to break. "Guess you're off the hook, too. Probably a relief, right?"

I'm sure I said something, but my mind was a million miles away. After lights-out, I lay awake for too long, trying to remember the last night I'd spent not talking to Emily. She had every right to hate us for what we'd done to her, but our connection had been real. I was sure of it.

And they weren't together anymore…so it was bad, but not totally unforgivable, right?

Who was I kidding, really? Ana had never cared about me. Never lay awake wondering how to do right by me. She had taken so much. I wasn't going to give her this.

When I was sure Ana was fast asleep, I slid her phone out from under her pillow, the glitter fish-tank case familiar in my hand by now. I pulled up Emily's contact—still saved under *bb girl*—and typed the text.

Can you meet me tomorrow? I asked. I know it's over, but there's something I need to tell you.

The reply came almost immediately: Sure.

We set the time and place—nine in the morning, a hiking trail just a mile from downtown—and I stayed up all night thinking about what I could possibly say.

When Ana asked me where I was going the next morning, I lied. Maybe there was more of her in me than I'd ever thought. Regardless, I had no loyalty left for her. After pretending to be her for so long, she'd entirely lost her luster. She was shallow and mean, and she took advantage of the people she loved.

My big mistake had been refusing to see it sooner. Thinking she had something I didn't or could give me something I wanted. It was time to grow up.

I just had to hope it wasn't too late.

The sun was already heating up by the time I reached the trailhead. Emily was already there, sitting on a bench reading a book, two paper coffee cups beside her.

My heart raced, my palms were sweaty. I deeply considered running. It was ridiculous, I thought. I'd spent countless hours sharing my darkest secrets with this girl, but I couldn't sit down and have a cup of coffee?

It had been so much easier being Ana. Now it was time to be myself.

"Hey," I said, hummingbird heart in my throat as I walked up behind her, standing in front of the bench, not wanting to sit if she was just going to send me packing.

"Hi," Emily said, and it took me a minute to realize she wasn't surprised. Her smile was knowing, and a little smug.

"Wait," I said entirely wrong-footed. "How did you...?"

"Know it was you?" she said, smirking, getting to her feet. "Come on, Jamie. I knew the first time you took the phone."

"So why did you play along?" I asked, reeling. Of all the possible outcomes I'd predicted, this hadn't even made the list. "We were...manipulating you. Tricking you. It was rotten and miserable, and you should hate me, and I'm not sure... why you don't?"

Emily smiled, then held out the second coffee to me. "Drip coffee, two sugars," she said, and I took it, unable to help myself from smiling. She had really been expecting me. She had really known. Even my own *mother* couldn't tell Ana and me apart. No one ever, ever had.

"I liked you, you know," Emily said. "For ages. And then Ana said you didn't like me that day with your fake breakup, and I was so bummed..."

There was nothing left in my head. Just a blank buzzing.

"Ana's fun," Emily continued. "A little wild, but fun. I figured it'd be a fling. Help get my mind off you. But then you got on the phone that night, and I knew I'd always been right about us. That we could have had a real shot."

"So..." I said, sipping my coffee just for something to do. It was the perfect temperature. "So really *you* were using *me*?"

Emily laughed. Bells and wind chimes. "I prefer to think of it as a very protracted meet cute."

It was my turn to laugh. She had known, all along. All those nights she'd been talking to me. "What do we do now?" I blurted out before I could stop myself.

She stepped forward, smelling like coffee and caramel and lavender. "We live happily ever after, of course."

And then she kissed me, and I'd never, ever felt less like someone else.

* * * * *

CANCER

Venus in Cancer

* *Protective, caretaking, and loyal*
* *Initially guarded and private until they feel secure enough to open up*
* *Extremely sentimental*
* *Ride-or-die mentality which can be seen as clingy*
* *Possibly overly attached to the past*

L(Train)iminal
Karuna Riazi

Most people don't like to be on the last train of the night.

Most people have other options.

Mia wasn't thinking about that, though—not then. Not for once.

This guy across the aisle was staring, and that never was a good sign.

He was the type of good-looking, ambiguously brown guy that another girl—a girl who didn't ride the L enough to know about stares, and which were okay and flattering and which were heck no, get your eyeballs back in your head before I shove them there—might subtly snap a photo of and upload to Twitter so he could go viral in the way cute guys tended to.

Mop of curly hair, pencil shoved behind the ear, those brown-rimmed glasses that had to be standard issue for any nerdy job you could think of—and wide, wild-looking gray eyes fixed on her clenching hands, her tight jaw, her forbidding glower.

Or, as much of a glower as she could muster. That was probably why he was fixated on her to begin with, after all.

Testimonials from close friends: *You're so sweet!*

You're too nice!

Don't let guys think they can get to you!

So today, she was trying out the glower and direct eye contact. It felt uncomfortable, but looking down at this point would be asking for more trouble.

Depending on what type of weirdo he was, that might seem like a gold-inked invitation to step across the aisle and take a seat next to her.

He was more normal than the usual *late-late* night crowd of troublemakers—not quite the type that seemed he could lurch forward and grab her by the lapels and slur in her face about his Lord and Savior Jesus Christ—but you could never quite tell on the last train to nowhere.

It didn't help that she was throwing out the wrong signals today: to him, to the train, to the universe. She should have gotten on the train sooner, earlier in the day when it was easier—safer—to be both Black and witchy.

But then again, you didn't end up on the *late-late* train if your day had gone well.

And hers—well, frankly, it'd been the pits.

Mia sagged, the day washing over her. She'd been feeling so confident that morning that she'd never even considered that she would be sitting here now. Yes, she woke up on a borrowed couch, but for once, the old springs kneading her back like a grumpy auntie prodding at her posture felt reassuring.

She'd stretched out her arms and limbs and wondered if it was what cats felt like when they woke up: smug and warm and satisfied and like everything could only turn up roses (or, well, whole cans of fresh sardines).

It wasn't a day to think about late trains.

It wasn't even one to think about the morning ones she'd missed, or shifts at part-time jobs that she might have been late for.

Outside the window and beyond the rusty fire escape, there was rich sunlight and bright blue sky.

And a job interview.

Usually, the thought of that would have given Mia a knot in her stomach, anchored her enough to feel the firmness of that old couch, bring up the station app and maybe think… Well, not the midnight train, but at least the 8:00 p.m. one.

Think some realistic how-you-gonna-get-home-girl vibes instead of floating around on cloud nine and not seeing the whole day through.

But she was so freaking confident. And cute, thanks to the tenured witches at the library—the East 84th location, out of the two she was a part-time page at and the one where she mostly did back-room organization assistance—who insisted they couldn't send their Mia-girl off to a life-changing opportunity without a little primping up.

Hannah Jo lent her a blazer, and Libby fluffed up her curls so they tumbled artfully out of the silk scarf tied about her head.

"Oh, look at her," Isa crooned, leaning over the desk with her head on her hand. "Do a twirl for us, baby girl."

Mia—blushing, beaming—spun with all her might, and all the librarians crowded in the back room clapped and cooed.

"So professional," Libby beamed, as though she was Mia's mother and not one of her supervisors. "They won't know what hit 'em."

"They better, or they'll have to deal with me," said Hannah Jo. "Your résumé is one of the best I've seen for a library assistant. You have what it takes, Mia. Show them."

Mia looked at her friends' faces, warmth bubbling up in her chest.

They were the favorites of the ones she worked with: not too good to supposedly forget her name every five minutes and supplement it with something they deemed ethnically close—Marisol? Meera? Ah, yes, Margarita!

They saw her. Not Mia, the girl with her high-school graduation—a year past—practically stamped in the empty space at the top of her résumé's education section like an old expiration date.

Not Mia, the first-generation failure.

But Mia who could, maybe actually did, have this interview in the bag and could get everything back on track the way it should be.

And then Lorraine, with the blond braids and the elite hippie skirts from the gentrified boutique where everything was five hundred dollars *on sale*, sashayed by and gave one of those tight, little quirks of her lips that Mia always tried to optimistically take as a smile but Isa hissed over as *condescending*.

That was Isa's favorite word for Lorraine, who liked to lord it over everyone else that her finance-wizard daddy—like, her actual daddy and not a weird euphemism—gave her a small loan, as she called it, of fifty thousand dollars just to help her scrape by, and that she spoke Latin with the right inflection when casting an archive spell.

"That's very nice, Mia. You almost look like you could fit the part. I hear competition is stiff, so I know that'll help make up for your résumé gaps. Chin up, okay, babe?"

Lorraine didn't linger, moving on quickly with the stack of books she was organizing still floating before her. The other women stared daggers after her.

"She," Hannah Jo said tightly, "better watch that her braids aren't too near my scissors when we cut out the kindergarten crafts later. Honestly. Did *she* even graduate from kindergarten?"

"It's okay," Mia said cheerily. She was good at that. Her mama said she always had been. She was the kid who always put on that quick, bright smile, like turning on a light bulb.

It's okay!

It's fine!

It'll all be okay!

And it had to be. Lorraine could be dealt with.

After all, as Mama always said, "There are worse girls than Lorraine out there. At least she keeps it to the catty remarks."

So she didn't let that burst her bubble or cast a shadow on her warm sunlight and big hopes—that moment or the morning after, when she easily found an empty seat on the morning train and a spot where she could snag the Wi-Fi and wheedle some energy for it to keep streaming her favorite instrumentals.

The very tracks seemed to jostle a little less than normal, as though the wheels themselves were greased with every spark of earth magic the tunnels could give off.

She rode to her interview with the magic cradling her and the sun smiling through the smudged windows.

But maybe she should have taken it to heart: looked up when Lorraine passed by and seen the expression in her eye properly. Taken in the look of a person who saw the borrowed clothes for what they were and her day for what it would be: not at all good enough.

That made it sound like the interview was bad. Mia was sure that, once she looped back around to the library, everyone would tell her it went fine.

But it didn't.

Not to her.

She could tell she got some brownie points for a good, solid handshake. The lady fielding the questions was the assistant director of the main branch. It was a serious step up from her first screening: handing over the initial questionnaire to a harried reference librarian, who skimmed her résumé while shaking a salad in one hand and keeping her head craned toward some snickering boys clustered around one of the research computers.

But apparently, with that step up came more intense stares, more looks at that wide hole where her high-school experience was supposed to come to an end, and then—of course—that fateful response.

"I love your enthusiasm, Mia, but we're looking for someone with a little bit more…"

She waved her hands about, apparently waiting for the right word to land in her hand.

Mia didn't need for it to appear, though. She could fill in a blank for herself now.

Experience, maybe.

A degree, obviously.

Clothes of her own to wear to an interview?

She could tell the woman would never say it aloud, but again, she could fill in a blank for herself now.

And then, the part that her friends would probably gasp over, say "You see? It's not over yet" while squeezing her shoulders and rubbing her back as though she'd caught a chill instead of been turned down for a job that offered everything she needed right now: support, a solid footing, some spare cash to start socking away so she didn't have to wake up another day on someone else's worn-through furniture.

"We are going to be looking for some part-time help, though," the woman offered after Mia numbly shook her hand and turned toward the office door. "It's a bit like page work, honestly. Filing and phone calls. But you never know when it would lead to an opening."

She said it with a bright smile, like she really, truly believed that.

Like she was the first person to offer Mia something like that, for Mia to force a smile and say *Okay* and write down her contact information and be offered the part-time work and come in and file papers and refill shelves and throw away old books and never, ever be allowed to step foot behind Circulation or Reference unless it was to leave a requested title or gather more papers to file.

Those words—that smile—brought not Lorraine's catty comment back but Amara's final words as she leaned over and tugged Mia's borrowed jacket into sharp and snazzy smoothness.

"She doesn't know an inch of who you are," she said fiercely, tugging her collar into submission. "She doesn't know why we're doing this for you."

Mia winced, her hands digging into her legs.

That was what it came down to, every time, with every person.

The guilt.

The expectation that Lorraine understand that Mia needed respect not because of her being a person but because she was a person *with problems*.

They were closer to understanding her, in the way Black and brown girls the world over bond over taking off their shoes at the door and having enough sense to not step into a haunted house, but not entirely.

She wanted them to do things for her, without it being a guilty thing.

A *You're special to us because you've been through so much* thing.

Usually, she didn't let knowing everything she had was a pity possession: borrowed or *borrowed* in that meaningful way a friend would press it on her and never, ever dare to ask for it back.

Usually, she did her best to feel grateful for the endowed clothing, secondhand books and foster familiars that tried their best to work with her only feeding them magic through stray sparks and borrowed energy off the tracks.

That was why she spent so much time on the L, after all, taking the long way instead of the express train that went to the center of the city like a direct vein to the heart.

Picking up on the magic around her, from her coworkers and particularly from the train—the only place she spent enough time in to really feel like a home, or something close to home—kept her confident enough to carry on.

To feel like a proper witch, a witch who had a home to go to and parents who were triumphant leaders of their coven and family heritage, rather than piecing it back together through menial labor and interviews to try and secure proper papers.

But tonight, it was hard.

Just like magic, there was very little hope to scrape up off the seats and floor of the late train.

The train lurched to a stop, and Mia jerked up, heart pounding.

The staring boy was gone. Other slouched, exhausted figures made their way through the open doors.

She followed, pushing down the part of her now very aware of her discomfort in form-clutching tweed and blotted-on perfume that hadn't lost the sharp bite of alcohol.

Tomorrow morning, there would be the warm, sunny early ride to the first library. Tomorrow there might be a spot to snag the Wi-Fi and wheedle some energy for it to keep streaming her favorite instrumentals.

Tomorrow, the very tracks might feel like they jostled a little less than normal, as though the wheels themselves were greased with every spark of earth magic the tunnels could give off.

Tomorrow, she would be able to keep up the pretend of being a somewhat witch, and try again.

Throughout magical history, witches have always done decent magic while in transit.

Hedge witches, wizards fleeing prosecution and refugee witches and wizards have done incredible things.

Incredible but temporary things.

For permanence, you need to yourself be permanent. It is what tempted Merlin to set down roots in Camelot—though, of course, it is always and has always been easy for white magical men to find favor at the hands of kings and nobility and gain status, citizenship and homes.

Always, always, at the very core of a witch's heart, there is a need for home.

They may enjoy traveling over ley lines, spending nights snuggled up in blankets within fairy rings and making brief excursions to places and covens unknown—

But at the end of the day, there needs to be a particular home.

And everyone in Mia's city who was magical seemed to have one. Except her.

Ten years after her parents escaped from their father's country with upheaval nipping at their heels like a rabid dog, with her in their arms, she still would start another morning on her best friend's couch, consulting a list of part-time jobs and openings on her phone, and laying aside the borrowed clothing to take to the Korean-American family downtown who knew how to keep the residual magic crisp as the collar.

Preparing to spend most of the day on the train.

Looking forward to it, though none of her friends would understand.

She was going to spend most of the day on the train. She was prepared for it.

It doesn't bother her—not really—that Agnes shakes her head and says, "One day, you won't need to be on the train so often."

The smile on Mia's face is genuine when Miranda grasps her hand and sighs over dinner, "I feel so sorry this is necessary for you to do."

Mia doesn't mind. Great things have been done in transit.

Or so she keeps telling herself.

* ◊ *

Tomorrow, as it turned out, sucked even more majorly than the day before.

It wasn't just clothes Mia's friends loaned her, after all, or food they insisted their parents made too much of, or business cards for good immigration lawyers to be tucked away without admitting that she called them up and was gently informed they couldn't take new clients months ago.

It was trouble.

A little skittering in her pocket made Mia cringe and stiffen up.

"Darn it."

She'd borrowed some other things today as Agnes—since-elementary-school bestie and owner of the terrible couch with the old springs—had anxiously insisted upon her doing when she mentioned that she might pop into Bee's hive and ask if anything was new.

Bee was the hiring manager at the East 84th Library, and she was one of those rare people who really leaned into the ready imagery her nickname brought up. Hence the bee clips currently tucked into Mia's curls, the gold-rimmed glasses balancing on the bridge of her nose.

And the...thing squirming in her pocket.

Every witch, after all, had her uniform to indicate where she belonged—if she belonged anywhere at all.

And, of course, part of that uniform was a familiar. Until recently, when she borrowed off all-too-willing and overly concerned friends, she had luck in the familiars she ended up fostering for a day or two: more than a few cats, one dog, even a little owl that liked to perch on her shoulder and watch *Divorce Court* reruns without a hoot of judgment.

That was a sweet little owl. The majority of them were scowling, cold little things who would rather you leave on the History Channel at all times.

But even one of those sour, old-lady owls was better than what was in her pocket right now. She peered out of the corner of her eye and flinched again as she saw a little whisker. Ugh.

A mouse.

The little mouse familiar in her pocket was not welcome at all. She hated mice.

But it was so hard to say no to Agnes, especially when she pulled out her secret weapon.

"I worry about you," she said, wringing her hands. "Look... I know you don't like to talk about it, but...your magic..."

Mia, in the middle of slipping a hoop into her ear, shot her a look.

"Agnes, you know how I feel about you worrying about me. I'm fine, girl. Really."

"Mia...there's nothing wrong with being in between places. A lot of witches have gone through that, historically. If you feel like there's a stigma..."

Honestly? Mia bit the inside of her cheek. And people called her the glass-half-full one of their best-friend duo.

Mia didn't feel like there was a stigma. There actually *was* a stigma.

When other witches heard you were homeless, they got this look in their eye. This raised brow.

This expression that all but screamed, *"Oh. And what did you do for that to happen?"*

Agnes saw the look in her eyes and backed off.

"Okay," she said softly. "I'm sorry. Like I said, you don't want to talk about it, and I shouldn't have overstepped."

Mia softened.

"Sweetie, you didn't…"

"But—" Agnes said, raising her finger "—at least let me send a friend along with you. You know, for some luck. You could always use some of that, right?"

Mia's heart sank. No.

"What do you mean, a friend?"

Agnes only smiled, in that *You know you love me even though I'm going to foist that annoying rodent into your pocket* way.

And so, the mouse.

It had a name, thanks to Agnes's younger sister—who was pretty and also pretty spoiled and had thus begged to have said rodent until she realized that she didn't like mice after all—but Mia hadn't bothered to learn it.

Agnes kept trying to make her bond with the thing. She claimed that, like Mia, it was just so cute and alone in the world, and maybe they both needed each other.

Honestly, maybe Agnes needed to change tracks in university from pre-med to writing. She was missing her calling in making Hallmark movies.

Mice were not any part of the magic that Mia worked with. She could admit that to herself now, just as she could now admit the blazer bit in a little too deeply at her sides and her hair was pulled up so tight to be "respectable" that she was getting a headache.

Back in the old days—

But she couldn't think of the old days now.

But back in the old days, her parents had never tried her on mice, in the way parents with indulgent hearts and enough money and status and a country where they were recognized as valued dwellers and not second-class citizens laid trial familiars at their children's feet to see what worked.

There were giddy-hearted bunnies and long-bearded goats and even one or two chickens that squawked irritatingly but had a keen glint of magic in their eyes and could be counted to peck up one or two artifacts when let loose in a shadowy corner of the courtyard.

Never mice.

Mia held still, held her breath, hoping that it would settle.

The train took a turn and swung over St. Martin's Graveyard. In spite of the name, it was one of the graveyards full of magic folk—not just the varied witches that had lived and died in the city but part-time werewolves, full-time gremlins and the stray staked vampire as well.

Rather than a place of rest, all those last glimmerings of power had made the ground restless—a gradual ley line. The humans onboard wouldn't feel those little tendrils reaching out and up to the vehicle they rode in.

Many other witches—the type that didn't have backgrounds that required them doing more than rolling their eyes and summoning an appropriate charging cord when they were worn down at the end of the day—would.

But they would also snort in disgust, flip over the page of whatever they were reading and wait for the train to move back into some more aesthetically pleasing magical force field that didn't release tufts of barely there, decaying magic like a mushroom releasing spore clouds.

Mia's entire background was turning over what was ravaged, torn through and gutted and finding the remnant ghost of what used to be there: home, love, family.

And magic.

Like her, that magic was wandering, homeless and free.

It rose up, like dust motes, and danced around her head. It felt like the ghost of a hug. She leaned into it.

Relished it.

Let it embrace her for what she was. What few people still recognized her as.

A witch.

The mouse settled in her pocket, giddy and glutted on the slightest scraps of magic as tiny familiars tended to be.

. Thank goodness.

The train dipped toward another curve. Wanting to relish this last little bit of magic, Mia inhaled and closed her eyes.

And then, someone settled next to her.

"Excuse me," said a boy's voice.

Mia's eyes flew open.

How did she know, before turning her head, that it wouldn't just be any boy—but that boy? Cute but weirdly staring boy?

He wasn't staring so hard today, but he was looking at her. Sitting next to her. Leaning up in her space, muddling her sunlight.

This was just *ridiculous*.

"Um," he said after a moment, "hi."

The magic dissipated from Mia's skin like heat being chased off by a shadow.

She pressed her lips together hard and stared.

He held out his hand. "I'm Anthony. I… I saw you the other day, and I'm sorry… It was an off night for me but—"

"Do I look like I want to know?"

Anthony's hand froze in midair. "Excuse me?"

Mia sputtered out a laugh. Excuse *him*?

"Why are you doing this? Do you have something for thrift-shop chic? Afro puffs? A librarian fetish?"

"What? No! I mean… I mean, no!"

The boy spluttered, pulling his hand back.

The old lady two rows down had raised her head. Some smart aleck who wasn't going to intervene but could see the way the wind was blowing—which was, of course, in the direction of a viral video—held up his phone, smirking.

Usually, this would set every nerve in Mia's don't-cause-a-fuss body on edge. But there was a freaking rat-cousin squirming in her pocket, she could already hear the *We don't have an opening* letdown waiting ahead of her, and this boy had kept her from soaking up the little magic there was in her life anymore.

Now he was going to get an earful.

"Look, I'm usually really nice," Mia spat. "But you've picked the wrong girl to try and talk up. I'm not interested. Now, move."

"Is there a problem here?"

Mia's heart sank. She knew that grouchy, biting tone, even if she couldn't put a name to this particular conductor. And she also knew, sure as that scowl would curl his lips and the mole to the right of his nose would twitch upward in response, that he did not like her.

At all.

The boy glanced anxiously at her face as she turned it downward and then up at the conductor.

"No," said the boy. "I… I'm sorry."

"I didn't mean you, son," the conductor said. "You. Is there a problem here?"

"Yes," Mia said. "I mean…he was staring at me…"

"I'm patient with you because I know you have nowhere else to go and that's why you park yourself here day in and day out, but I'm going to draw the line at hysterics. Okay?"

Mia's gut clenched. She hated this man, she hated this man, she *hated* this man.

But she hated herself more for not having anything in her hands—not the strength to clench them into fists, not the magic that she should have had to shock him silly—and only being able to say, "Okay. Sorry."

The conductor turned to the boy. "Look, I'm sure this was all a misunderstanding, but you're going to need to move on to the next car."

"No. I'll go." Mia stood up, cheeks burning. She needed to get away from here. From being on display in front of other regulars, looking back and forth, murmuring.

Trading notes: *Yes, she is always on here, isn't she?*

Homeless, probably, right?

That's sad.

A flock of white, preppy witches looked at everything going on, eyes wide. She could tell they knew her, in the way all witches knew each other.

But there was also a look on their faces, under the pity: they *knew* her.

Or else, they thought they did.

An unmoored witch with nowhere else to go, surviving off the sheddings and leavings of her betters.

A pitiful creature. A leech.

The train coasted to a stop at that moment, two stops ahead of where she needed to be. It was good enough. She pushed past the conductor.

"Wait!" he called behind her, and maybe the boy did, too, but she pushed out, inhaling the steel-tinged air of the platform. The train doors slid closed behind her, taking him—them—away.

If only everything bothering her was that easy to shake off.

What Mia hates:
—Being asked, "Where do you live?"
—Being asked, "Why aren't you going home yet?"
—Being asked, "Shouldn't you be going?"
—Being asked, "Where are you headed?"
—Being asked, "Are you still in transit?"
Yes, she is still in transit.
Now and always.
Never resting. Always leaning her forehead against the smudged window and letting that cold seep into her skull.
She knows it. She doesn't need to be reminded of it.
But everyone always seems to think she does.

The mouse wouldn't let go of her knee.

It was the most annoying thing. Agnes thought it was cute.

"Just get someone to pry it off at work," she said mildly.

"Hannah Jo's off from work today," Mia said grouchily. It didn't feel like a magical morning, not like the previous day. The sky was as gray as a polluted snowdrift, and there were projected delays—particularly for the L.

Agnes waved that away. "Seriously, though, I'm glad you two are bonding. You needed this."

"Did I? Did I really?"

"He brought you that key, didn't he?"

Mia looked dubiously at the wrought iron key lying next to her purse on Agnes's kitchen table. Indeed, The Mouse (she still couldn't remember the horrible thing's name) had practically flung it into her popcorn bowl last night during a particularly fraught moment in *A Nightmare on Elm Street* and scared the living daylights out of both her and Agnes.

She wasn't sure where it had found the key or why it felt so strongly about her having it, but one social-media post later a friend of a friend's cousin was reaching out and saying that it was the cellar key he'd lost while showing a potential client a house and could she stop by his realty office and return it?

As though reading her thoughts, Agnes called out, "And it's going to get you a reward! So the luck is working already."

"He didn't say anything about a reward."

But there was no use arguing with Agnes—or, well, any witch—when the word *reward* entered their brains. In the old days, if you handled a few quests the right way, you could have a whole parcel of land handed to you.

(Hard now to imagine, as the daughter of two undocumented parents who wouldn't dare cross the threshold of an office like the one she was off to, for fear that their lack of papers would be smelled on their skin.)

She doubted there would be a reward. She doubted there would be even an offered chair or a word of thanks.

But she hopped on the train anyway—the early-afternoon one with a stop in the middle, not the bright and beautiful morning ride—and spent a few minutes bouncing her knee just for the sheer pleasure of watching the little white annoyance grip as hard as it could.

That came to an end when a group of elderly nuns gave her The Look, implying she was going to be mentioned in some very unkindly worded prayers against animal cruelty later.

It felt relieving, though, to get the kind of stares that acknowledged she was a witch, or that whatever not-normal thing she was doing should be knocked off without having a conductor looming over her.

The normal stop-being-abnormal treatment she expected anywhere, without any extra judgment that assumed she was homeless or helpless.

Instinctively, Mia craned her head, but the boy wasn't where he had been the last two times she was on a train, two seats back and to the right.

She relaxed.

Enjoyed that warm, sunlit train where magic swirled around her ankles and she could pretend it belonged to her and wasn't merely slinking up like a tentative stray cat to the nearest person with the right gene and soul-marrow to accept it.

It was fine.

She was fine.

And she stayed fine as she was ushered to a chair at the realty office—a good one, with a plump cushion—and the Realtor hemmed and hawed over the key.

"I appreciate your bringing this here," he said. "I'm not sure if I could have shown it, otherwise."

Mia's eyes lingered over the listings, and he noticed.

"In the market?"

"Not right now."

"You know where to find me if you are."

He didn't have a reward, unless you counted the themed paper fan and melted chocolates his receptionist slid her with a sympathetic smile.

Mia wandered back out, sucking on one, and stopped short.

There was a bookstore next door. She didn't really pay much attention to how it looked. It was the window display that caught her attention: an adorable explosion of paper-craft work, elegant cuttings and lovely, large fans.

She smiled. It looked like the type of thing her mom would have liked to have in their apartment window, back in the town she grew up in—back before a neighbor who didn't mean well, not at all, even if they said she did, called ICE and tentatively whispered, "I don't know if those people next door have their papers."

And then they started having to move, constantly. It caused a little ache in her chest, just remembering it. Thinking about all the days she skipped school under that dour woman's watchful eye, wondering if she was the tip-off she needed to make the call—and she wished she could give it to her mom without her mom's eyes filling with tears, without the usual questions.

Are you still blaming yourself?

Can't you just come up and see us?

She sighed and was about to turn away, when someone rattled out of the door behind her.

"Wait! Don't go!"

Oh. My. Gosh.

It was the boy from the train.

The boy. The cute, staring boy. The boy who nearly got her kicked off.

Mia turned on her heel and kept moving.

"Hey! Train Girl!"

That got her to stop. She whirled around. "Don't. Call. Me. That."

The boy raised his hands, eyes wide. "Whoa! I'm sorry."

"What do you want?"

"Look, I… I think we got off on the wrong foot yesterday. I'm not… I'm not mad."

Mia's eyes narrowed. Was he kidding?

"*You're* not mad? Shouldn't that be my line?"

"No… No, I mean…"

He pushed a hand through his hair.

"Look, I'm sorry. I know that looked really, really bad. I just wanted to ask you something."

She snorted in spite of herself. "Did it hurt when I fell from Heaven? Do I come here often?"

"Do you?"

Mia stared at him in disbelief as he spluttered, "No…wait… Really, that is what I wanted to ask but not that way."

"You look like the type to have a mama that taught you better."

"I do. She did. I…"

"Go ahead."

He leaned in closer, and she quickly leaned away. What was up with this guy?

"What's your sign?" he hissed.

Mia stared at him a moment, mouth wide. And then she started laughing.

"What?"

His face reddened, and he sharply rapped out, "What?"

"Are you trying to ask me if I'm a witch?"

He gave an awkward shrug. "All the magazines say it's more polite to ask for your sign. That witches know."

"That's so old-fashioned."

She smiled at him, reluctantly. He was such a dork, she couldn't help it.

"I'm a Cancer. If you must know. And yes, I'm a witch."

He brightened. "Cool. I'm a Virgo. Nonmagical." And then, to her surprise, he suddenly blushed. "And...what do those two signs make together?"

For a moment, Mia stared at him, his bright eyes and the freckles over the bridge of his nose. This boy, who belonged here and didn't have to wander on and off the L.

"Utter incompatibility," she lied and made to leave. He grabbed her hand.

"Wait. At least stay for coffee."

"I'll pass."

"Come on. You just got here."

He dragged her behind him as she spluttered protests. And then, she stopped dead. The words were ash in her mouth.

Because she was in the bookstore, and it was gorgeous. Mahogany bookshelves lined every wall from ceiling to floor, and the places they weren't leaned up against revealed beautiful, exposed brick. The floor was polished wood, lined here and there with elegant, aged carpets and open crates with books spilling out like a just-opened Christmas present left by an excitable kid.

"This is…" Mia gasped, trailing her hand along a shelf. "I've never been in a bookstore like this in my life."

"Do you like it?" the boy asked anxiously.

Mia turned to look at him. Again, she couldn't help that smile.

"I love it."

He exhaled, as though it really mattered to him—as though it made a huge difference for him. So weird.

But weirder than that…

Mia stopped and stared down at the line of little neat miniature houses. There was a small avenue of them along the small check-out desk.

"Are those…?"

"Familiar houses?" The boy puffed out his chest proudly. "Yep. I've seen some on the street now and then, and I thought it would be nice to offer them sanctuary."

"That's so cool."

Mia bent down and then startled as the mouse darted out of her pocket and into a house. It popped its head out, whiskers twitching.

"Look at that!" the boy crowed. "One already!"

Mia smiled ruefully at the little pest.

"Look at you. That's pretty cozy."

If only it was so easy for everyone to find a home like that. She lifted herself to her feet.

"I gotta go and nestle down myself. It's getting dark."

"Oh." The boy frowned, and then, when she reached for the handle, blurted out one word.

"Anthony."

"Huh?"

"Oh…uh…my name. It's Anthony. Remember?"

Mia paused for a moment, remembering they'd done this part before. Or, at least, he had. What could it hurt to reciprocate? What could it hurt?

"Mia. Not Train Girl."

"Noted. Sorry about that." Anthony fidgeted for a moment and then said, "Come back and visit. I'm sure your friend would like it."

Mia looked down at the mouse in its little house, and her heart ached.

"Maybe," she said softly.

Maybe. If she could stand the sight of someone lost finding their way home, when she never would.

* ◊ *

It was Christmas when their house burned down.

And that wasn't even the worst time. Or the first time.

It just happened to be the time that was Mia's fault.

Her parents never said a word about it. About the fact that she should have known better than to put a paper towel into a toaster oven, should have scalded her own fingers on the hot toast and sucked them sensitive and soft again rather than done a fool thing like that when they were both away at jobs with bosses who didn't raise their brows at their lack of paperwork.

But the house burned. And they didn't have a deed to their name or good friends to turn to, and the old lady next door was raising her eyebrows at how hushed it got when an unfamiliar van passed by.

So they wandered.

They wandered, and everywhere they went, a child turning out herself to go to school and showing up to banks and insurance companies on her parents' behalf and always, always finding the right words to explain why she couldn't go on a trip or apply for anything solid and grounded brought eyes.

Watchful eyes. Narrowed eyes.

And then, she started losing her magic. And even though her parents hadn't said a word—they never would—she could see the lines carving into their foreheads, the heavy sighs, the nights she would startle from sleep to find her mother staring down at her through an unfamiliar mask of fear and sorrow with her heavy, calloused hand on Mia's head.

They worried for her.

They were held back by her.

So she broke off and learned how to wander on her own.

She broke off and—hapless and homeless—learned how to find a space to briefly call her own in crowded train cars, just enough to keep up her magic so she wasn't siphoning off theirs, just enough to stay alive so they didn't worry or look for her and had time to feed themselves and keep going.

And that was where it all began.

It was always hard when Mama got sniffly on her about her not coming to visit.

"You promised last month!"

"Ma," Mia sighed. "Really, I'm trying. I really am. I am so sorry it's so disappointing, but, well…the library's busy."

"They can't spare you just for a weekend so your mama can make sure she can't see your ribs?"

"You can't see my ribs, Ma. I eat."

She held the phone away from her ear, looking at the line of applicants for this job ahead of her. It was a disheartening sight, as much as she tried to talk herself out of it: not even a top-tier data-entry job, just some part-time spreadsheeting and documenting for a little hole-in-the-wall furniture warehouse.

And yet, every spare chair in the waiting room had someone in it.

Someone was gushing about this being her gap year, and even with Mama yammering on about how thin she was sure Mia had gotten since she last saw her, she couldn't tune it out.

This was her gap year, too.

Or, well, the second one in a row.

She'd been in the process of finishing high school since she moved here.

She wasn't fancy enough for the witch preparatory, and public school kind of let the witches move about unmoored— not bothering them, but not giving them the training they needed, either.

She was working her way along on both sides: picking up spare tome-title recommendations off this coworker, rushing to take a seat in the back of a GED class wherever she could.

She was trying.

"I just want you to be grounded at some point," Mama said, and Mia sighed.

"Me, too."

She held back the instinct to remind her mama that she wasn't exactly grounded, either. Bouncing between relatives' basements and guest bedrooms or wherever she and her dad could get squeezed in wasn't exactly an anchored, easy life, either.

She headed in after Gap Year Girl and faced a hostile-looking group of supervisors. They noted her lack of an address right from the get-go, and she sighed.

It was going to be another one of those days.

It wasn't until she was trailing out with a curt "We'll be in touch" at her heels that she realized she knew where she was.

The bookstore was three blocks down.

She hesitated, looking in that direction.

It was going to be out of the way. She had promised Agnes she'd help with dinner.

And, most importantly, it was going to make Anthony too hyped to see her.

Mia looked between the subway entrance and the street. She sighed.

The doorbell jangled over her head as she stepped over the threshold. And, of course, with the worst timing in the world, Anthony was right there by it, rearranging some paperbacks on a rotating bookshelf.

His face lit up when he saw who was hovering in the doorway.

"Mia! I didn't know you'd be this way today!"

"Oh, um…" Mia stumbled over her words, face flushing. Why did he have to be so ridiculously cute and happy all the time? "I had an interview a few blocks down…"

She waved her hand in that direction, realizing a moment later she was pointing the wrong way.

Ugh.

But Anthony didn't laugh. He didn't ask how the interview went. He just…smiled.

"Well, I'm glad your feet found their way here afterward."

Before Mia could read too much into what *that* meant, there was a loud exclamation of joy behind her.

"Girl, you're my lucky charm!" An elder woman rushed up to her, graying dreads swinging as she beamed and reached out to squeeze Mia's shoulder. "I thought I was going to leave here without the first edition I was looking for, and it was right on the end of the shelf."

Anthony's eyes widened. "Whoa, really? I looked there for you twice!"

The woman nodded, looking gratefully at Mia.

"You're magic, aren't you?"

As though responding to the mere word, Mia could feel it suddenly: a sudden, strong swell, like a breeze picking up and flinging itself confidently into a gale. It swirled beneath her feet and up her arms.

Yes. Magic.

Magic that recognized her, wanted to be tapped into by her.

The woman was strolling off to the register, but Anthony stared at Mia.

"Did you feel that?" His smile came back, even wider than before. His eyes shimmered with wonder, for her.

At her.

Yes. She did feel it.

"That hasn't happened in a while," she mumbled dazedly.

Anthony reached out and gently put a hand over hers.

"Maybe it's a sign that you're meant to stop in more often," he said. "Bring us some magic we need around here."

"Maybe," Mia said slowly. "When I have time."

More time spent at the bookstore, less on finding jobs.

As it turns out, there is time for Mia to linger.

It's dangerous for a witch to linger. It means she's letting moss gather on her back. It means she's attaching herself to a place because she has nowhere else more important to be.

For once, Agnes has a frown on her face—a thoughtful one, but a tight, little line that is at odds with her dimples.

"You haven't taken the L so much."

Why is there a reason to take it when magic sparks off the walls at the bookstore, when she can stand on a stool under a customer's awed stare and find the cozy mystery they've wanted for months without knowing exactly what their reading appetite needed?

"I have another place to be."

"You're putting down roots," Agnes says. "Is it because of the boy?"

A cute boy always helps. But it isn't that. Not fully. Not really.

More time spent at the bookstore, more time spent seeping in magic.

Agnes frowns, worry lines visible around her eyes.

"If you're not ready to put down roots, be careful of where you stand. It'll be hard to pull yourself back up when the time comes."

When it's time.

Sometime.

But for now, more time at the bookstore.

Agnes's concerns niggled at Mia's chest as she stacked books on the shelf, letting Anthony's idle patter about whatever movie he watched last night flow in one ear and out the other.

Usually, she would be feeling some kind of way about the fact that he was supposed to be two shelves down but had insisted that two heads were better than one (Just for rearranging a shelf of romances? Anthony, please.) and settled down right next to her so their shoulders touched.

He had such nice, broad shoulders.

But Agnes's voice was in the back of her head.

She'd waved off her friend's concerns, but now, she couldn't. Was she really putting down roots without even realizing it?

Then again, though, what did Agnes know about any of it? She had a cozy brownstone apartment with a sweet (if Mia said so herself) roommate who...well, didn't always pitch in rent as she should but could cook nice meals to make up for it, and a gorgeous sorcerer boyfriend in pre-med just like her who planned to propose next year.

She had a cute familiar, owned nice clothes to lend to friends who didn't have them, and only took the train when she wanted to.

What did she know about roots, when she had so many of them already tethered and never had to worry about them being pulled up?

A knot formed in Mia's stomach.

Wait.

The L. When was the last time she took the L?

When was the last time she took the train? To be honest, she'd been walking to the bookstore most days. It was a bit of a trek, but...well, Anthony pretending he had something to do in the vicinity of Agnes's apartment and then asking if she wanted to help him cart back the groceries or books he had with him or whatever was a great incentive to not take the train.

"Mia?" Anthony looked concerned. "You okay?"

Mia forced a smile. "Yeah. Yeah. I just…"

She was trying to tally the days in her head the same way she would for a late period. Two weeks? No. It had to be more, considering that one branch of the library had cycled her out for their summer schedule and the other was undergoing renovations.

How could she not have realized?

"You sure? I…"

Anthony stood abruptly, forgetting about the stack of books at his feet. Mia flung her hands out, eyes wide.

"Anthony!"

Anthony was already tumbling backward, though, eyes wide.

And then—he stopped. In midair.

For a wild, wonderful moment, Mia thought it was her. That her outstretched hand had done something.

And then, she felt it. The thrumming of the shop. That strong, powerful, intense energy. Not through her. But of its own accord.

Holding him up.

Mia stood up herself, eyes wide as Anthony spluttered.

"Mia… Mia… I…"

But his voice trailed off. He knew. He knew, and now he knew that she knew that he knew.

"Oh," she said hollowly. "So the store is…"

A ley line.

Just like the train. Just a stronger, older, more reliable one.

One that could convince her that she was doing the magic, right alongside the boy egging her on with those sweet smiles to believe that she was actually a witch getting her power back.

"Mia," Anthony said, reaching out for her. He stumbled as she backed away, but the store steadied him.

"Goodbye, Anthony."

"Mia! Come on. Really, it's not what you…"

Mia turned on her heel and walked out the door. She could hear Anthony behind her, and she just sped up.

She took the turn into the subway entrance, walked down to the platform, and watched the L pull out without her on it.

She sat there, staring at the trains coming in and out.

It wasn't her.

It never was.

She's tried to be brave, all this time, but she's tired.
She's tired of the L.
She's tired of wandering.
She's tired of being disappointed—by people, by jobs, by magic.

* ◊ *

Another day, another interview. Mia wasn't in the mood to borrow blazers or tights. She wore one of her own sweaters, nearly outgrown jeans and Tilda's gold hoops.

She slouched in the chair and didn't look up as the woman

hummed over that spot on her résumé. It would be the same. It always was.

But then, there was a surprised sound. A flicking of papers.

"You work at the little bookstore on Fifth? I love that place!"

"What?"

Mia leaned over, staring down at her own résumé. Surely it wasn't really... But there it was, in neat print: *Bookstore witch (weekends)*.

Agnes!

"I... Well..." Mia fumbled. How could she possibly explain that her roommate had put it on there when she didn't even know why she would? As a joke? To make a point?

But to Mia's surprise, the woman laughed.

"That's so charming! I haven't heard of a bookstore witch before, but it sounds so right. I'm sure they're glad to have such an accomplished one, too."

"A-accomplished?"

"Working at several libraries, freelancing, volunteer work?" The woman shook her head. She looked...impressed. Astonished.

No one had ever looked like that during an interview before.

"Honestly, you're so good I hate to tell you this, but I'm pretty sure the position is going to be filled internally. Not something I agree with, but..."

"I see." Mia bowed her head. So, it was going to end the way it always did. "Thanks, anyway."

"Now, hold on." The lady slid a card across the desk. "That's my personal email. We might not have an open position yet, but I'm willing to make one open for you. It's not every day a bookstore witch comes in and wants to take a job like weekend data entry when she could be behind a check-in desk. In the future, at least."

Mia's eyes widened.

"Really?"

The lady's eyes twinkled. "I look forward to setting up another appointment with you, Mia. We'll see what I can do to help."

In a daze, Mia wandered outside, still grasping the card.

What had just happened?

It took her a moment to realize someone was waiting by the wall—and when she recognized him, her back stiffened.

"Whatever you want to say, I'm not interested," Mia said coldly. "You can go right back to Agnes and tell her that I'm not interested in anything she has to say, either, until I get a new résumé and an apology."

Anthony flinched. "Look, I know you're mad…"

"I am. Very."

"But," he pushed on, "I need to take you somewhere. Somewhere important."

"I'm not going back to the bookstore. Not when you— when it was fooling me all this time."

"It's not like that…with the store, I mean. If you would just listen… Anyway, just come with me."

Mia followed him, reluctantly, down the street and stairs into the subway platform. She stopped short at what waited beyond the turnstiles.

Mia gasped.

"Why…is this the L train? What is it doing here?"

"It's going to be retired," Anthony said grimly.

Mia could only stare at him in horror.

"What?"

What would she do without the L train? Out of every shock she'd gotten today, this hit the hardest.

"Look, I... That can change. I just need to show you something inside, alright? I need you to trust me and just follow my lead."

Mia stared at him. "Must everything you say sound like it's from some Disney Channel movie?"

He flushed.

"Look, just...come here."

She let herself be dragged in and then stopped short.

"Is that—"

Anthony beamed, throwing his arm out grandly.

"Ta-da!"

It was her seat. In her car. Well, it wasn't her seat, not completely, or her car—not at all. But it was the one she liked to plop into the most when it was available, leaning her head back against the window and letting the sun and magic sparks soak into her hair.

It was glowing, with magic, in the exact outline of her body.

Mia stepped forward, swallowing hard. There was no denying it. She could feel the magic pulsing through her body, and for once it wasn't anonymous, wasn't that tasteless crackle across her lips and skin, like Pop Rocks without any sugar to them.

It was her aura. Her signature.

Her, like she hadn't been able to feel her own magical presence in years.

She had done that. Well, maybe the train had helped. Claimed her. Given her a space.

But how was that possible? It wasn't a house, or an apartment building, or the department of a library.

How could it even choose her as its witch?

She put her hand on the seat and felt it warm her.

"I went to see Tilda," Anthony was explaining. "I was trying to reach you, and she had your phone. She said you forgot it this morning, but I really needed you to see this. See that the train missed it. It was waiting for you."

Mia felt her eyes stinging. It missed her?

He cleared his throat.

"The bookstore…is thinking of making an investment. In the L. They want to park it on the lines and make it a second location, for witches particularly who like hanging out near a designated ley line. We were wondering—well, I really suggested it—we wanted a bookstore witch. We wanted you to be…our witch. It'll be paid. Whatever you want, the manager said. Benefits, too. He was really excited about it."

Their witch.

Mia felt her jaw go slack. She couldn't find the words. But Anthony tumbled on, his mouth full of them.

"You see that seat? Everywhere you've been between the shelves glows so much brighter than that. Your familiar showed me how to look for them. Okay, not really, but watching it made me realize. The store droops when you aren't there. It's like…it loses all its starch. And when you're not on the train, it loses all its warmth. All its magic."

"The magic gathers around me," Mia mumbled. "Because I'm a witch."

"Yes," Anthony said and rested his hand on top of hers. "Because you're a witch. A wonderful witch. You know that song, where the birds just want to be close to you…the way the singer does? It's like that. The magic just wants to be close to you, and when you're not there… I feel like all the magic has gone out of the world."

Mia gave a watery laugh.

"Oh my gosh, you have to be kidding me with that corny stuff."

Anthony blinked, affronted.

"No! I mean it! I… Mia, have you ever *seen* yourself? I know you feel you're some bad witch, but you're amazing. I mean, why else do I feel like I need to do a handstand or learn some card tricks to impress you?"

Mia blinked.

"You…what?"

"I-I didn't mean to say that," Anthony mumbled. His ears were steadily turning pink. "I mean, okay, well, I said that, and it's true. One hundred percent. When you're around, all I can think about is making sure you stay. You shine, Mia. It never was the store itself that made that burst of magic when you stepped in. It could only do that because it was trying to show off for the witch that stepped in. It likes you. Loves you, even… Me, too."

Anthony was clinging to her hand now, and Mia was clinging right back. Neither of them could look each other in the eye.

This was just…ridiculously Hallmark.

"I knew when you told me your sign you'd be trouble."

"Totally incompatible, right?"

"Maybe not."

She let his hand linger above hers and brushed her hand across the seat again beneath it. She looked back up at him, life in her eyes.

Is this what Merlin felt, when Arthur asked him to form a seat at Camelot?

She could see it all unfolding in her head: a steady job, a good paycheck, time to study for the SATs with him at her side, time to lay down roots when the time was right and help her family set down their roots, too.

"Okay." Mia exhaled and smiled. "Let's make this happen."

*   *   *   *   *

LEO

Venus in Leo

* Loves spoiling and being spoiled
* Drawn to drama and grand displays
  of romance
* Requires honesty, integrity, and loyalty
* Needs fun and attention
* Pushed away by any perceived
  ambivalence

Alternative Combustion
Kiana Nguyen

Princess didn't do crushes because she was a sucker for love. It had to do a little with the thrill of being scared and a little with the way Lala spoke as if each word was carefully chosen for Princess to hear. To be fair, that could be the simping talking. She liked the good ol' comfortable IG stalk from afar on a baddie whose TikTok she came across on her For You Page at three in the morning. Not this real-life *I'm gonna see you in the halls every day and at my girl's girlfriend's place every weekend because we're in a close group of friends*. The only light in the dark tunnel was that they hadn't dated any of the same people as far as Princess knew. The thought of Lala hooking up with any of her exes while she hadn't gone past second base was something she hid in a dark vault in an unwritten diary entry sprayed with holy water.

"Cheer up, buttercup. You look like you got socked in the throat." Her best friend, Nami, jostled her shoulder with her skateboard. Looked a little too cool doing it, too. Nami had never had an awkward stage.

"'Snot far from the truth, my dude. You didn't tell me they were gonna be here!" Princess pointed wildly at Lala, feeling sweat begin to gather beneath her boobs. Lala did a kickflip off the roof of someone's busted SUV, their long locs flying behind them as they sailed through the air and somehow managed to land wheels to ground. Nami had the nerve to act like this wasn't an act of war against her mental health when Princess found herself at a loss for sense around the nonbinary heartthrob.

"You're dragging it, Princess," Nami said, eyeing her from her curly mane to her holey Vans. Clocking Princess's BS like only a best friend could.

"You love sabotaging me, and it's getting old."

"How did I sabotage you when you're out here pointing and hollering?"

Princess steepled her hands over her eyes and silently screamed into her lap.

"We gotta get you an Emmy for that performance." Nami clucked her tongue.

The problem: across the empty parking lot, where their friends regularly parked to skate, hang, and stir up drama, the hottest person she'd ever known was having the time of their life completely ignoring her. Not even on purpose. The idea of Lala knowing of Princess the way she knew of them was high-key the worst thing she could ever think of.

"The thing isn't that you're afraid to talk to them, it's that you're afraid to like them." Nami announced this like an award, a gift of fortune.

It made the anxiety prickling in her belly worse. And it didn't make any sense being afraid of something that already happened. But Princess's feelings never made sense as they bubbled and curdled within her at any sign of encouragement.

"I am not doing this again," I said. It was a lot of work, connecting with the person you liked, getting to know them, sharing parts of yourself you hadn't really confronted on your own. Had never confronted. Never even acknowledged.

That's what blogs were for, but Tumblr was played out.

"You still haven't done it first."

"Chill out. You get wifed and all of a sudden you're the guru of romance." Princess clucked her tongue.

"Ay, don't do my girl like that," Keema piped up from where she lounged against the back of Nami's rusted third-hand Toyota. Nami pressed her cheek against her lil' stud girlfriend and sighed.

Insufferable, truly, to learn that under the bad-bitch personality, Nami was softer than the Sugar Plum Fairy. Ever since she started dating her girl, Nami was swooning all damn day and swerving the reckless lifestyle they'd once shared. No more midnight runs to Kennedy's after getting high and watching *Jeepers Creepers*. Not that Princess was bitter or anything, she just wouldn't go down like that. Hadn't so far either, but she had terrible taste in partners.

The slick kiss of wheel to asphalt hit like a shock to her

system. She was quaking by the time Lala braked in front of her and kicked their board into their hands. Tony Hawk could never.

Lala dapped Keema. "What's good, baby?" Voice low and gritty, sinking beneath her skin.

Princess nodded like she was the one being spoken to. If she could, she would rub herself in poison ivy. It would feel better than the prickling itch of embarrassment.

Lala tilted her head to Princess. They said, "Hey," as Keema leaned forward to answer.

"Trying to get my girl to leave the streets, but her loyalty is unmatched." Keema wiped away a fake tear.

Nami dropped her board and, before speeding off, said, "The streets of where, Keema? Binghamton barely has a Main Street."

"See what I mean? Cruel and unusual."

Crueler to Princess who was left alone to fend for herself with Nami's girlfriend, who she still barely knew because the two were constantly ditching her to huff each other's air or whatever, and the person who kept her up all hours of the night writing sad poems on scraps of paper about because she refused not to have something to show for her suffering.

"Them Geminis. Can't hold 'em down." Lala pulled back the locs framing their long face and tied them with a frayed satin scrunchie.

"Say less, man." Keema shook her head.

"You seeing what's on the wall and cricking your neck to run away from it. SMH."

And they said it exactly like that: s-m-h. Each letter gliding from their tongue in a honeyed wave. She normally hated acronyms, especially so when people said out loud what was meant for texting. But something about this struck a note within her, and she had to stop herself from giggling. So that's why she chose to speak up, to dampen the urge to find completely arbitrarily annoying things cute in one person.

"Y'all gotta be kidding with this," Princess said.

Keema huffed. Lala turned their deep-set brown eyes on her and waited, but Keema shivered and thumbed her mouth.

"My baby's Cancer moon makes up for it," Keema said, not clearing up anything for Princess. That was the embarrassing thing, attempting to decipher the codes flying from their mouths, over her face, and through her ears in incomprehensible patterns.

"You can go 'head and tell ya girl I mean that." By the steady eye contact, dude wanted her to go over right now.

"Nah, I'm good," Princess responded, patting Keema's shoulder as the latter scratched her nose and slumped back against the car.

"Tell me what you mean." Lala stepped closer, invading her senses.

There were three problems with being the sole focus of their attention. Lala had heavy brows set low over droopy hooded brown eyes that made Princess feel like her skin was being peeled away to reveal the soft wants she was too afraid to say aloud and make real. To run away from their eyes, she ended up looking at their nose, which was strong and broad and pierced with a silver hoop that brought out the deep blues in their rich brown skin, which typically made her too flustered to breathe so she ended up letting her eyes fall—only to be completely taken in by Lala's wide smile, the way the Cupid's bow dipped low over their teeth.

It was hard for Princess to mean anything when it felt like everything only existed when Lala looked at her like that.

That was what a crush felt like for her. The idea that love could compound this feeling was terrifying. And that fear gave her enough ammunition to say, "You can't seriously believe in astrology."

Keema snorted but waved away Princess's passing glance.

Lala let their board rest flat to the ground, lashes dropping low as they scraped Princess clean from her holey Vans up to her dandelion fluff of curls.

So when they asked her what her birthday was, she answered quickly, hoping they'd forget what they might have seen in her.

"April twenty-fifth."

Keema squawked, no joke, but Lala idly held up their finger. God, it was somehow the hottest thing she'd ever seen. One of the shitty lot's lights caught the glint of the silver chain around their neck, and Princess longed to hold it in between her teeth for a faint taste of their skin.

"Ruled by Venus." Lala said this deeply, a rasp that melted over Princess.

"And what does that mean?" Princess asked, irritated. Wanting this to be over, to be done with, wanting this moment to never end. Wanting to feel the way her heart slowed for fear this moment wasn't real at all. But it could end, at any moment, and she didn't want it to. Dangerous.

Lala grabbed her hand, palm steady and warm as they wrapped their fingers over her hand and brought Princess's palm to their chest, the beat of their heart so strong Princess no longer felt her own.

"It means, baby, that *this* wasn't meant for you." Lala dropped her hand and shrugged.

It didn't matter that Princess was staunchly avoiding any attempts by her silly little heart to undermine her will in resisting crushes and love and the way Lala made standing still interesting, her heart fucking plummeted. She wanted to be meant for someone, particularly the person she currently wanted to kick in the shin for not knowing the power of their astrological rejection.

"Tauruses and Leos, Princess. Not good," Keema offered up, probably seeing the tears wrenched in her soul.

Before Princess could even ask for a guided tour through their cryptic riddles, a lone, weather-beaten security car drove into the lot, popping off a short siren. Most of the group didn't need more warning than that, belting off on wheels and feet out of there as a dud of a man in a cheap uniform exited the car.

Unfortunately, they couldn't leave Nami's car here to get her plate read and were forced to interact with a guy that had nothing better to do than harass kids on a Saturday night.

"Alrighty there. Let's pack it up." He held his thumbs in his belt loops, relaxed with not a care in the world.

"We're not doing anything. We're just hanging out." Princess bristled, a lump in her throat. With nothing to do in this no-good town, he really wanted to get up in arms about skateboarding in an empty, unused parking lot?

"I need this clear in sixty seconds, sweetheart." The guard twirled his finger as he popped a stick of gum.

"Alright, you got it, but we can only move so fast." Lala moved between Keema and the guard, as the girl started to get visibly upset, and made sure to shift so Princess was guarded with their shoulder. "We have to wait for our friend to get here for her car."

Quite frankly, Princess almost shriveled up and died from a burst of full-blown idolatry. Which she was blaming, for now and forever, on panic.

Before Keema could speak, flashing red and blue lights glided over them as a couple of cop cars rolled into the lot. The three of them shifted, and Princess sighed in relief as Nami bustled over to them, but Keema had had enough.

"Y'all really draggin' it," Keema got in as the cops came to a stop.

The security guy bared his teeth. "Go."

Just as Nami reached the car, just as a can of Arizona iced tea smashed into the windshield of their car, just as Princess realized Nami would need a few moments to get behind the wheel and drive off without her license plate getting clocked.

"I love cardio." Princess grinned at the guard, faking out an attempt to grab his radio to give Nami a chance to start her car. As soon as the car peeled off, she darted away and toward the back lot where there were trees, almost stumbling from admiring how graceful Lala was on their board as they hurtled away.

Per reality and her love of sitting, lounging, and napping, because she was a liar and did not love cardio, Princess was out of breath well before she reached the trees, but it was worth not getting fucked with by some chump-ass mall cop with a raging hard-on for ruining children's lives.

She couldn't see anyone by the time she got into the thick

of the small forest but caught stray pairings of footprints in the dirt. Princess had no business cheating during the mile in gym, and now look at her, stranded.

Her phone rang, and she picked up Nami's call to subject herself to worried chiding. "Where are you, man? It's dark as hell, and you have those ankles that break when you kick twigs."

"I can and will argue that you got away because of my quick thinking."

"Quick thinking? Dude, you looked like you'd caught a muscle spasm."

"Well! I was just trying to distract him, damn! Stop yelling at me, please. *I'm* the one alone!"

"I'm right here."

Princess screeched and jumped away from Lala, who had the nerve to be startled that she was startled. "You were not *here* a second ago," Princess said. Her freaking heart was about to fly out of her chest, it was beating so fast.

Lala thumbed their mouth, eyes flitting to the ground. Princess thought it was sweet until she realized they were holding back a laugh. "I circled back once I couldn't hear you huffing behind me."

Huffing could be good; huffing could remind Lala of other things…which would be worse because Princess was pretty sure she was demisexual, and who knew how long it would be until she was that connected to Lala to want to get hot and heavy. She'd just made it to wanting to hold hands and kiss what she'd heard from her dreams were pillow-soft lips.

"What a savior. Don't know what I would do without you," Princess said. But she knew: she'd get a good night's sleep and stop daydreaming.

"Heh, I'm sure you'd be able to figure something out."

"Princess? Who's that?" Nami's voice filtered through the phone still squashed to her ear, pulling her away from the soft, fluttering feeling that had sprouted in her chest like new flower buds tickled by a gentle breeze. Most people thought she was useless, incapable of anything other than getting into trouble. Lala didn't think that?

"What's up, Nami." Lala leaned in close to Princess to pass on her message.

"You stay lying, P. Alright, just meet us over at Kennedy's."

"You gonna order me one with cocoa bread, right? Hello?" Princess peeled the phone back to see her screensaver staring straight back at her. Useless. Best friends were useless.

"Nami says they went to Kennedy's for beef patties and headed to Keema's place after."

"Dope."

Princess didn't actually think it was dope. She thought it was court-ordered torture. So she said, "Yeah," and swallowed past her dread.

"Waiting for you, Princess." Lala gestured into the thicket that would take them toward the east side of the town, toward Kennedy's.

Princess instantly started moving, as she said, "The problem with that is that I am navigationally inferior. I wasn't a Boy Scout." She broke out her phone to bring up the GPS.

"I didn't know they taught skills along gender lines." Lala slinked alongside her like the cool anime character with a broody past would. If it wasn't for the board tucked to their side, she was sure they'd have their heavily ringed hands in their pockets. Better to slouch their shoulders with.

"To be fair, I don't know a lick about the scouts. Is it fucked up that the girls are only known for their cookies?"

"Sounds like a you problem more than their image problem. They do mad humanitarian work and outreach."

Seriously, the fact that Lala knew anything at all about a children's organization that Princess never had the opportunity to enlist in because of a childhood split between daycare and Boys & Girls Club was oddly charming.

"Were you a scout?"

"Nah. I just got a thing about organized children's activities. You putting mad energy into this one thing that basically directs how your personality grows, and we're not even talking about little-league sports and what that does. It trips me out thinking about how much impact and influence it has on you. Not like anything as hopeful that you're a more selfless person, but, like, how much more goal- and achievement-oriented you are versus someone who was never in."

This was the most Princess had ever heard Lala speak—well, spoken to *her*—and it was absolutely not a good thing. Before, Lala was just a hot person with fucking bedroom eyes, a sick boarder with a goofy-foot stance; now that she'd gotten a peek into their spirited thoughtfulness, Princess felt cheated. By her feelings, by Lala's inability to be admired and not heard, by the goddamn freaking stars. The great thing about being from Binghamton was that she could flip off those big, juicy diamonds firing misfortune upon her weak soul. So she did.

"So, what regulated childhood activity leads you to astrology?" Princess asked Lala when she'd gathered what was left of her dignity.

Lala stopped walking and rested their skateboard on their

wide shoulder. "I've been waiting for you to bring that up." Something about the stance was screaming f-boy but was simultaneously breathtaking. They closed their eyes and shuddered like they wore a heavy weight.

Princess had never regretted saying anything before more, alarmed that a joking question was leading somewhere else.

"Being queer," Lala said with a straight face that lasted the five seconds it took for Princess to catch up.

"I'm so done with you," Princess declared, stomping away.

"You've barely gotten started with me," Lala said lowly, which was possible because they were once again toe-to-toe with her. Lungs of steel on this one.

Luckily, it was dark, and shadows hopefully hid the way Princess glanced around for a bush to jump into and never come out of.

Princess flicked her own forehead. "Crap, I forgot to look up the directions. I've never walked there from this far out."

But she only bought herself the few seconds it took to plug in the address and get oriented. "Cool, we've been walking in the wrong direction for a couple of minutes," Princess said, shrugging, as they looked over her shoulder.

"From God's lips." Lala then, in the most thrilling way that felt unreal, licked their lips and made eye contact. Which felt like a kiss, pretty damn near as good as one.

After turning around and reorienting, they finally cleared the end of the thicket onto a residential sidewalk, clear of crap security guards and neighborly entities. Just Princess and Lala with enough streetlight to gawk and be smooth about it.

"Do we think ol' boy has a mouth? Like in the sense that there's a physical body attached?"

"Don't care enough to think about it," Lala said.

She didn't know why, but that made them even more attractive.

"Notice how I haven't asked you about your relationship with lying?"

Notice how I'm six seconds away from being in love with you? She wasn't going to keep it together.

"I can't, for the life of me, figure out where you got that question from."

Lala put her hands to her ear like she was using an early-2000s cell phone. "Nami got a loud voice."

And Nami's got a first-class ticket to these hands, too.

There was no way to avoid it, though, as Princess's brain faltered for anything even mediocrely interesting to say around them. It sucked being your own worst wingperson; she had a feeling avoiding the question wouldn't have the results she wanted.

"If you're really feeling a way about it, you don't have to share. I'm just teasing you." Lala reached out, the amethyst on their middle finger glinting, then pulled back. "Are you cool with being touched?"

That's when Princess's heart stuttered, stopped, and sped up like it was rebooting and recalibrating to a new state of function. She'd never been asked that before. Touch was one of those things most people took as a given, a mandatory part of normal communal existence. But it meant something for Lala to ask that, that requesting was a part of their lexicon rather than blithely taking something from Princess she wasn't confident in restricting. There were so many parts of her taken without her permission, it never occurred to her that she could withhold. Or that she could consent to sharing something of herself and take joy in it.

"Yeah, I am. Thanks for asking." Her words were soft as she said them, shy and earnest. Words that she didn't for once want to shove back between her teeth.

Lala smiled, their dark brown eyes clear and focused on her. It was unnerving. Not that she hadn't been seen before, but that Lala looked at her without seeming to count down the moments until they had to look away. Whenever Princess looked at them, it felt rushed and forbidden, like she needed to memorize every little detail from the beauty mark above the left curve of Lala's mouth to the ridged scar on their chin.

Lala looked at her like they had all the time in the world.

"Sweet. You have a cobweb on your shoulder, I think." Lala reached for it while Princess died a thousand times.

They only wanted to touch her because of a grubby fugging spiderweb on her hand-me-down pullover. How ideal.

"There we go," Lala said when they finished. "All clean, storyteller."

That's when Princess resumed walking, avoiding the smug dimple that presented itself on Lala's face.

"You don't even understand! This story is easily the most anticlimactic thing you'll ever hear, and if you pass out from boredom on me after midnight on one of these shitty streets, I'll leave you there and think of you fondly."

"You'll be thinking of me," Lala said as they got into step and shrugged.

This is the part where fourth-grader-level-you're-yucky flirting left Princess ill-equipped to decipher. Lala could be being funny or could be implanting the seed of wanting Princess to think about them. Then again, Lala was pretty upfront, as she was learning, so wouldn't they just say that? Though, telling someone to think of you sounded straight out of fools town and not something they'd say or mean.

Anyway.

"I want to preface this by saying that I blame Nami. Mostly for not realizing how little street smarts I had because I spent too much of my time reading manga at that age. We were fourteen, though, so still highly embarrassing."

Lala nodded, then grabbed Princess by the shoulder to stop her from stepping into the street as a car whizzed by.

"I see what you mean by lacking street smarts," Lala quipped, and it pained her in the most delicious way as she laughed. Couldn't help but laugh.

Bad jokes were her undoing.

"Let's just stop here," Lala said and promptly took a seat on the ground. Princess almost tripped over them, it was so sudden. Then they had the nerve to look at her expectantly, shooing her.

"Get to the story, Princess. You can turn off the GPS, too. I know where we're going from here."

Which was great because Princess honestly forgot she even had the app on. She didn't remember the last time she heard a direction alert.

"For Nami's birthday, her grandma took us to see the Harlem Globetrotters at the Arena, and we were, like, mad excited."

Lala nodded. "Who doesn't love the Globetrotters?"

"We don't mention my enemies, alright?"

"Say less, I got you." Lala made a noise in the back of their throat, though.

"You know how they do their halftime shows? They asked if anyone could sing."

Lala crowed like a fiendish witch. Princess covered her ears, the only way she could get through telling the end.

"And I really said to myself that they were talking to me, so I raised my hand and was led down to the court and then I sang 'Genie in a Bottle' like I had a frog in my throat."

After Princess got out that excruciating sentence, there was a fleeting second of silence. Where Lala was sat on the dirty sidewalk, their legs crossed around their board, hugging it to their chest, and looked up at her. Where Princess noticed the dry patch on their knee and the scar that ran along the front of one shin. Where she anxiously, desperately, obsessively wanted to sit on the grody sidewalk next to Lala and talk for hours.

Lala clapped. "You weren't kidding. We have to get you some better stories, babe."

And there it was.

Princess knocked her thigh with her fist, bit her lip, then locked her knees against her fear.

"I'm really not sure, but I have to ask or I might never. Can I kiss you?"

She couldn't look up from the toughened glob of pink bubblegum next to her shoe. Her brain was even nice enough to conjure up the possible expressions that must be flying across Lala's face. She'd liked people before, had kissed people before, but had never quite felt so unbearably vulnerable.

"You might have been waiting to ask me, but I've been waiting to answer."

Princess didn't respond, sure she'd actually been hit by that car and was blacked out in the back of an ambulance hanging on for dear life.

Then she felt a hand wrap around her ankle, sending sparks up her leg. "Look at me, eh?" Lala asked her. "And come down and kiss me when you get the chance."

She heard that, she definitely heard that; her brain could never imagine the good stuff and wouldn't be able to come up with this.

Princess swallowed, and nodded, and knelt on the gross ground on that hardened glob of gum and balanced herself with a hand on Lala's leg.

There's something about first kisses that make you come undone. The moment before your lips touch, and a sigh brushes your lips, and you finally accept that this is happening. You never thought you'd have this and can't quite figure out how this person you've seen effortlessly exist wants to share this touch with you. You won't even give yourself the kindness of believing the moment is real.

Lala leaned forward, held her elbow as she laid her hand on their shoulder, pressed the tip of their nose to her cheek as if to steady themself. That was what broke the thin film of fantasy that Princess hid behind, the one that narrated their movements like they were distant characters in someone else's book. Lala was just as nervous as she was, hesitant. And Princess chose to be brave, to fall.

"Just to be clear: I don't believe in astrology."

Princess let that promise leave her lips, then kissed Lala and thanked those god-awful stars for their incompatible charts.

*   *   *   *   *

VIRGO

Venus in Virgo

* *Practical and unflirty*
* *Seeks out the perfect relationship, potentially to their detriment*
* *Needs order, directness, and dedication*
* *Not into boastfulness or arrogance*
* *Potentially insecure in relationships*

Sometimes in September
Byron Graves

There's something terrifying about not knowing what comes next. Especially for an idiot like me.

Should I really write that in my journal?

No. Well maybe the first line, that's just me being honest; the second line is that negative self-talk that I'm supposed to stop. I rub the eraser on the top of my pencil back and forth on the *idiot* line until it disappears, then set my journal down on my bed.

This addiction isn't my fault. That's what they're always telling me. The counselors at the group home I have lived at for the last five months. I ended up here after getting pretty badly addicted to pills. I was in a dark place until I got help here. It's a place for kids like me who have battled with alcohol or drugs. It's a safe place where we can stay sober and work with counselors in daily group sessions and sometimes just one-on-one. Those are the ones I like, away from a crowd. The group home is tucked away, deep in the forest on our reservation, and sits on top of a hill overlooking a lake.

In our evening group sessions they remind me that I'm not a bad person. Addiction is a sickness, not who you are. That's what the counselors are always telling me.

I need to remind myself of that. I open my journal back up and start writing again.

Smile. Smile. Smile. One choice at a time.

One day at a time. One. Day.

There's a knock on my door.

"Hey, Waabooz, it's time for your exit interview," says my counselor, Jacqueline.

She's wearing a Minnesota Vikings jersey and some track pants, fresh braids falling just below her shoulders.

I stash my journal under my pillow.

"Well, what are you waiting for?" she asks.

"I'll be right there."

"I have a surprise for you. I'll be in my office."

"For real?"

She nods, and I race after her down the hall.

Not gonna lie, Jacqueline's been cool as hell. She's taught me a lot about these feelings inside me, the ones that tell me to chase that next high, to run from reality, to destroy things.

"So what's my surprise?" I say, taking a seat.

"Holy, nice to see you too," she says but smiles her *just messing* smile.

"Uhh, I mean it's good to see you. I'm sorry, I'm just excited."

She opens up one of her desk drawers, then slides a small cardboard box across the desk. I'm nervous to pick it up. Not that I'm afraid of what's inside of the box, more like I'm afraid of what's inside of me. My eyes start to burn. I turn my head away and stare out at the lake. It's quiet still. A couple of loons float along the water. A squirrel jumps onto the ledge of the window, acorn in its mouth, staring in at us.

"You okay?"

I nod and try to do everything I can to bottle up this flood of emotions.

"I can't remember the last time… I got something from someone. Ya know?"

"It's okay, Waabooz. Remember what we've been talking about. Breathe the happy feelings in, exhale the bad ones out. Let the good feelings you deserve come in."

After a couple of deep breaths, I take the box and cradle it in my hands, like it's an injured baby bird.

"Thank you," I say, staring at the box, ashamed to look up and show my teary eyes.

"It's nothing big. But it has meaning to it. Open it."

I crack it open, slowly, wanting this moment to last as long as it can.

I open the box to reveal a copper chain with an old-fashioned bronze skeleton key on it. It looks antique, almost magical, like you could put it into any door and it would open up to some other place. Maybe some better place.

"I know you're leaving in a couple of days and you have a lot to figure out. I wanted you to have a little reminder that you have the power to open whatever doors you need to open."

"Miigwech," I say. It means *Thank you* in Ojibwe, our language. "Can I wear it?"

The office phone rings on Jacqueline's desk.

She nods, answering the question that I wasn't even sure she heard me ask. She grabs a pen and some paper, scribbles something down, then says into the phone, "Yeah, okay. Send her in."

"Waabooz, you've done so much better this time around. Stay out of trouble now. No fighting. No silly business. Let's finish these last three days out and get you started with your new life. Okay?"

"Yeah. I'm so ready to get out of the group home and back to the real world. I'll be good. I swear."

"I'm proud of you. I want you to know if you ever need anything, even just someone to talk to, I'll be here," Jacqueline says. She looks at me in that weird way adults do when they really want to make sure you agree.

I want to say something nice, but the words get stuck in my chest. They never make it to my mouth. Instead I nod and smile before I bounce.

I walk through the living room and stare at the floor as usual. I avoid eye contact as much as possible, 'cuz that's just what I do. It's easier, takes less energy than giving a fake nod, a little smirk or making small talk. This lets me pass by like a ghost, invisible.

Beat-up Chuck Taylors with stars hand-drawn on them stroll by.

Skinny, brown legs, a short plaid skirt, a tattered T-shirt. Scar marks that run sideways on both wrists. Black curly hair and a septum piercing. I've never seen someone with that part pierced in real life before. Just on the Gram.

Shit.

She catches me looking at her.

React, Waabooz. Smile or something.

She rolls her eyes and shakes her head as she walks into Jacqueline's office.

"Don't even think about getting any ideas, Bunny. You know what happened last time you got all heart eyes about a girl in here," Aaron says, before pinching my nipple.

Waabooz means *rabbit* in Ojibwe, but Aaron loves to use every variation that he can think of. Well, it actually means *snowshoe hare* if you google it. But *rabbit* to my family and friends.

"I don't know what you're talking about," I say.

Aaron gives me the *Yeah okay* look.

He pulls his glasses off and rubs them clear with his shirt. He throws his head back to move his hair from his face, then puts his glasses back.

We've been roommates ever since he arrived a month ago. We've spent a lot of nights talking quietly enough that the overnight counselors wouldn't hear us as we shared each other's biggest secrets and our wildest dreams without fear of judgment or snarky remarks. I've never felt as comfortable, or as understood, by anyone else ever before. Basically, he's the best. And I hope we stay friends when we get out.

"You want to sneak a smoke behind the garage? I scored a pack on my weekend break." He opens up his palm and shows me a cigarette. "The staff is switching between the day and night shift, and Irene is running on Indian time, like usual."

"Nah, man, I'm good. I only got three days to go, dude. I appreciate the offer, though. Not trying to get stuck in here again."

We both laugh. His grayish-green eyes glow from behind his crooked glasses.

"All right, your loss. Keep watch for me?"

I nod, and we walk outside. I hop onto the ledge of the front deck and watch Aaron walk behind the garage.

"Boo!"

My limbs flail in every direction like a giant starfish as I leap off the ledge of the porch.

"Dammit, Boo."

She laughs in that beautiful, maniacal laughter of hers. She holds her stomach like her guts are going to fall out. When she finally recovers, she crawls up the side of the porch and sits next to me.

She's my little cousin. We call her Boo because she's as quiet as a ghost. Her favorite fucking thing to do is jump-scare people. Plus she is the palest Native any of us have ever seen. So there's that.

Boo has been a client at this group home for the last few weeks after she drank enough vodka one night that she got alcohol poisoning and ended up in the ER. But before that night she had been sneaking out and drinking with older kids on the White Earth rez, which landed her in the group home out there.

Yeah, it usually takes more than a few mishaps to end up here.

"What's up?" she signs, before tucking her long black hair behind her ears.

"Keeping watch for Aaron," I sign.

"I'm going to miss you," she signs, then picks at a string that's dangling from her hand-me-down baggy shirt that hangs low enough to be a skirt.

"Same."

"Thanks for watching out for me, cuz. I'll miss feeling safe," Boo signs.

"I'll get a cell phone when I get out of here. I'll make sure the staff give you my number. Call me if you ever need anything."

"You better have a couch for me somewhere." Her brown eyes stare at the chipped black nail polish on her toenails. A rattling, clanking sound works its way down the winding dirt road.

I whistle to Aaron.

Me and Boo watch as Irene's rusted-out rez bomb bobs up and down due to the dips in the road. A cloud of dust surrounds her car as she parks.

Irene walks up to the porch, then claps her hands. I nudge Boo. "You two done with your chores?" Irene verbalizes with lazy, I'm-just-learning signs. But her words sound more like a threat than a question. Irene is second in command at the group home, but she seems to get a kick out of bossing us around. She told me her actual title one time. I think it was some fancy-sounding words, but for some reason, when she talks I tend to blank out.

"No, we haven't been assigned them yet," I say.

"Well, let's get to it," Irene says and waves us inside. Her frizzy black-and-gray hair reaches out in every direction like a mad scientist as her black-and-turquoise ribbon skirt blows in the wind.

"It looks like Boo has the bathroom as her chore tonight. Go grab the mop bucket and get to work," Irene says.

Boo's shoulders drop. She hates cleaning the bathroom. Sometimes all of us here will switch chores for small favors, like we'll give up a dessert in exchange for not having to clean the bathroom.

"And it looks like, Waabooz, you have after-dinner cleanup with... Who's Alexis?"

"Me. You can call me Lexi, though."

"Okay, Lexi. I'm Irene. I work the evening shifts here. I am the residential program coordinator here, so what I say goes. This is Waabooz."

I'm about to jokingly point out that technically she's Jacqueline's assistant, but Lexi looks over at me and suddenly my mind goes blank and my hands get all clammy.

Why am I like this?

She's just a... Maybe the most gorgeous human being I've ever seen IRL.

Lexi reaches her hand out. We shake hands, and I can't help but notice how soft her skin is.

"Nice to meet you, B-Rabbit," Lexi says.

"Huh?"

"You know, like that old-ass Eminem movie, *8 Mile*? His name was B-Rabbit. I just... Never mind."

I force a laugh, finally getting her reference, but it's awkward. Her and Irene both stare at me.

"So do you mind showing me around this place? I was told that you're the OG here. I heard you set the record for the longest stay of all time. They said you've been here like twenty months."

"Weeks. Twenty weeks. But yeah, I've been here a minute. Only three days left, though. So anyway, down here is the hallway." I point with my lips and nod down the hall. "This is where we stay. The three rooms on the left are for girls, the three on the right are for boys. Last room on the left is the shared bathroom."

"Gross. We have to share a bathroom with a bunch of nasty-ass boys? No offense."

"The girls usually get in there first because the boys here all sleep until we get yelled at. We have to be out of our rooms by six for morning chores and breakfast."

"Six?" Lexi asks in disbelief. Her perfectly shaped eyebrows push together, and her forehead crinkles.

"I know."

"That's usually when I'm about to go to bed. So what are you in for?" Lexi asks, as we walk to the kitchen.

I've attended group discussions for months where I am an open book about my drug problems. But looking over at Lexi, I'm embarrassed to tell her. Even though I know she's probably in here for something similar.

"Earth to B-Rabbit…"

"Pills. Pills and drinking," I say so quietly that I wonder if I only thought the words.

"Same," Lexi says with a look in her eyes like she didn't give a fuck who heard or what they thought.

"So this is the kitchen area. The table over there is where we eat. Plates, cups and the forks and stuff are all in the drawers in the corner."

"I like your necklace," Lexi says.

"I like your necklace too. It's dope. Looks kind of like the Roman numeral for the number two...but it's an astrology sign, right?"

"Look at you. Yeah, it's the sign for Gemini. It symbolizes twins, because we tend to prefer to do things in pairs, not alone. What's your sign?" Lexi asks.

"My sign?" I stop walking, like it's going to help me think harder.

Lexi steps in front of me, her eyes grow super big.

"You're really into this stuff, huh?" I ask.

"Well, duh. So what's your sign?" Lexi asks.

The aggressive blank stare that I'm sure is on my face right now pushes Lexi to continue.

"What month were you born? Wait, let me guess... It was in September."

"Yeah. How did you know?"

"And hold on a second." Lexi closes her eyes and presses her fingers to her temples, looking like she's Jean Grey or some shit. "You were born...on September seventh."

"Holy shit. How could you know that?"

"I'm not done." She fights back a smile and closes her eyes again. "Your favorite rapper is Lil Peep, you miss playing *Pokémon Go*—that's embarrassing—and you want to blow up on SoundCloud."

"What?" I ask, wondering why Lexi's face is about to explode into laughter.

"And you already low-key have a crush on me. Wow!" she says, her eyebrows rise in disbelief.

I spin around to see Boo bent forward, slapping her knees, damn near hyperventilating.

"Nice, Boo. Real nice." I bury my face into my hands, wishing I could disappear. When vanishing into the void doesn't work, I turn around to Lexi. "Wait a second. You know sign language too?"

"Yeah. Me and Grace here spent a couple of months together at the Whispering Pines treatment center in White Earth. You call her Boo?"

"Yeah, that's the nickname my family gave her forever ago. She's my little cousin."

"Cute. It's fitting."

I turn back to see if Boo agrees, but she's gone.

Typical.

"You aren't fraternizing, are you, Waabooz?"

Irene's shrill voice comes out of nowhere, even more startling than one of Boo's jump scares.

"Don't you even dream about rolling your eyes. This boy loves rolling his eyes at me," Irene says to Lexi. "It's got him extra chores more times than the government has broken our treaties."

"I'm sorry, I just—"

"I'll take it from here," Irene says. "We're all done checking your bag, so take it down to your bedroom and get unpacked."

"Uh-oh. I think she likes you," Aaron whispers to me as we watch Lexi sling her bag over her shoulder and walk down the hall.

"Dude, you smell like cigarettes," I whisper.

Aaron links his arm into mine like we are a prom couple and pulls me to our shared bedroom.

"Figure out where you're going when you get out?" Aaron asks. He digs out a can of body spray from his dresser.

"Pretty sure I'm going to crash at my grandma's."

Aaron sits beside me on my bed. "She still in the hospital?"

"In and out. But she called me last week and said she will be at home for the next couple months."

"I hope she's okay." Aaron runs his hand across my back. "I lost my grandpa to cancer. It was rough."

We stare ahead and don't say anything, but having Aaron next to me, leaning against me, makes me feel just a little bit better.

"What's for dinner?" Aaron asks as soon as we walk into the kitchen. "Please don't tell me it's the slop."

Boo signs, "How did you know?" then gets on her tiptoes and reaches as high as she can to grab a bowl down from the cupboard. She dips a ladle into a big metal pot, then dumps the grayish sludge of what we think is beef and gravy into a plastic bowl.

It's what we eat most Wednesdays. I'm super sick of it, plus I'm not really feeling hungry, so I grab some crackers and a cup of water.

Great, there's only one spot left at the table, and it's next to Big Clint.

"Is that all you're going to eat, you little fish? Some crackers?" Big Clint asks.

Fish is this stupid word some people use on our rez. It's usually meant as a dis to someone who is soft, or gay, or whatever. I hate it.

I try to act like it doesn't bother me. If Big Clint sees any sort of reaction he'll keep on teasing.

"Not that hungry." I stare at the cracker in my hand.

"What's wrong with you? Sad to be leaving your boyfriend Aaron?" Big Clint asks.

I look at Aaron. The sting in his eyes says it all.

He has only come out to me. He hasn't even told his family. But it's hard for him to hide that he's not the typical, macho, straight guy. And Clint's bitch ass has made sure to make a point to say something about it every chance he gets.

"Yeah, I'm gonna miss Aaron *and* my little cuz. But not this slop. Not the early wake-up calls. And I'm especially not going to miss your trashy-ass jokes."

Clint stands.

I stand too, hoping to give myself a chance in case he hits me.

I tilt my head back to look up at him. His wide shoulders and brick wall chest are the size of two of me.

"What?" I ask, trying to sound tough but praying to the Creator he doesn't swing on me.

He smiles, which is weird because Clint never smiles. "Waabooz is all tough now that he's about to leave, eh?"

We stare at each other. His hands ball up into fists. I wait for him to throw a punch. My hands start to shake.

"What about me? You're not going to miss me?" Lexi asks, cutting into the moment. Her eyebrows arch and her arms cross.

Clint picks up his empty bowl and walks off to get more food.

"Well?" Lexi asks again, her eyes still burning holes through me.

"Yeah. I mean, we just met, but yeah." I sit back down.

"Ask her more about astrology," Boo signs, hiding her hands before Lexi can see.

"So astrology, huh?" I ask.

"Yeah?" Lexi asks.

"Cool…" I say, then notice Boo and Aaron both turn into face-palm emojis. "I don't really know all that much about it, but it sounds cool."

"I could lend you a book if you want. It's called *Astrology for Dummies*."

Everyone laughs, even Clint, who almost chokes.

"I'm just messing," Lexi says with a smile big enough that her dimples show.

"Nah, but for real, it's an astrology book for beginners. I'll lend it to you if you're actually interested and not just trying to flirt. But you'd better return it. I only have a couple of books with me and a *Sailor Moon* graphic novel, which I've already read twenty times."

"Speaking of moons… There is no moon in the sky to-morrow night *and* there's going to be a meteor shower. That's what they said on the news this morning. They said it would be at its peak at about ten o'clock," Aaron says in between bites.

"But curfew is at nine. Do you think Irene would let us sit out there?" I ask.

"Maybe if we all ask real nice and promise to get all of our chores done right away this week," Aaron says.

"That'd be cool," Clint says, never looking up from his bowl.

*   ◊   *

"Make a wish, B-Rabbit." Lexi points up at the first falling star of the night.

I close my eyes. I wish that I get to see Lexi again when she gets out of here.

"I got next," Aaron says.

"What did you wish for?" Lexi asks me.

I laugh, an awkward choppy laugh.

"I can't tell you. Otherwise it won't come true. Right?"

"Tell me," Lexi says, in a voice that spot-on mimics a death-metal growl as she shakes my shoulders.

We all bust out laughing.

"Why don't you use those psychic powers again?" I ask.

Lexi closes her eyes tightly, fingers back to her temples. "Okay, I will." A smile grows on her face. She opens her eyes and looks at me. "That's a great wish."

"Oh, yeah? What was it?"

"I can't say it out loud either. Or it won't come true." We look into each other's eyes. Lexi scoots a little closer, never breaking eye contact. Her leg rubs against mine.

The world around us disappears. Time stops moving. My lungs stop bringing in air, but my heart is working overtime. I can even feel it beating in my neck.

With our eyes still locked on each other, I wonder if we are about to sneak in the fastest kiss in the history of kisses.

What if we get caught? I'd be stuck here all over again.

I look at Lexi's lips. She catches my gaze, smiles, then leans in toward me.

Boo gasps, and we all look up. A stream of shooting stars fall like fireworks. We count them.

One. Two. Three. Four. The fifth one burns the brightest and then fizzles out.

"What did you wish for, Aaron?" I ask.

"Well, I can't tell you, or it won't come true."

I roll my eyes, then look over at Boo and sign to her, "What did you wish for?"

"A pet unicorn. And some Sour Patch Kids."

"Nice," I sign back.

I scoot away from Lexi just a little. Some breathing room in case one of the counselors looks down at us. "I read some of that book last night, but there's no way I'll finish it by tomorrow afternoon. I'm sorry," I say.

"Power read it," Lexi says.

"Christ, this is boring as hell. I'm going in," Big Clint grumbles.

Aaron lays back, suddenly at ease, and puts his hands behind his head.

Boo pops up and walks over to the dock, then dips her bare feet into the lake.

"So how'd you get into astrology?" I ask Lexi.

"Kind of by accident. I was in a bad spot. Everything in my life was spinning out of control. Bunch of shit happened all at once. My mom went to jail, and I hardly ever saw my stepdad. He was gone for a week at a time partying and shit, and when he'd come back he was acting...weird." Lexi pauses, her face scrunches up, like she's trying to either forget or remember something. "Then one day, I was digging around in my mom's stuff, hoping to find her stash, if you know what I'm saying."

"Yeah, I hear you."

"My mom was into Oxys, Xanny bars, sometimes Vicodin, whatever she could get her hands on. That's how I got hooked, sneaking hers. I was just doing whatever to find another. Started hanging with an older crowd. They convinced me to steal some shit and pawn it. So I did. Then I stole some more shit, got caught, got in trouble."

"And that got you into astrology?"

"Oh, sorry. I get all gabby when I tell stories. I end up going in all kinds of directions. So that day I was digging through my mom's shit, I found an astrology book, and I started reading it. I learned about my sign, and it just kind of like, clicked. It felt like there was something that explained the madness around me. It kind of just explained why I was me and why I felt the way I felt."

"That's deep."

"Yeah. So, SoundCloud rapper, huh?"

I laugh.

"What's funny?"

"I thought you were messing with me. People usually laugh about that. I know it's like, impossible or whatever, and everyone who has any flow thinks they can blow up. So I get why people like to crack jokes on it."

"Psshh… Fuck them. When did you know you wanted to rap?"

"You for real want to know?"

"That's why I asked," Lexi says with a wink.

"I was really struggling, in this dark place. I couldn't find any Oxys, couldn't find anything. My teeth were grinding. I was feeling super alone and sad, but I couldn't say anything to anybody. Then this Lil Peep song came on, and damn, I just felt like everything I was feeling he was saying. Felt like I could have written that song, word for word. It made me feel less alone. Eventually I started writing my own lyrics and got hooked."

"I hear ya. I go mad geek mode once I'm obsessed with something. Once I got into astrology, I got hooked. It helps me feel like there's a GPS guide to the universe. It helps me slow down the chaos. You know what I mean?"

I look at Lexi, and it feels like I'm looking in the mirror for the first time and not hating what I see. And her looking at me makes me feel seen, like she's the first person to really see me.

We both scoot close together, enough so that our legs touch again. Lexi nods at me, and now it feels like I'm the one with the psychic powers. I'm pretty sure she's telling me we should kiss. I lean toward her, heart threatening to explode.

I've never kissed anyone before. I'm not even sure what to do exactly. But I think I've seen it in enough movies.

Don't judge me.

I'm picky.

My face instantly starts to feel flushed red, like when you slam one of those five-hour energy drinks on an empty stomach.

"Hey, you two! You are way too close," Irene yells from the porch, waving her arms around like she's batting away mosquitoes. "Matter of fact, let's call it a night. Get inside!"

Lexi has an embarrassed but happy smile on her face, then she points up at the sky at one last falling star.

I finish the last page of the astrology book Lexi lent me. I shut it and sit with my thoughts for a minute. That's definitely the fastest I've ever read a book before. I think that's what some people call *cramming*. Everything I just read is flowing through my mind like crazy. Almost like it's flooding. Feels like I need some time to process it all and just be with my thoughts for a minute.

I stuff Lexi's book into my dresser drawer and grab my journal and a pen and make my way down to the lake, avoiding eye contact along the way.

Sitting on the dock I pull off my shoes, then my socks, and dip my feet into the cool water of the lake. This little wave of relief comes over me, calming my mind. I get lost watching the water move toward the shore.

Then some music starts flowing into my head. I never know when it's going to hit, but when it does I try to capture it before it leaves. Music, like almost fully written songs just come into my head, like tuning into a radio station or something. It's like they're playing somewhere out there, and I'm just able to capture them if I listen carefully.

I grab my notebook and start scribbling lyrics as fast as my hand can move. All these feelings about Lexi start pouring out onto the page.

Sometimes in September, ~~she makes me fall.~~

Nah. Not that. Umm…

Sometimes in September, she tells me what it—

Hold up. I got this.

I close my eyes and listen carefully to the beat playing in my mind. I start nodding my head as I hear the bass, the snare. Even though the sun is shining down on me and it's hot outside, I still feel chills scatter down from my neck to my fingertips.

The piano chords of the song start to construct themselves. I'm really feeling it now.

I start the song over again in my head.

Sometimes in September, she tells me what it all means, even my disasters.

One time in September, she made falling stars and wishes matter.

"Where are your headphones?" Lexi asks, cutting into my song like a record scratch.

"Hey!" I quickly shut my notebook and set it aside. I already know I've got a big, stupid smile on my face.

"Writing your next big hit?" Lexi asks.

I laugh. "Yeah, right. I wish."

"That's the first step. Mind if I chill here with you?"

"Nah. Not at all. I'd like that."

Lexi is wearing short tattered jean shorts and a black tank top that says *Strong, Resilient, Indigenous* on it. She pulls her shoes and socks off and dips her feet in the lake as well.

"Yo, miigwech for letting me borrow that book. Believe it or not I finished it this morning. Blew my mind. For real."

"Yeah? Prove it."

"Prove it?"

"Yeah. Tell me your thoughts about it." Lexi splashes a little water on my legs.

I smile, then look down at the water.

"It was just kind of like this epiphany. Like, remember how I was telling you before that Lil Peep lyrics sounded like words that could have come from my own mind or my own life? That's just how it felt reading about all the stuff about being a Virgo."

"I had a feeling you'd appreciate it," Lexi says.

"So much of it just made sense about how I am. How I act and think. I do internalize a lot, shit…everything. Other than what's in this notebook. And people always tell me I overthink things, like I'm forever looking back wondering about how I end up where I end up, and how so many things could have been different, if any of my decisions had been slightly different."

Lexi softly slaps me on the arm. "You really did read it." We laugh hard until our eyes catch each other's again, our laughter slowly fading off.

"I told you I did. I wouldn't lie to you."

"Oh, really? Said every guy ever."

"You know what other epiphany I had when I was reading it?"

"What's that?"

"You."

"Huh?"

"You. Being here. You being you. You telling me the things you do. You sharing this book with me. And…making me feel the way I do. It all feels like it was sort of meant to be. Like where I'm going to go after this. I can already tell, it's changed 'cuz of you. For the better."

Lexi smiles. Her dimples show. This time she's the one to look away.

"You're dope. You know that?" Lexi says.

"You're…"

"I'm?"

I want to tell her she's the most amazing person I've ever met. The most gorgeous person I've ever met. I want to tell her how bad I wish I could kiss her.

"You're pretty dope yourself."

"Typical Virgo," she says, and we laugh again.

"Come on. Let's get back into the home before someone thinks we're doing something bad and I get stuck here for ten more weeks."

*   ◇   *

"What's up, lovebird?" Aaron says as I fall back onto my bed.

"What are you talking about?" I ask, already knowing he knows.

"I'm no detective, but I saw you and Lexi down on the dock. You're lucky Irene isn't working today. She probably would have written your asses up just for being a boy and a girl alone together."

"Alone together," I say, then jot it into my notebook. "Stealing that."

"Oh my god," Aaron says.

"Shut up," I say, throwing a pillow at him.

"So what's up with you two, though?"

"I don't even know. I've never felt like this before. It feels like electricity flows through my entire body every time I think about her. It all feels kind of like a dream or something."

"That's cute. Like really cute. I'm happy for you. But you leave tomorrow. What are you going to do? Even if she makes it a perfect ten weeks, that's forever from now."

"Man, like for real. I don't care about the ten weeks. I waited this long. Lexi is my person. I know it. I'll just be out there, staying sober, making my music and waiting."

*   ◊   *

"Waabooz, your uncle is on his way. Should be here in about fifteen minutes," Jacqueline says. "You got all of your belongings?"

I stuff my notebook under all my clothes in my duffel bag, then zip it up. "Yeah, I'm all set."

"I'll be down in my office. When your uncle gets here, we'll have some release paperwork for him to sign. I'll also provide you with some resources for maintaining your sobriety on the outside, okay?"

I nod and grab Lexi's book off my bed.

"Did you really finish reading that whole book last night?" Aaron asks as he brushes his hair.

"Yeah. Tired as hell, though."

"Don't forget about me when you are on tour with Wiz Khalifa."

"Psshh… Yeah, right. I wish."

"But seriously, don't forget about me out there, okay? I hope we'll stay friends."

Aaron sets his brush aside and gives me a long hug.

"I'm going to miss you," he says.

"Same," I say and squeeze him hard.

We push apart and smile at each other.

"I'm going to run this down to Lexi before my uncle gets here," I say, holding her book up.

"Hey, Lexi. Here's your book," I say. She hops up from her bed and comes to the door but doesn't reach out for her book.

"Is it weird that I'm going to miss you?"

"No. I'm going to miss you too. Sorry I'm leaving right as you're getting here."

"Probably a good thing. We'd be trouble together."

"Waabooz, your uncle is here," Jacqueline yells down the hall.

"I better get going," I say.

"Yeah, you better," Lexi says. She reaches out and takes her book.

"I wish I could give you a hug goodbye or a…you know," I say.

"Me too. But it's not worth you being stuck here another ten weeks. How about we give each other our first hug when I get out of here. Hello again, instead of goodbye?"

"Okay."

We stare at each other. Probably longer than we should. But I've lost a lot of family members and a lot of friends, as I'm sure Lexi has. That's just how it goes on my rez.

If it's not a car accident, it's an overdose. If it's not an overdose, it's someone getting shot or stabbed at a party.

Too many times I've walked away thinking I'd see someone

I cared about again. I want to stay here, just like this. Looking at Lexi. Wondering about what might be.

"Waabooz, let's go get your papers signed," Jacqueline says. She looks at Lexi, back at me, and shakes her head with a knowing smile.

She puts a hand on my shoulder and says softly, "Come on."

"Uncle!" I say, throwing my arms around my uncle Joe. He's in the same worn red-and-black flannel and torn jeans that he's probably been wearing since Kurt Cobain made that look cool.

Sure, my uncle might drink every day and disappear for weeks at a time. But when you really, really need the dude, he'll be there. He's clutch like that.

He pats me on the back and pulls away from our hug, both hands still on my shoulders. He looks me over like I just got shot at. "Dang, neph. Really missed your uncle, eh? You good?"

"Yeah, I'm good."

We sit down, and Jacqueline slides over my release papers and starts explaining to my uncle what each one means. I zone out as my uncle signs the papers. Then I'm snapped back to reality when I hear Clint's voice booming from the living room.

Fuck.

I don't even think about excusing myself. I jump up from my chair. Feels like I'm hypnotized or something. Thoughts scatter like birds after a gunshot.

I open the office door and see Clint in the living room, standing in front of everyone, holding my journal in his hand.

"'Sometimes in September, she tells me what it all means,

even my disasters.'" Clint reads my lyrics, then busts out
laughing. "What kind of gay-ass, corny-ass shit is this? This
dude ain't no rapper."

"Clint. Give that back."

"Fuck you going to do about it?" Clint says.

"I said give me that back, you fucking asshole."

"What's going on out here?" Jacqueline asks, storming out
of her office, my uncle right behind her.

I grab my journal, but Clint grips it more firmly. I yank
hard, hoping to rip it from his hands. Clint pushes it toward
me, then takes it away.

The momentum sends me onto my ass. I jump to my feet,
my legs feel like Jell-O, and my hands are shaking. My teeth
are grinding. My hands ball up into fists.

Fuck this dude.

I cock my fist back, ready to punch Clint.

No other thoughts flow through my mind.

Two arms grab ahold of me from behind. I feel Lexi's forehead press against my shoulder. "Don't," she says.

Clint opens my journal back up and starts reading again,
"One time in September, she made falling stars and wishes matter."
His eyes never leave the page. Each word he reads steals air
from my lungs; my chest feels all heavy from the embarrassment.

Lexi shoves Clint, sending him toppling over the coffee
table behind him, and my journal flies up into the air.

Lexi catches it and hands it to me, and suddenly I can
breathe again.

"Here."

"You. In my office. Right now!" Jacqueline yells at Clint.

"And Alexis, you go wait in your room. We do not tolerate violence here."

"You okay?" my uncle asks me as he picks my duffel bag off the floor, zips it shut and slings it over his shoulder.

"Yeah. I'm fine. Hey, did you finish signing my release papers?" I ask.

"Yeah. We are all good to go."

"*All* the papers?" I ask.

"Yeah. You're a free man."

"Lexi," I call after her as she's walking away.

"Yeah?" she asks, stopping and turning back.

"I'm no longer a client here. I can't get in trouble."

"And I'm already in trouble anyways..."

Lexi puts her hands on my face and pulls me in close. Our eyes close, and our lips touch. I don't care that my uncle is standing there. I don't care that Boo is probably covering her eyes.

I don't care who sees.

Lexi kisses me. Soft and slow. Her fingers run across my face. I wrap my arms around her.

I already know I'll remember this kiss forever.

"Giigawabamin, Waabooz," Lexi says as she breaks away from our kiss.

In Ojibwe, giigawabamin, means *See you later.*

In Ojibwe, there is no word for *goodbye.*

*   *   *   *   *

LIBRA

Venus in Libra

* Easy-going, gentle, and kind
* Easily pushed over or taken advantage of
* Requires balance and diplomacy
* Prefers keeping the peace over any conflict
* Loves love and romance

Fake Scorpio
Mark Oshiro

"Efren Torres, Guide to the Stars, is now open for business!"

Tracey scoots closer to me on the bench, and I am thankful she is here. Somehow, it's less embarrassing to not be completely alone at this moment.

I stare out at the student body of Arlington Heights High School, all of who pass me by without stopping. It's the beginning of spring, so the shorts are back. The tank tops. Spaghetti straps. Most people have on bright colors—that's back in style this year, like the '90s regurgitated over everyone. It's all I can focus on, because otherwise, I would be panicking. The weather is perfect. The spring dance is coming up, too, and normally, there would be a long line of people snaking away from me, eager for one of my readings.

I started providing horoscope readings last year. I withstood skepticism when everyone (except Tracey, my ride or die) said that no one would ever pay for a horoscope. I survived the Arlington High Recession, too, when all cash-sending apps were banned completely on campus. We just found other ones that the administration didn't know about and couldn't block. I even survived Harmony and her mathlete friends, who all tried lying to me about their birthdays in order to discredit astrology as a whole.

But this? This new threat? I think it has *completely* killed my business.

"Maybe you'll get a couple before the lunch bell rings," says Tracey, twisting one of her dark brown locs. "It's Friday. People are busy." A pause, and then, "You never know."

What I do know is that if I look at Tracey right now, I'll see pity on her face. I can't blame her. This is pathetic. Perhaps the worst day of my life. Kids drift by our bench, which is completely empty aside from us, and no one even seems to know that we exist. At this point, I'd even take a sympathetic glance.

I tap my fingers on the wooden table. "You know that's not true," I finally say to Tracey. "They're never coming back."

"Don't say that," Tracey says softly. "Maybe—"

She doesn't get to finish. The words hitch in her throat, and now I'm looking at her, and her eyes are wide and—

"Hey, Efren. You still giving readings?"

Nah.

Nope.

I know that voice.

Sal Benevides.

Soft and buttery, like velvet.

Velvet? I think. Why do we say that? Can the inside of a throat feel like velvet?

I am so consumed by this deeply cursed thought that I don't fully register who is standing opposite me.

And who is now crouched down, waving a brown hand in my face.

"Efren? You there?"

Tracey nudges me—too hard, but what else is she supposed to do when I'm thinking of Sal's *throat*?—and I nearly fall off the bench. My gaze shoots up to Sal, and...damn.

See, Sal is... He's a lot. You ever meet one of those people whose skin always seems perfectly moisturized? Or who always seems to have a perfect fade, a perfect line-up, and grew facial hair before all his peers? (I don't understand clean-shaven faces. Well, mine is bare because I still can't grow anything to save my life, but we're talking about Sal here, okay? Focus!) And we're not even gonna get into how good he looks in his football uniform.

I'm well aware how much of a cliché that is.

But I am not aware of any reason why Sal would want a reading.

"Is he all right, Tracey?" Sal asks.

I snap out of it. "Um... Hi, Sal," I say, and I offer a pathetic smile. "Sorry. Did I hear you right? You want a reading?" And then, because I can't bear to avoid saying something utterly useless, "From *me*?"

Sal looks around for a moment, and the meaning is clear. It's not like there are a ton of astrology-loving queer boys at this school who sell readings for money or gifts. "Yeah," he says. "I mean, if you're still doing them."

Tracey presses the heel of her shoe on my toe. *Hard.*

Oh, I must have my mouth open again. I do this a lot with Sal, and Tracey has my back.

"Sure, sure!" I say, and I spread my arms out in front of me. "Sit down and…take a…load off?"

That pitches high into an apparent question because I have become another cliché: the boy who can't speak normally when faced with their crush. *Take a load off?* Who do I think I'm talking to?

Sal sits down hesitantly, gripping the edge of the table as he does so. Oh. Great. He has *forearm* muscles. Is that hot? I guess it is. I'm a forearm guy, I've decided.

"How do you do this?" Sal asks. "Are you like, a fortune teller or something?"

I laugh at that, and then he smiles *at* my laugh, and Tracey makes a gasping sound that I have to ignore or I'll start making one, too. "No, no, not like that," I say. "When's your birthday?"

"April twenty-seventh."

"Oh, it's coming up soon!" says Tracey.

He grins wide, and… Well, guess I'm a teeth guy now as well. This sounds terrible in my head (I can already hear Tracey chanting, "TEETH, TEETH, TEETH, TEETH," at me), so I move on. "Okay, so you're a Taurus!"

"Oh, right!" he says. "I *did* know that. But…what does that *actually* mean?"

Finally, familiar ground. "You're an earth sign," I tell him, "so generally speaking, you tend to be really grounded. Practical. You are probably the most reliable sign."

"Reliable?" He beams. "Mami would love to hear that."

A momma's boy? Oh, my Scorpio heart can't handle this.

"Some people might see you as stubborn, but a Taurus actually just tends to be able to commit to things long-term."

Sal's face droops. (Even *that* looks cute.) "Well, no long-term anything on my end," he says. "Except football, I guess?"

"That counts," says Tracey.

"I could keep telling you about the features or qualities of a Taurus," I say. "But…was there a reason you sought my services out?"

He grimaces. "I don't know. I just… Well, you know there's that dance coming up, right?"

Tracey's foot is on mine again. It's a strange way to communicate, but I know exactly what she's trying to say. Alarms are going off. We're in uncharted territory now.

"Yeah, of course," I say. "Do you have a date to it?"

"No," he says, shaking his head. "And you'd think the star running back would have a date, but I'm just…too confused to pick someone."

Tracey squeezes my leg, and it takes everything in me not to yelp.

"Well, would you like to know who you're likely to be compatible with?" I ask.

Sal pulls out his phone and starts scrolling through it after opening it. "Sure. I went ahead and downloaded Star Chart and—"

There is no hesitation from me *or* Tracey. We groan at the same time. Hell, pretty sure we harmonized there for a moment. Sal's eyes go wide.

"I'm sorry, did I do something wrong?" he says.

I sigh. "I just… That *app*." I put my head in my hands, and for a moment, Tracey takes over.

"Ever since Star Chart came out, Efren here...well, he's had some trouble getting clients."

"*Some* trouble?" I shake my head at Tracey. "My business has never been drier."

"Just from an app?" Sal looks back down at his phone. "I mean, I wouldn't say I really learned anything from it. It told me I'm most compatible with Scorpios."

Oh.

I'm a Scorpio, I think, and when I look to Tracey, she manages to have an expression on her face that is both an encouragement and a manifestation of her extreme terror. She's talented, I'll give her that.

Who cares about Star Chart? I tell myself. He's here in front of you *NOW.*

"Well, the app isn't *wrong*," I start off, nodding my head. "But you need more guidance than that, right?"

"Exactly!" he says. "Like, am I supposed to just find a Scorpio and ask them on a date?"

"You could ask Efren," Tracey says under her breath. Well, she intended for it to be under her breath, but she hasn't historically been good at whispering.

I ignore her, though. "So, as a Taurus, you're looking for reliability, too. You can be kinda stubborn, so it's best not to be with someone who is like...immediately argumentative. Sometimes, Capricorns and Leos are like that. But the point is you need someone who probably is a lot more flexible or empathetic than you."

Sal nods his head. "That makes sense."

"And loyalty is big with you. Or at least I'm guessing it is."

He nods, but his mouth turns down. "Yeah. I've been cheated on before, so that's *very* important to me."

"Boo, who the *hell* would cheat on someone as fine as you?" Tracey clicks her teeth with her tongue. "Absolutely not."

"Tracey."

"I'm not wrong, Efren!"

"Thank you, Tracey," says Sal. "I appreciate that." He pauses. "You wouldn't happen to be a Scorpio, would you?"

My disappointment crashes in my chest, but only for a moment. "Aw, Salvador Benevides, I am flattered," says Tracey, "but while I *am* bisexual, cis men are *not* included in the folks I am attracted to."

And then she does…this thing. With her eyebrow. I think she's trying to lift it up suggestively, but it just looks like it's heaving in its final throes of life.

"Well," says Sal, locking eyes with me, "do you know who else is a Scorpio on campus?"

There's no subtlety from Tracey this time. She just back-hands my chest. *Hard.* So hard that when the air rushes out of my mouth, I sound like I'm deflating.

"Whoops," says Tracey as I devolve into a coughing fit. "Sorry, he was choking, had to help him, you know. And I'm sure he'd *love* to be choking on—"

"I'M FINE!" I yell and swat her away. Sal has an odd look on his face. Confusion? Suspicion? Maybe both. I try to give him my flashiest smile. "Yeah, there are quite a few Scorpios around. Would you like to—"

They're like a plague of locusts: Sal's teammates descend on him, covering every inch of his body with fist bumps and squeezes and that desperate straight-boy eroticism that an-

noys people like me, because most places in America would
devour me if I ever touched another boy like that. Sal mutters
a brief goodbye and waves to me as he is swept away by his
teammates. To do what? I don't know. Bump chests together?
Throw a ball around? I don't know what straight boys do!

I watch him leave.

He has nice calves.

Is it bad that I seem to like every part of his body?

"Well, you had a chance," says Tracey. "Sorry for accidentally assaulting you, by the way."

"You really should try out for the tennis team," I say. "That
backhand is dangerous."

Silence falls, though, because there's no one else in line.
No one here for advice or guidance or just a simple reading.

Was Sal just a pity concession?

"He didn't even pay," Tracey says, her voice low.

Fuck.

He didn't.

* ◇ *

Tracey and I make it to my house just as Mami is getting
home from work. She hops out of her old sedan—we haven't
been able to afford a new one since Papi left five years ago—
and her scrubs are bright and colorful set against her dark
brown skin. Today, she's got her hair pulled back tight and
into a bun. "Te extrañé, mijo," she says, kissing me on top of
my head. "Hello, Tracey!"

"Hola, Señorita Torres," Tracey says, waving.

"Señorita?" She pulls Tracey close and hugs her. "See,

Efren? You could learn a thing or two about respect from that one."

"She calls you *old* when you aren't around," I say.

"I definitely know she doesn't," Mami says, heading into our tiny home, "because she's a Taurus *and* loyal."

"That's right!" Tracey calls after her.

I've been betrayed. Thrown under the bus by my own Mami. Which is fair, since I just tried to toss Tracey under first.

Our home is on the far edge of Riverside, just snuggled up with the wildlife preserve and Norco. We don't go to Norco... well, for a lot of reasons. To give you an idea what that place is like, the city decided to do something completely unnecessary way back before I was born: *all* of the dividing lines painted on their streets are red, white, and blue. Also, you can get a speeding ticket in half a second for going one mile per hour over the thirty-mile-per-hour speed limit because they care more about horses than anything else there.

Anyway, we've got a big backyard here in our neighborhood, even though the house is small, which is great for nights when Mami and I lay a blanket out on the grass to stare at the stars. Tracey is the only person I know on this side of town because pretty much everyone over here is...well, I'll spell it out: not Black like her, not brown like us. Papi moved us into the "nice" neighborhood, but then he left us, and Mami can't move us on a nurse's wages.

So here we are. Tracey's mom is all she's got, too, so the four of us...we're a team. Two Tauruses. A Scorpio. A Cancer.

It's chaos. But it's *our* chaos.

Tracey is deep in conversation with Mami about what she's

singing in the spring recital, and soon, the two of them are trying to sustain fifth harmonies. Mami shoulda been a singer, but after Papi left… Look. He's gone. I try not to think about him all that often, but clearly I'm not very good at it. It's just that I can't ignore that he changed our lives. Mami couldn't pursue music, we got stuck here in this tiny-ass home in a city that doesn't really care for us…but I guess we do what we can.

"How was your business today, papito?"

I sigh. "Does it count as a business if you only have one customer, who didn't pay?"

"Aw, I'm sorry," she says, setting a kettle to boil on the stove. "Still competing with that app?"

I plop down at the table. "Unfortunately."

"It's just an app," says Mami. "Why don't *you* use it?"

"Ugh, *why*?" I lie out over the table dramatically. "There's not even a person behind it! It's all automated garbage."

"And who wants their horoscope from a robot?" says Tracey. "It doesn't have that Efren flair."

"Well, I downloaded it today. It's not that bad."

I don't move for a moment. I hear Tracey fidget in the seat across from me.

I raise my head. "I'm sorry, I think I misheard that."

Mami has frozen near the stove, holding the kettle in her hand.

"Oh, no," says Tracey.

"Did you say you used Star Chart?"

"Papito, I—"

"The very app that has ruined my entire life?"

"That's a little exaggerated, don't you—"

"Do you want to replace your son with a machine?"

"Efren Torres!"

I wince. Yeah, okay, maybe that was too far.

"Just download it. *Now.*"

"Oooh, she's mad," said Tracey. "And you basically called her a bad mom. I think you're the *best* mom after my own, Ms. Torres."

Mami smiles at her. "Thank you, cariña." But then she turns back to me. "Seriously, mijo. Download it. Try it. It isn't that bad."

"Fine!" I pull out my phone and seconds later, this awful, useless app is downloading. "It's not gonna be worth it."

"Maybe you can use it in your favor," Tracey says.

"How am I going to use a badly programmed app that everyone at school is addicted to?" I counter.

The app and its trash icon are there, on my screen.

I tap it.

Welcome to Star Chart, the intro text says, and then it whooshes away to the side. Please enter your birthdate.

"Okay, okay," I say. "So demanding."

"What's it asking for?" says Tracey.

"My birthday. October. Twenty. Third."

I hit Enter.

For a more accurate reading and with proper star and planet alignments, please enter the exact time of your birth.

I squint at my phone. "Mami, when was I born?"

She laughs. "Wow. Didn't expect you to start losing your memory so young."

"No, silly. I mean *literally*. Like the exact time on the twenty-third."

"¿Exacto?" Mami wrinkles up her brow. "Ay, no lo se."

"How do you *not* know?"

"Efren, I do not recall the exact moment I shoved you out of my body," she says, pouring hot water over a bag of chamomile, her afterwork routine. "I might have been in a little bit of pain!" She's quiet for a moment. "Con esa gran cabeza tuya," she mutters.

I throw my hands in the air. "My head is the normal size for boys!" Tracey is cackling way too hard at this for my liking, but I have more important things to deal with. "Where's my birth certificate? Doesn't that have the time?"

"Oh, yes, of course!" Mami is off, and I know she's headed for the fireproof file case she has in her bedroom closet. "One second!" she calls out.

"Look, Efren, I think there's still something you can do with this," says Tracey. "Think of it like…you're spying on the enemy. Getting their intel."

"I guess," I say. "But how am I gonna compete with this?"

"Well," she says, reaching across the table to grab my hands, "what do you have that it doesn't?"

It takes a few seconds before I realize that Mami is standing still at the end of the hallway. She's got a piece of paper close to her face.

"Mami? ¿Estás bien?"

"Efren."

She just says my name. It's even. Kinda lifeless. Tracey wrenches herself around.

"Mami?"

She slowly walks toward us, and her face is all twisted up. "Umm."

I stand up. "What's going on?"

Mami *laughs*. It's high and nervous. "Well, this is a funny thing," she says. "You know, I guess maybe I never looked at this thing."

"Why?" My heart leaps into my throat.

"Well, according to this, you were born at 11:59."

"Okay..." I say.

"P.M."

"Oh. Oh, no."

"On October twenty-second."

No. *No*.

My legs go weak. But...but that's not possible. I'm a Scorpio. I knew I was on the cusp, but... I'm a *Scorpio*.

I'm tough. I'm witty. I am determined. I'm all the things a Scorpio is.

"This isn't possible," I say, and then *I* laugh, because clearly, Mami is playing a joke on me. "Are you filming me, Tracey? Did you two plan this?"

But when I look at my best friend, she isn't laughing.

Mami isn't laughing anymore, either. She hands me my birth certificate.

And sure enough, there it is, on my certificate of live birth.

My name. My parents' names, Miriam and Gerardo Torres.

Date of birth: October 22.

Time: 23:59.

I'm not a Scorpio at all.

I'm a *Libra*.

My legs give out, and I'm wobbling, and Mami is calling

my name, she's at my side, and my whole world is ripped out from under me.

I'm a fucking *fake Scorpio*.

I don't get out of bed the whole weekend.

Okay, that isn't exactly true. I don't wet the bed or anything, and I manage to eat a couple meals with my mami's urging. She keeps apologizing, saying that my birth was difficult, and she just assumed that I was born *after* midnight because that's when she was lucid enough to register that I was now in the world. So she never looked at my birth certificate. Why would she have to?

I don't blame her for that. I tell her repeatedly that I'm not mad at her, because truthfully, I'm *not*. She didn't do anything wrong. And after Papi left... Well, it would be hard for me to *ever* be mad at Mami. It's just us two, you know?

I'm mad at myself. I burrow deeper underneath my cobija, shrouded in darkness, because I can't face anyone. Not Tracey, who finally left when I refused to get up off the floor. She's texted me a few times, and I've given her one-word responses. Not anyone at school, since this has to be the nail in the coffin. Who is ever going to trust my advice or my guidance again? Not the fake Scorpio. Not the astrologist who didn't even know their own birthday.

It's times like these that I start thinking about Papi. Times where I'm stressed, or sad, or panicking about something. I don't know what that says about me. Or *him*. But sometimes, I wonder: When he left, did he tie a tiny thread of my life to him? And as he moves further and further away, deeper into his new life and his new family, does he unravel me a bit more?

That's how I feel. Unraveled, like when the bottom of a sweater starts to come undone.

Oh. Great. Now I'm thinking in Weezer lyrics.

I spend Sunday trying my best to not think about this new revelation, which of course means I think of it constantly. Even my last reading was flawed. It's because I have been faking it this whole time, right?

God, and of course it was with Salvador Benevides. I can't face him. *Ever.* He was already a little skeptical, but now? Oh, I'm going to be the laughingstock of *everyone* if I go back to school.

Will he tell his football buddies? Will they all gather around in one of those huddle things and laugh about me?

And why does this thought crush me more than all the others?

So I've decided: it's time to drop out. I'll drop out and get a job over at Stater Bros., packing groceries into paper bags and walking older women out to their cars while they bark orders at me because they're used to bossing around brown people. Then I'll develop a crushing addiction to late-night infomercials and waste away all my paychecks on crystals, Groupon deals, and those overpriced compilation albums that only seem to be advertised between 1:36 and 5:12 a.m. Mom will force me out of the house, and I'll get a studio near La Sierra and waste away because there is no way anyone will ever trust me again.

Certainly not Sal. Sal, who is looking for a date to the dance, who is best paired with a Scorpio.

Which I am definitely *not*.

I tell this to Tracey over video chat on Sunday morning.

"I know you're normally pretty dramatic," she says, squinting at me through the phone, "but this is a *lot*, Efren."

"Is it?" I whine. "I'm pretty sure I'm going to be expelled tomorrow, so why bother showing up?"

"Efren."

She says my name with force behind it.

"Tracey."

"I know this sucks, but…but it's not the *end*."

"Then why does it feel like it?" I sit up in bed and brush my curls to the side. "Why does it feel like I'll go to school on Monday, and everyone will like…tape me to a flagpole or something?"

"No one has *ever* been taped to a flagpole at school, Efren."

"Well, someone has to be the first!"

She makes a grunt of exasperation. "Come on, Efren. I get why this is upsetting, but it's not like anyone even *knows*. Just don't say anything for a while."

You know that emoji? That one with the teeth bared in a straight line? I always use it to represent the face I'm making now, which is an expression between a grimace and embarrassment.

"Efren," says Tracey, "did you do something?"

"I assume you haven't been on Instagram yet," I say.

She groans. "What did you post?"

I wait for her to look. I'm sure she'll see it soon: the posts announcing *I am a Fake Scorpio* and that all business is suspended indefinitely. Or maybe she'll go to my Stories and see the screenshots I took of the only two notifications that Star Chart gave me after signing up:

Saturday Morning: People do live double lives, so beware.

Sunday Morning: Why are you so nervous?

Clearly, because Star Chart *knew*. They knew I was a fake Scorpio.

Tracey is quiet for a few moments as she reads. "What did you once tell me about this app?" she finally asks.

"That it's garbage?"

"Uh-huh. And?"

"That it's programmed to be random, which makes it useless."

"So why do you suddenly take it at face value? It's not real."

"Well, first of all," I say, "it *clearly* knew I was living a double life."

Tracey drops her phone, and I hear it clatter on the floor, followed by a string of expletives. "If I could come over right now, Efren, I would take you out in your backyard and put you out of your misery."

"Thank you, mi amor."

"It's not a compliment!" she shouts. "Listen to yourself! Suddenly, this garbage app is ruling your life. Why are you letting it have so much meaning?"

"Because—"

She holds up a hand. "Actually, I don't want to hear it. Just…think about this for a moment. How do those notifications count as a reading? How are they helpful? *Why are you so nervous?* Really, Efren? You know it's bullshit!"

Tracey is right, but it stings nonetheless.

"Well, what if the app is *coincidentally* right, then? What does that say about me?"

"I'm more concerned with what you're saying about yourself," Tracey shoots back. "This idea that your whole life is going to end is ridiculous. On top of all that, you're melting down over a boy who hasn't even shown any romantic or physical interest in you."

"I am *not*!"

"Efren."

"What?" I say to her, and I can't help it when my voice cracks. "Okay, so maybe it is possible I am freaking out over… over a boy."

"Duh!" she says. "Look, if Salvador Benevides is even remotely interested in you, this isn't going to matter to him. Even if it does, that's not the kind of guy you want in your life."

There's a knock at my door, and Mami opens it a little bit. "¿Estás ocupado, mijo?"

"Hey, Tracey, I gotta go," I say. "We'll talk later?"

"Of course, boo." She smiles at me. "And be kind to yourself, okay?"

I nod and hang up, and then Mami comes in and sits on the end of my bed. "How you doing, Efren?"

I sigh loudly and then drape myself over the bed. "Better, I guess. Maybe thinking that I've gone too hard in grieving my lost Scorpio identity."

"Mmm." That's all she does is make that sound, and she runs her hand over my cobija a few times.

"Mami? You okay?"

"That's an interesting word you used," she said. "Estás afligiendo."

I don't hear that word in Spanish often. Some people say "lamentar," but that's tinged with regret. Am I regretting anything?

I twist my mouth downward. "It's just that... Well, what am I if I'm not a Scorpio? How can I be a *Libra*?"

"Why does that matter?"

My hand goes to my chest. "How can you say that? You know how important this is to me!"

"But does it change who you *are*?"

She raises her eyebrows when she says this, and I don't immediately fling back the first thought that comes to mind. I want to argue with her, but...she kinda has a point, doesn't she?

Mami reaches out and brushes her hand through my hair. "Papito, you're still Efren. You're still perceptive and observant. You're still able to tell what kind of person someone is from just talking to them, right?"

"I guess," I say.

"No guessing. I *know*. And just because this part of you has changed doesn't mean who you are at your core is any different." She laughs, and then she rubs her right shoulder with her left hand. "At least you didn't get a Scorpio tattoo or anything."

Maybe she didn't quite mean to make the connection, but I know why she's rubbing that spot. Gerardo's name was once there, and after a handful of laser treatments, it's mostly a bad scar.

She catches me staring at her shoulder. "Ay, mijo, it's not the same," she says. "I didn't mean to say it like that."

"No, it's fine," I say to her, grabbing her hand. "I guess it puts things in perspective. We're not really different people after *that*, are we?"

"Maybe a little," she said. "If anything, we're a little closer."

I make that closeness literal as I lean in to her. "Thank you," I tell her. "For reminding me."

We don't say anything for a while after that. The silence is enough.

"Efren Torres, Guide to the Stars, is open for business!"

It's Monday.

It's warm out.

The earth is spinning.

I might not be a Scorpio, but I'm still Efren Torres.

And there is one person in my line, waiting for me.

"So, about that reading you gave me on Friday," says Salvador Benevides. "I realize that you didn't really get to finish, and I didn't actually pay you, either."

Tracey scoots off the bench. "I'm gonna give you this moment alone," she "whispers" to me, and as she walks away, she turns around and makes a terribly vulgar gesture.

I don't know what I'd do without her.

I turn back to Sal, who is staring at me in anticipation. "Well, I don't charge if I don't finish," I say. "Maybe we could pick up where we left off?"

"I'd like that," Sal says, and he flashes that killer smile at me as he sits down. "And I'd love to know if I'm compatible with a Libra."

My mouth drops open a little. "Oh. Okay, well..." I gulp. It's a coincidence, right? The timing is so perfect, though! "So it kinda depends. Tauruses and Libras *can* pair well, but it takes work. Libras... Well, I guess we can be attracted to things that are pretty, like a sort of instant attraction."

"You said *we*," Sal says.

"Uh...yeah. I did."

"So you've already adapted to being a Libra, then?"

I nearly choke. "I'm sorry, what?"

"I saw your Stories from this weekend," he says. "What a shitty way to find out you're a different sign, but it's cool you're just going with the flow. I like that."

"Wait, you saw that?" Panic is ripping through. Does Sal follow me? No, I would have noticed something like that!

"Yeah. I check your page from time to time."

There's a gasping sound behind Sal, and Tracey is at a bench not too far away. It looks like she's busy dying.

But I have to focus. I have to. "So...so you know about me, then."

He smirks. "I mean, who doesn't? Efren Torres, Guide to the Stars. You were here before that app. You'll probably outlast it."

And then he reaches across the table.

Tauruses tend to like touch. Taste. Smell. They usually use their senses to make a connection with someone.

Is...is that what he's doing?

"So tell me."

Oh, I'll tell you *anything*.

"Does Efren Torres have a date to the spring dance?"

I am not sure I heard any of that correctly.

"Because I don't think I'm all that confused anymore."

A Taurus.

A Fake Scorpio.

Maybe it could be love.

Maybe it couldn't.

But I squeeze Salvador Benevides's hand back, because the risk is worth it. He is the prettiest motherfucker I've ever seen.

"JUST KISS ALREADY!!" Tracey shouts, practically falling off her bench.

Sal tilts his head to the side. "Sounds like we should give the people what they want."

I breathe the word *Yes* into his mouth as he leans in.

"Yes *what*?" he says, just inches from my face.

"To the dance," I say, and then he pulls me closer.

A Taurus.

A Fake Scorpio.

No, no, no.

A *Libra*.

I could get used to that.

And I could get used to the feeling of Sal Benevides kissing me.

✳   ✳   ✳   ✳   ✳

SCORPIO

Venus in Scorpio

* *Focused and intense*
* *Deeply committed and connected*
* *Mysterious and hard to read*
* *Hates feeling slighted and can be vindictive because of it*
* *Demanding, suspicious, and jealous*

The South Street Challenge
Eric Smith

"Miguel, there isn't enough Lactaid *in the world* to save you from this," my best friend Dario says, our legs dangling down and swinging from where we're sitting in Headhouse Square. He's got a Rita's water ice in his hands, bits of sticky blue sugar water coating his tan cheeks.

"Bro, come here." I reach out with a napkin to wipe some of it away, leaving a trail of red. I look at the napkin, already coated in my own water ice, blackberry.

"Did you get it?" he asks, tilting his head up, blue and dark purple slicked across his face. His sharp Colombian cheekbones leave a near-perfect straight line for more drips of water ice to slide down, like raindrops on an angled roof.

"Um...sure." I shrug, tucking the napkin under my thigh.

I've always been a bit jealous of how staggeringly handsome Dario is and never quite understood parents and teachers saying things like, "Look at that jawline!" when we were in junior high. But these days I get it. At least his lush hair matches my own thick Peruvian curls.

The Headhouse Square fountain pumps water up into the air, and little kids are running around in the middle of it, their parents chasing them about the gold-and-blue-patterned tiled surface. It's a typically hot Philadelphia summer day, the kind where you can see the heat rising off the Old City bricked sidewalks in waves, and the spray of mist from the fountain feels amazing. I watch a few kids skateboard by, one of them doing a jump right in front of a No Skateboarding sign. I nod approvingly.

"But seriously. It's a wildly bad idea," Dario says, eating another spoonful of his Rita's. It's mostly liquid at this point, and a bit dribbles down onto his shirt. "Dammit." He wipes at it with his hand, making it worse.

"I think I can take it." I shrug again, closing my eyes as a breeze carries some water across my skin. I rub my hand over my face, a little water stuck in the stubble I desperately need to shave. I definitely have my father's scratchy facial hair, the kind that looks terrible after a day, amazing around three days, and then terrible again by the end of the week. I wish my face could just live in that in-between stage where things look and feel perfect.

Kinda like this summer.

"Listen, I know you're fueled by spite, but this is just going to make you feel worse," he says, shaking his head. A little kid nearby squeals at something or someone, kicking up water.

"I don't think you should do it. You really want your last big Philadelphia memory to be us rushing to find a bathroom up and down South Street? Cuba Libre is like four blocks away. We could at least go dancing or something. The girls are here."

The rest of our little crew, Farah and Kim, ditched at Rita's in favor of getting some ice cream a few blocks away. I look over at him, and he gives me a knowing smirk.

"It'll be fine," I scoff and wave his implication away.

"I'm just saying, maybe you need a little more Sprite and a little less spite in life. And in your stomach." He hands me a soda like we're in the world's worst commercial.

"Shut up." I laugh, swatting at him and his drink.

He's right, though.

But I don't like being told what I can and can't do.

Over the last month, me and my closest friends have spent the days doing just about every single Philadelphia cliché you can possibly imagine, trying to squeeze in a bucket list of items for what feels like a final goodbye but really isn't. It's all temporary, I know. After all, everyone who has ever moved away from the city has come back. More than a few friends moved away in grade school or junior high and returned just in time to wrap up high school, their parents unable to resist the siren song of our city. Two of my favorite teachers, Mr. and Mrs. Weir, moved away to the West Coast my first year and were back at the start of our junior year. It's the kind of town that has that sort of hold on you, the sort of city that proudly holds up advertisements like *Philadelphia: It's not as bad as Philadelphians say it is*. And with this move to California looming, just waiting for me at the tail end of the summer, there are just a few things left to check off.

My parents spent all of my junior-high and high-school career reminding me of all the things that could potentially get me in trouble. Smoking, drinking, sure. But the push against me dating anyone, the pressure to avoid ever going downtown, and to just stick around our hideaway in Manayunk, as if Main Street didn't exist as a hot nightlife spot… It was a lot. I feel like I missed out on so much, so many integral parts of being in high school and living in a big city.

One of my cousins joked that he was worried I might explode in college, and these last few days here in Philly, with my friends, have showed just how misplaced that concern was.

Because I think I'm going to explode *here*.

School is over. High school is a wrap. College is coming, and there are so many things I want to try for the first time before I'm off, while my parents are getting things settled out on the coast, leaving me to enjoy a final summer with my friends, courtesy of the guest room at Dario's house.

We already ran up the *Rocky* stairs and rode on electric scooters around the Philadelphia Museum of Art, two things my mom has always been terrified of. "What if you fall?" was the response to both activities. Farah talked to her older sister at Penn and managed to convince her crew team to take us out over the waterworks on one of those wildly long rowboats. One of those iconic Philly images that make for some of the most picture-perfect postcard photos of the city in the fall, little ships coasting over the water with autumn leaves exploding like fireworks in the background.

It should have been impossible.

And that only made me want to do it more.

I couldn't stop until it happened for me, for all of us.

"Just..." Dario starts and sighs, taking a sip of his soda. "Can you maybe just promise me you'll be a little less intense when you're off to college, or in whatever you end up doing out there?"

He looks over at me, his tan skin slicked with water ice and riddled with beads of sweat or droplets from the fountain, I'm not sure. I tug at my T-shirt, shimmying a little, cooling myself down. The two of us are gloriously tanned as is. Being out here in the summer sun isn't going to do much, but we're also both a hairy mess. Him and his long hair on his head, me with my ability to grow a full beard since eighth grade.

"We'll see." I glance at him and wink, closing my eyes for another spray of mist from the fountain.

"You'll never change." He exhales.

An abrupt blast of cold water pours down my back, and I can't help but scream, as does Dario. I jump up from the concrete wall we're both sitting on, stumbling a little into the fountain, my shoes and socks and bottom of my dark blue jeans drenched, and spin around.

"Oh. Hi," Farah says, tilting her head and grinning, looming above me, behind the wall we were sitting on. She's got a now-empty bottle of spring water in her hand and wiggles it around. Kim is next to her, a smile just as big and a bottle just as empty.

"You are terrible," I groan, walking out of the fountain. I shake my feet, water sloshing inside. Dario joins me but looks a little less upset. He's wearing his usual sandals and shorts, and I can't help but glare at his choice in footwear, a bit jealous.

"If you wore shorts and reasonable shoes in the summer like a normal person, you wouldn't have this problem," Kim says, hopping down.

"I have a look," I snip back, gesturing at myself. Tight jeans, combat boots, band T-shirts. The Philadelphia group mewithoutYou is written on my shirt today, and glancing down at the slightly damp shirt, the band's name has a bit of irony. That's basically going to be me in a few weeks, without my crew, and now I wish I'd worn something else.

"Yeah, your look is *wet*," Farah says, jumping off the wall. She runs her hand through her thick black hair and glances over at Headhouse. "Did we want to hit the antique market first before we do…" She gestures at me and then off at South Street, groaning. "Ugh, this *thing*?" Her and Dario share a smirk.

"Pretty sure they have antique flea markets in California." I shrug, looking over at the square, where a bundle of fold-out tables are propped up, along with big racks of clothing, old furniture, and steamer trunks.

"Yeah, but let's rummage anyway," Dario says, looking at his phone and then glancing up at Farah. He shakes off his sandals. "Maybe the camera guy is there."

"That's exactly what you need." Farah snorts, nudging him. He's been collecting vintage cameras at these things since I've known him. The flea markets around the city, the antique markets, any kind of we're-selling-junk-outside market, and he is there, trying to haggle for cameras he doesn't even know how to use.

"Listen, one day I'm going to get amazing at photography, you'll see," he says, walking toward the square. Kim gives me a side-eye, and we follow him. Farah hurries along and catches up to him and bumps him with her hip, the two of them laughing as they walk ahead.

"You think they'll finally get together once you move away?" Kim asks softly.

"Maybe," I say. "Might as well. Been waiting years for it to happen."

"I'll be sorry you missed it."

"Yeah." I sigh. "Yeah, me too."

We enter the outdoor market, large brick pillars forming a narrow space of shade, surprisingly cool. The various open junk markets around town in the spring and summer have a certain smell to them, like pages in old library books mixed with crispy leaves in a campfire, the scent of age. There's something about that, combined with being in one of the most historic cities in the country, that fills my heart every single time.

Probably why I'm off to study history and become a history teacher.

I love the feeling of being tethered to a place.

I glance up at Kim, who is already stopped at the very first stand in the antique market, running her fingers through a large wooden crate of what looks like fashion jewelry. Her green eyes are wide as they survey the chains and bracelets and charms, her sun-kissed freckles standing out against her golden skin. Her eyes flit up to me, and she smiles and shrugs.

Tethered to a person.

Though I suppose that's a conversation that we're probably never going to have.

"Hey, come look at this," she says, motioning me over. I

stroll back toward her, having already walked up a few tables, and she pulls out what looks like a leather necklace. "Bend down. You know you're enormous."

I laugh and lower my head. I'm six feet tall, which means I'm exactly one foot taller than she is. She ropes it over my neck, and I stand back up, looking down at it. The charm on the end is a little silver outline of the state of Pennsylvania.

"So you'll think about us from time to time." She smiles, flicking a finger at the charm.

"I love it." I smile. Though the idea of not thinking about Kim almost feels ridiculous. She's an ever-present thought, as much a part of me as Gritty is to Philadelphia, the feelings strange and wonderful. Again, like Gritty.

She turns to a man behind the table, handing him a couple of dollars, and I glance back up the corridor leading toward the end of the Headhouse Square market. I can spot Dario and Farah down at the end, talking to one another. They turn back, looking at me, and wave before walking off to the side someplace, disappearing behind a brick column and some racks of old clothing.

Those two are up to something.

"So besides this cheesesteak mess you're determined to do—" Kim starts.

"I am."

"Ugh." She rolls her eyes. "What else is there?"

"Oh, I don't know..." I shrug, thinking. We keep walking, poking at the various tables. There's one full of old paperbacks, a mix of books that look vintage, and others just brand-new and on the cheap. I run my hand over their spines, spotting a few historical novels, and glance up at the sidewalk bookseller, who just nods at me. I grab an Erik Larson paperback and an Adele Griffin novel and pay her using Venmo.

I want to buy more, but all my bags and boxes are already out in California with Mom and Dad, a lone, small, rolling suitcase my last bit of luggage to fly cross-country with. I hope I can find a good used bookstore out there in Oakland. I'd say I hope I'll find friends as good as these, like Kim, Farah, and Dario but... I'm not holding my breath. Thank God for social media and texting.

"Wait, look at this!" Kim shouts, plucking another book out of the stack. It's the latest novel by my favorite author, Meg Medina. "That's an awesome find."

I open it up, and it's signed.

"Oh my God," I gasp, holding it out to her. "Look!"

"Oh, wow! What are the chances?" She laughs, smiling. I look up at the bookseller and hold it up.

"How much is—"

"On me." She smiles, shooing me with her hand. "It's buy two get one free, anyway."

"What? But it's signed."

"Enjoy."

I press the book to my chest and slide it under my arm, and Kim walks up closer, nudging against me.

"Pretty sure whenever we come to these things, you scour books for signed copies." She shrugs, grinning. I nod. She is correct. One time I found a Michael Crichton novel inscribed to someone named James, and it thrilled me to the point that I considered briefly changing my name. I could be a James.

We keep walking, Kim stopping at every other table to flick through jewelry and rummage in boxes full of old video games. She plucks out a few old cartridges for ancient systems she's got lined up in her bedroom, an old Super Nintendo, a Sega Saturn. Nothing she doesn't have already, but it's always a thrill to find this stuff out in the wild, waiting to find someone who will appreciate them again.

I twirl the Pennsylvania necklace around my finger and feel the weight of the book under my arm. Kim's eyes are piercing into me, her auburn hair bright against the green leaves of street trees and faded old brick surrounding us.

"What?" she asks, putting down a game, pushing against me again. We walk to the end of the market space, and I shrug. I can smell her orange-vanilla shampoo as she moves about, jostling her hair, and it twinges at something in my chest. I remember when she first starting using that in like, eighth grade. And a body spray that smelled the same. Dario had said she smelled like his grandmother's candles, and we all laughed about it, as best friends who bust each other's chops do.

But now...

But now I wonder how it might feel to wrap myself up in all of that. My arms around her, her hair tickling my neck.

"Nothing." I sigh, looking back out at the city and the street, cobblestones, and a Wawa looming before us. But it's not nothing. I leave tomorrow. The flight is in the morning. And this is maybe my last chance to really tell her how I've been feeling. How I've felt. All these years as friends. I can feel all of that, just welling in my chest, like one of those creatures in those *Alien* movies.

There's a pause here, between us, among the rickety tables and surfaces full of old junk. Items packed full of unspoken history, in a way, just like us. All these trinkets can't talk, but I can. I know I can.

But instead of digging deep, I clear my throat and look around.

"Where did Farah and Dario go?" I ask.

"Not sure," Kim says, pointedly looking puzzled. "Let me text them."

She pulls out her phone, taking a few steps away from me, and then quickly looks back up. I follow her gaze and catch Dario and Farah walking out of the Wawa across the street, little bags under their arms.

"Hey, there they—" I start, taking a step.

"Why don't we—" Kim says, walking up to me quickly "—go walk down around Spruce Street Harbor? Take a few photos on the oversize chairs, maybe? See if we can grab one of those hammocks that swing over the water?"

I look back up at Dario and Farah, who disappear around a corner up toward South Street. Those hammocks are always taken, full of snuggling couples or people pretending to read while on their phones. But something about the hope of finding one empty, just for me and her, sends my heart absolutely racing.

"Sure, just..." I look toward Dario and Farah and then back. "Sure. They're just being weird."

"I think Dario had to pick up stuff for his mom." Kim shrugs, nudging me away. "Come on."

Her hand is out, as she walks ahead of me. I reach out for a minute and then shrink back. Maybe...maybe if we get a hammock. Maybe then.

* ◇ *

Spruce Street Harbor Park opens up like a strange little oasis smack in the middle of Old City, or maybe on the edge of it. I guess it depends on who you ask. Suddenly you're leaving a concrete walkway that passes through a war memorial with a trio of eyesore condos in the background to a place full of trees, hanging lights, and life, right on the Schuylkill River.

It's a little more packed than usual, and that's saying something. In the summer months, it's nearly impossible to grab a seat or even some standing room. The lines for food, served up from makeshift restaurants inside large shipping containers, are impossibly long. But the smell of fried chicken and sugary funnel cake fills the air around us, making my stomach rumble.

"I wonder what's going—" I start, looking at all the people. But then I hear it.

Music.

The sound of an acoustic guitar and some microphone feedback.

"Sorry, everyone…" a familiar voice says, booming through the park, echoing on the water. Kim looks up at me and shrugs, as we continue down a brick walkway toward the small area where they occasionally host a band or two.

We weave in between a few people, an open space clearing up a little farther in. A guy stands in the middle of the small amphitheater, guitar in hand, with someone next to him, holding another guitar.

"No… No way," I whisper and look down at Kim. "Did you know about this?"

She shrugs again, a sly little smirk on her face.

I want to cry.

It's the singer of Hideaway and, I think, maybe their guitarist. My favorite group. The guitarist swipes at the strings with a *schikt, schikt, schikt* before ringing out a chord that sends the audience into loud cheers.

I've never seen them live before. Just in videos on social media and streaming concerts. They're local but don't play out all that often, for whatever reason. There are all kinds of near-conspiracy-theory reasons for why all over Reddit, but one of my cousins told me it's because the singer is actually a high-school music teacher at his school.

I like the mystery better.

God, not only have I never seen them in person, but I don't think me and Kim have ever gone to a concert together before. She's not into my particular brand of indie rock, sticking to her pop singers. Which is fine, but I've never been able to convince her to check out any of the Philly bands I like. The War on Drugs or Dr. Dog or The Wonder Years…

She planned this.

The performance kicks off, and I feel this chill sweep over my whole body, and it's not from the breeze coming up over the water. I feel something flicking at my wrist, and I glance over to see Kim grabbing my hand, lacing her fingers in between. I have to…inch my back down a little, to properly hold her hand, but oh my God.

I look at her, and she glances up at me for a second before looking back at the band.

"Kim," I whisper.

She stares ahead, but I see her eyes flit my way.

"Kim?" I almost plead, and her head turns a little. I swal-

low, a little lump in my throat. I leave tomorrow. *Tomorrow.*
"Why now?"

"If not now, when?" she asks.

I look back at the band, and she squeezes my hand.

"It's not fair," I manage to get out, as the singer belts and
the guitarist keeps jamming.

"I know."

* ◊ *

"Are you sure you still want to do this?" Kim asks, as we
make our way back up South Street, holding my hand.

"It's the last thing on my list. I *have* to." I shrug, the two of
us letting go of one another and grabbing onto one another
in a series of beats, as people cut between us. But I immediately know that isn't true. The last thing on my list was to
tell Kim how I felt. To finally get it all out, before I hop on
a plane, leaving my friends to be replaced by long text messages and video calls.

"I know," she says. "I just hate the thought of you lying
around Dario's the rest of the day, with a messed-up stomach. That's no way to spend a final night. And then you'll
be all out of sorts on the plane. That's a long plane ride to be
uncomfortable."

"I took my medicine!" I press, smiling at her. But now I'm
torn. We finally had that moment. A moment. Maybe I should
be spending my last night here in Philly with her and my crew,
instead of at Dario's full of self-loathing and video games.

"Okay." She shrugs.

I spot Lorenzo's in the distance and know that Jim's isn't far behind.

The South Street Challenge is one of those things that everyone talks about but no one does. You order a cheesesteak from Jim's on South Street and walk over to Lorenzo's and order one of their slices of pizza. If you're not from Philly, or you've never been to this particular stretch of street, you don't know that a Lorenzo's slice of pizza is basically three entire slices put together. It looks like over a quarter of a pizza.

You wrap that monster slice around the cheesesteak, and there you have it.

The South Street Challenge.

The South Street Taco.

It has many names, this legend.

I can already taste it and can already feel my stomach hurting. But right now, it feels better than my heart. I know how bad leaving is going to hurt, and I need something, anything, to distract from it. I finally know how Kim feels about me, and we didn't even have to talk about it. I can feel it. The way I've felt it all these years of being friends-that-could-have-been-more.

When we get to Lorenzo's and walk inside, I'm surprised to see Dario and Farah there already, hanging out in the wildly small pizza place, the interior only big enough to host a line and maybe one or two people awkwardly eating near the window. No one likes those people, though. Tourists, usually. And mercifully, it's not as packed as it tends to be.

They've got cheesesteaks in their hands and are grinning.

I point at them, as Kim nudges up against me. Dario looks at the two of us and smirks, before holding one out.

"For you," he says, smiling.

"We're not ready for this day to be over, just because you're out here with something to prove." Kim grins, nodding at the cheesesteaks. "Yours has pepper jack on it."

"And this…" Dario nudges a slice of pizza my way, but it's all red "…is tomato pie. Figure we blast it with a bunch of parmesan cheese, and it'll work just as well."

I look at the cheesesteak and the pizza slice, confused, and all four of us move toward the front of Lorenzo's. Photos of the South Street Taco usually show a traditional cheesesteak, with Whiz or provolone cheese, and a huge sopping slice of pizza wrapped around it. This…does not look like that. But I'm not sure it matters.

"Did you guys all plan this out?" I ask and notice the Wawa bag in Dario's hand. "Is that what the Wawa trip was all about?"

"Some of it," Dario says noncommitally. "Jim's didn't have the pepper jack, so I had to get some. I know it's low in lactose. Wikipedia taught me that. Kim called Lorenzo's and had them make a whole tomato pie, since you can't exactly order one lone slice as a surprise for a stubborn friend."

"And Kim here distracted you while we got everything wrangled up," Farah says, smirking. "The perfect plan."

"The whole South Street Challenge Taco thing," Dario says, grinning. "It just says a slice of pizza from Lorenzo's wrapped around a Jim's cheesesteak. Doesn't specify any other rules."

Farah points at my tomato pie slice and the pepper jack cheesesteak. It looks so horrible, and I love it. Part of me feels like I'd cry if I wasn't smiling so hard, to the point where I'm pretty sure my cheeks are squeezing against my tear ducts. I love this bunch.

"This still counts." She lowers her gaze and raises her eyebrows at me. "So where are we going to construct these monsters?"

"I know," Kim says.

"Good, 'cause there's a line, youse kids." I turn around to spot one of the guys working behind the counter giving us a *It's time to get going* look, but he's clearly amused by the whole thing. His smug smile even seems to have a Philly accent, if that was even possible. "I hear the pizza sucks out there. Good luck."

Farah gives him a glare, but I can't help but laugh.

I'm gonna miss this.

* ◊ *

We make our way back down South Street, crossing Front Street and heading toward the bridge that crosses over the wildly busy Columbus Boulevard and overlooks Penn's Landing, the Delaware River right in front of us, Camden across the water. Dario and Farah sit down against the wrought iron fencing that circles the overlook, the busy highway below us, people zooming by on their way to wherever.

The two of them start unwrapping their cheesesteaks and take out the huge slices, laughing awkwardly as they try to wrap them up. I take mine, the tomato surface bright red with huge basil leaves, and slap it against the cheesesteak they got me. The sauce makes a wet sound against the bread, and Kim lets out a loud laugh as she makes her own.

Mom and Dad would absolutely hate this, though neither of them are exactly known for home-cooked meals. Just the cliché plate of fruit whenever I have friends over.

"A toast!" Dario says, holding his pizza-wrapped cheese-steak in the air, like we're a bunch of South Philly muske-teers. "To happy travels."

"To good friends," Farah says, leaning against Dario.

"To being more." Kim grins at Farah, who blushes in-tensely. I look down at Kim, who stares up at me, beaming. A smile on the perfect face I've been smitten with the entirety of high school. A smile that tells me maybe it's not too late.

"To us." I nod, and we all awkwardly press the cheesesteaks and pizza slices together, and a large dollop of grease, ketchup, cheese, and tomato sauce slaps loudly against the concrete around our feet. We all dart back a bit, laughing.

I take a bite. The tomato sauce, basil, and Italian spices blending...not exactly well with the spicy cheese, hard seeded roll, and chopped-up steak, but it's not terrible either. Like someone overdid it on the ketchup and spilled some oregano. While I'm chewing, I watch Dario, Farah, and Kim's faces as they try their own, the way their expressions twist and turn.

I want to memorize every bit. Every second.

I glance over at Kim, who laughs a little as she makes eye contact with me, trying to wave me off, her mouth full of sandwich. I reach up and press a thumb against the corner of her mouth, wiping away a splash of sauce.

And in that moment, I know.

I'll be back.

*   *   *   *

OPHIUCHUS

Venus in Ophiuchus

* *Ambitious, dominant, and authoritative*
* *Passionate and intense*
* *Enjoys being a protector and provider*
* *Seemingly cold or uninterested*
* *Potentially vengeful, conniving, and ruthless if spurned*

Formation
Cam Montgomery

"Once upon a time, a starry Black girl was born beneath a white moon, and a boy named for the darkness of the night sky joined her…"

Spiritual Bae. Working the Roots. Maker of spiritual bits and pieces. Student and slave to Black spirituality. 1 of 5. Ase.
Venmo: thewhitemoon   Cash App: $whitemooon

There are only so many times you can change your Instagram bio before it starts to become an obsession. And I'm not saying I've changed my bio seven times today. But I've absolutely changed my bio seven times today.

Would have been six, but I just couldn't bring myself to deny the angels' number since I found seven smooth stones outside in the tall grass behind my house. I collected them all, placed them in a jar, whispered over it and tucked that right into my pack.

Sevens are good. Mama Dukes down on the corner always says so.

Angels' numbers are little taps on the shoulder, she'd say. Taps on the shoulder that any angel might send you. A little hey-how-are-ya, or sometimes even a hint that you need to check yourself.

The little taps aren't necessarily always from someone of your own ancestral line. But I always know when it's my people. I always feel it right there. In that same spot.

It's the space where, if I had two hearts, the other one would be. Sitting pretty on the right side of my chest. It was a dream I used to have. That I had two hearts.

I don't dream it anymore, but I still feel little pricks and pinches there on occasion. From the angels. From the stars.

I toss my phone onto my bed, double-check that my knapsack is secure, everything tucked away into it, phone charger *not* forgotten because holy hell, would it be hard to find an iOS-compatible charger up on the mountain without being clowned for loving Apple. So I checked that seven times, too.

We haven't known it for long, The Five. But the moment we all found out it was us—that the ancestors had chosen us—I think that's the point where we started to let go of everything. Knowing we'd be headed up on the mountain to follow this whole destiny thing. Me and four of my bests chosen to journey up the mountain, set up shop there and serve the people of the mountain city.

I live in a small Acadian Louisiana parish. Evangeline Parish.

This parish, with all its lakes, rivers, tiny huts and bayous, is who I am. My pops almost named me for it—Evangeline Paris LeBlanc.

Mama shut that shit down with a quickness, stuck me with a name that would tell the people who I am. Who I would become. Who would be the Étoile witch to carry the parish back into the light.

Destiny. Fate. One of *The Five*. The will of the ancestors. No matter what you call it, those are the cards I've been dealt.

Luna LeBlanc, Black girl, Étoile witch, French Cajun daughter of the Acadian bayou.

I was born on a bright night, but all the free will Baby Luna might have been allowed to have once was lost to a summer wind.

I try not to buck back against it. I try to embrace my lot in life. To understand and feel the luck of my life. I am the witch who will save her people. Katrina's stiff hurricane fingers still touch the walls and the cracked cobblestones of the city, and there's one way to get her back on her feet. Me. I am the way. One of five, anyway.

For a second, I stop and ruminate on the way I used to hate my fate. Controlling birth charts. That's what I do. As an Étoile witch, I'm supposed to manage the birth charts of others. Make sure they've been born under the right stars, and if not, I change that.

Felt supremely cool at first, but then I learned the ancestors' stories about encountering the one sign I'm supposed to contain if I find it. Don't like that part.

I am not the person to police the signs.

With one more check of my phone, waiting for the time to

hit 7:07 a.m., I drag all my earthly possessions out to the living room where Pop and his millennia-long best friend, Muhammad, and Muhammad's daughter, Nilu—my probably-going-to-be-millennia-long best friend—wait. I smile as Pop and Muhammad sit there, smoking their pipes, sipping slowly on chicory coffee.

It's a scent that perfumes the entire house, and I will miss it. Almost as much as I will miss him.

The second I drop my bags, Pop turns in his beat-down BarcaLounger. "There she is! I thought she fell face-first into her phone and wasn't gone come back."

Pop doesn't do anything quietly. Talk, laugh, sleep, drag people. All loud.

Muhammad laughs and stands to hug me, his too-big, too-loose, too-old button-down shirt swaying around us. "You ready, my girl?" Muhammad asks, accent thick. Muhammad's people hail from Senegal. He is estranged from them the way I'll be estranged from him and Pop. Only, his situation swims in bad blood, while mine swims in a tepid bathtub of necessity. Just the same as Nilu's. She, too, is one of The Five.

"I'm ready," I say, shouldering my pack. Nilu stands quietly in a corner. It's so unlike her.

I walk over and grab her hand. She is very still, staring at the floor, bags strapped tight to her back and chest.

When I squeeze her penny-toned hand, with the vitiligo dancing and jumping all over it, she finally looks up at me and smiles. Exhales. There's my girl. My twin flame. The Bonnie to my Clyde.

"Hey, Lu."

Her shoulder bumps mine. "Hi, Lu," she says back, sardonically.

Nilu and Luna. We weren't named to match one another, but we do. We were, however, born on the same day. Her chart is slightly different than mine, but it's the same in the ways that matter. I haven't altered her chart at all.

And her birth—that *was* on purpose. Intentional. The ancestors, the universe, commanded it.

All of The Five are born on the same day.

The Five. The entire reason we're leaving our parish and heading up the mountain to settle. To protect the people.

It is, on occasion, hard for me to reconcile with fate. Destiny. This ancestral mission I'm on with four of my closest friends who had no choice in the matter either.

Every seventy-seven years, a new group of The Five is born.

That's us. Me, Nilu, Sevan, and the twins, Beyah and Keturah. The magickal girl gang of your freakin' dreams. I tried to talk them into Sailor Scout suits, but it was vetoed pretty quickly.

"Your hand is hella sweaty. I'mma need for you to let go."

I glance at Nilu, who suddenly has come back to herself. I drop her hand, wipe it on my pants—because she's right—and mouth *Fuck off* to her.

Pop stands. "When are Sevan, B, and Keturah going to arrive?"

We're all traveling up the mountain together. As is tradition.

Nilu stretches her arms over her head, walks her vertebrae up their own set of spinal stairs. "We're meeting them at the mountain base."

"Good, good," Muhammad says, placing a kiss on Nilu's head, right in the middle of her space buns.

Both our fathers are nervous, and I can tell. Neither of our family lines have ever been called to The Five before. This is new and nerve-rattling for all of us.

We spend an inordinate amount of time hugging our fathers. And having each of them hug each of us back. We do another *Yes, Pop, yes, Baba, we got everything, we're ready, it's going to be okay* thing. And then we're walking off, waving back at our fathers like we're Frodo and Samwise setting out to destroy The Ring.

Who knows when we'll see them again.

This was my mother's favorite thing to say, and it stuck the day she died. *"If we knew which goodbye would be our last with a person, how different might that goodbye be."*

She was brilliant and beautiful and tough, and though she wasn't of The Five, she definitely stayed in her magick, forever settling me with the muddied visions that came to her every so often.

The last vision she shared with me is one I'm still figuring out.

"My darling dark-skinned thing, one day," she laughed. *"One day, baby, you will find yourself inside a dark sky, and you will wonder how that dark sky will guide your own starlight. The dark sky will be your perfect match. Unusual only in that the sky's darkness will be so very special to you."*

While the bayou of Evangeline is murky, muddy and incredibly misleading in its "tame" nature, the mountain is much different. Or so I'm told. I've never actually been. The mountain is for The Five and the *Others*. Those who may or may not be human. Those not necessarily meant for this astral plane.

It's not a place for humans, and that's the point. That's why, when The Five join and come of age, we get together and move our entire lives up the mountain. Up the mountain where we essentially stand sentinel for Celestials. Also tried to talk them into business cards with that stamped on them. Vetoed that, too.

Horrific taste on their part.

"You're smiling," Nilu says as we start the short trek to the mountain's base.

With a dancing hand, I wave her off. "Nah, I'm really not. This just feels right now. Proper. That's all."

"In five minutes you're going to change your flighty-ass mind."

I plant my not-even-a-little-bit sensible boots in the grassed-over trail and stop. "This doesn't feel right to you?"

"I'm not sure if I'm supposed to answer you honestly or just throw some witty quip in the mix. Middle finger to my thumb and snap and smile."

With a nod, I throw my locs up and tie a length of leather around them. Nilu's tiny button nose has this little up-turn at its tip. People pay money for noses that look like hers. Hers scrunches up tight now. I *know* she's 'bout to say something about my hair.

"You're so *rough with it*!" Called it. She walks back toward me holding her hands out. "No. Stop, here. C'mere. Let me help you."

Considering how much I'm carrying on my back, it shouldn't be so easy to evade her grabby hands. But I do. "No. No, no. It's fine."

She rolls her head around her neck, her eyes follow, and then a breath of air escapes her mouth, and even though it's just a breath, I swear it sounds like she's just whispered the word *exasperation*.

When she turns and continues toward our incline, she mumbles to herself, "I'm gonna have to get stuff for her hair *and* Sevan's. Maybe make some rose oil for the scalp. Avo paste for deep conditions. Gah, this is going to be so much work."

I used to flinch when she'd have these little reprimands-that-aren't-really-reprimands tirades. I thought they were a criticism of me. Of how hard it is to deal with me. Not anymore. Nilu's all bark, no bite, and she knows how to love on you just as hard as she bitches at you.

Pop used to say that it wasn't ever my fault that not everyone could swallow the parts of me that have sharp edges.

"Spending too much time in the linen aisle, cher. We gotta find you a comic-book store."

"A what?"

"Oh, cher. You know what comic books are. Right? Your generation knows what those are."

"Yes, Pop. But most of that stuff's online."

"Well, point stands. More comics in your life. More Man of Steel. *You deserve all of the iron-throated hearts that you can find."*

I laughed at the time, I remember. I didn't really get it then. Was too young. This was the magick Pop had. Maybe not traditional like The Five. But raw and powerful all the same.

He threw an arm around my shoulder and said, grinning, "We gotta invest in one of them metal detectors for you."

"Very funny."

"Who is laughing here, cher? Be surprised what you find then. All the tolerant hearts you can handle."

And he was right. The Five came together not long after that. I've had this super-solid girl gang full of iron-throated heart-friends ever since.

* ◊ *

Beyah, Keturah and Sevan spot us before we spot them. Sevan practically sprints up to us. She throws bear hugs, lifting each of us off the ground solidly before setting us back down. I smile back at her because hers is just that infectious. Sevan is the child of three Black hippie moms. If you thought *Timmy Has Two Dads* was a whole thing, just get a load of my girl Sevan. Her parents are polyam and happy and beautiful. Sevan is loved and cherished, and it's reflected in her magick. In her food.

Sevan is our Kitchen witch, while Nilu is a Gaia witch.

I mostly specialize in…well, at this point it's mostly just a gimmick for the 'gram. Haven't used it much. That's supposed to be for the mountain. But the Étoile lives deep in my bones.

Beyah is an Angel witch. The pedantic assholes who think they're right about everything (because they are, that's the whole point, but the rest of us don't gotta skip a beat for it) and practice magick that connects them with angels and other divine beings. Beyah's got the strongest connection to the ancestors I've ever seen.

Keturah, with her thick ringlets that used to be loc'd up before her Big Chop, sleepy eyes and Lisa Bonet vibe, is our Sigil witch. Words, symbols, sigils. That's her thing. Give her something to write with and something to write on—books, trees, your left arm that one time—and she's good to go.

We walk a path not many have taken, but the ground beneath our L.L. Bean–booted feet is still well-worn. The earth lays out stories and, on the odd occasion, emotions, evident in the way the sticky-thick moss grows up the spines of a few gentle magnolias with their leaves like fat tongues. Evident in the way the tupelo trees and their fresh-bruise-colored leaves seem to sway not left to right but up and down. Evident in the way we five can all hear whispers licking up our backs.

Keturah spots it first. The mountain town.

Mountain City exists on three levels. The first is occupied by your standard, everyday folk. The wandering souls who exist beyond any sex or gender, the Wild Men and the women who've swallowed stray Matagot, Oberon and the rest of the Fée. Those types.

As we make our way through the winding cobblestone streets of the first level, we do what we do.

I draw eighteen constellations on these really dope Sailor Moon Post-its I got on Etsy. I bless each of them and hand them out accordingly. The last one I hand out is for a baby. I place it in her mother's hands. She's going to be a star girl, too, someday. I change her chart only slightly. She's already got the stuff.

Beyah whispers secrets into the ears of seven people. All of them cry.

Nilu hands out a whopping forty-eight bundles of wrapped

herbs. Herbs she's lovingly prepared for just this. Sageing them and everything.

Sevan hands out small crinkly bags of hard rock candy. Each of them a sweet healing gift.

Keturah writes only one sigil. She writes it on the main entry gate to Mountain City. It's a blessing, yes. But it's also a protection. It's a message.

The Five are here. This is what we do, and it feels…like settling into clothes that finally fit. This is why we Chosen come here every seventy-seven years. To help those the world only sees fit to force into a system built against them.

The second level, dancing inside and just above the first like two rings sitting close to one another, is where The Five live. Immediately upon seeing it, I can tell it's not a huge patch of land. But it's enough. The house sitting at the top of the stairs we all trek to is two shakes away from its own very tragic death.

"Holy hooker, look at that ugly thing," Nilu says.

Beyah and Sevan disappear inside while Keturah walks a perimeter around the house, up through the black iron side gates, crawling with vines and their heart-shaped leaves.

"Do not insult our house, Lu. Jesus, no respect. Who raised you?"

"Wallahi, please. Your father, mostly. And even the house is insulting the house. My disdain is nothing new to it, I'm sure." She brushes past me, her pack jacking mine off-kilter on my back.

"Thanks," I mutter.

Inside is…well, not *better* per se. What's a word that's just below *better* but still means *lol, dayum*? Our house is that.

"I call this room!" That's Sevan, voice crashing through walls Kool-Aid Man–style from just beyond the kitchen. Figures.

Beyah and Keturah don't announce their room preference, but it's assumed they'll room together—because they will—and none of us ever question it. I haven't met many twin sets, but Beyah and Keturah are those fraternal sisters who get along so well it drives everyone else bananas. And I'm an only child. Never had a problem with it. Love it, in fact. I'm not great at sharing. So to say their relationship makes me jealous beyond belief is really a whole thing.

Nilu walks back toward me, having come from a hallway I hadn't noticed. Her pack is missing. "Found two adjoining rooms if you wanna scope and snag 'em?"

I smile, walk toward her. "I trust you," I say, then shove past her. "But I get whatever one has a bigger bed."

She follows quickly on my heels. "No, you don't! My ass is bigger than yours, and it deserves a throne. Your skinny behind will do just fine on a twin, let alone anything else."

Turns out both beds are fulls. So…although she has a point, it's moot anyway.

The third and final level of the city is private and houses one citizen. The divinity. Usually whatever extremely-should-not-exist-on-this-plane thing sets up shop. It changes with every group of The Five. Except for this time.

Rumor has it now there's a demigod in our midst. Rumor has it he's been around since the last set of Five arrived on scene and carved roots up through the city's darkest streets.

I've been more curious about him than any of the others.

Except for maybe Beyah, who, as an Angel witch, has probably had some kind of contact with him already. Who knows.

Been sitting for about twelve minutes before I decide the breezy thing I feel in my legs is calling me to explore. "I'm gonna go up to three."

All four heads turn in my direction. Even Sevan, who is at this point blasting Tears for Fears in the kitchen and seasoning a cast-iron skillet.

None of them even has to say any words. I leave before their *Girl, don't do it. It's not worth it* judgy looks get to me.

But, of course, Nilu never stays silent for long. "I'm coming."

I pivot, about-facing like my body's spring-loaded. "You're not."

"Lu, I feel like…"

"Like?" I counter.

She nods slowly, like her brain is reconfiguring itself. "Like I *have to* come with you?"

"Well, if it feels like a question, you probably shouldn't. Plus, I want—"

"A minute to yourself."

Nilu knows me like no one else ever could. I nod and send a closemouthed grateful smile her way.

Three is a whole thing. Like, the nature surrounding the cottage is actively moving.

I always thought the stories from Mama Dukes were just her being overly romantic about Mountain City.

But after having been here for all of thirty minutes, I know I'll never leave.

All that bass rumble in the earth has been calling to me

ever since we started up the trail. Here, I can be someone else entirely if I want to. And, in fact, I'll probably have to. The Five are, to the best of their magick ability, whatever the people need them to be.

But it also feels like I—Luna LeBlanc—can leave the rougher bits of Evangeline behind for a time.

Mountain City doesn't seem to care if you've left your house sans makeup or left your panties in the back of a cab one night or ordered two street hot dogs—yes, both of them for you and you alone.

This Luna taps gently on a dark wooden cottage door. This Luna forgets herself and enters when no one shouts a permission. This Luna dances languidly in doorways foreign to her and sings into the random black candlestick found just at her feet.

"Tell your stories to strangers, hear rivers below these floors, pounding like blood. Let the night sky swallow you into its warm mouth." A guy. My words? My...thoughts.

It's *him*.

I swallow hard, my head jerking up onto my neck with all the force of a tetherball on a fifth grader's fist. My forehead feels too warm.

The guy laughs, and even that is accented.

"I didn't mean to eavesdrop, but you fantasize very...loudly. Like, you shout a little bit."

FANTASIZE?

"Uhh..." I nod jerkily.

"You gonna say anything?"

"Uhhh..."

He nods. "This is my house. That you're in."

"Yeah, I'm sorry. Jesus, day one and already a B and E."

"Bacon and eggs," he agrees.

I itch the space on my chin where I maybe tweezed a little too heavily this morning. "No. Business and economics."

"Breakfast and fiscal responsibility aside, you're in my house. Like I said."

Mm-hmm. Yep. Jeez, he is, like—oh, my God, why am I, like, a little bit attracted to him—

Nooope. Not even a little bit why we're here.

But, low-key, he is, though. Devastatingly handsome. He's all sinewy muscle, hollowed cheeks and new-penny brown skin. Giant circular glasses kissed by long lashes, and too many freckles on his face not to remind me of the spots on a banana. Bridge of his nose and dusting the top of his lips.

He turns, noticing his door is still wide open, then turns back to me. But before he does, I notice what looks like a constellation swimming up the back of his neck. The pattern disappears into his shirt.

What feels like a few moments to me is, I know, really much, much longer.

"I very suddenly want to leave here and have to go," I say.

Before I turn to do so, he says, as though there is only time here for us in the world and nothing more, "Urges are the only trustworthy thing many of you have got. Might as well heed this one."

I've been warned more than once, by all the Black women in my neighborhood, by teachers, by our old Pastor—whose church we no longer subscribe to for this very reason—that I am *too fast*.

Pop wouldn't hear it. He balked at those people, but he

never talked to me about it. Never elaborated or smoothed the matter over.

I turn back to him. "Actually, maybe I lied. Maybe I'm fine just here. Maybe I'm here for a reason."

"A reason?"

Here we go. "*A reason*, my friend. And that reason is…" Damn. What is it, though? "I'm here to introduce myself. To offer you a gift. You're the demigod here and—"

"I'm aware—"

"Yeah, so maybe let me finish, b." I find that being a Black woman serves me almost as often as the people who are not Black women and femmes curse me. This is one instance. I know the power that exists within these old bones made new by time, by tradition, by the ancestors.

I know the ways in which Hoodoo prepossesses my future, my intention.

He takes a step back and yields the floor with this…like, sweeping arm gesture.

And although he's taken a step back to give me space, I don't want it. So I take a step closer. I like that we're pretty much the same height. I don't have a ton of it—I'm five-seven—but this feels good. Perfect.

"I'm of The Five. I am an Astro witch—étoile—and would like to offer you the gift of one jar of your choosing."

"A jar?"

"A root-work jar. A conjure jar."

"Of my choosing?" he says.

With a nod, I say quietly, "Yes."

His smile is so slow, all cold honey and condensation pooling at the sides of a glass mug.

"Can I rain-check it?"

"Is rain-check a verb, though?"

"I'm going to assume that's a yes. I'll thank you for the gift. I can offer you and the rest of your Five one as well."

"Amazing, I love presents. Can't and will not guarantee I'll share whatever it is, though."

He nods, knocks his head forward to indicate I should follow him and waltzes into a wide-open space. A galley kitchen. In such a small cottage, it seems outlandish and could-be-garish, but it's not because it's him.

I hear a metal stool scraping against the cobbled floors as he pulls it out before slapping an open palm against its seat. I sit, and he steps toward the sink, filling a metal teapot with water.

"Coffee? Tea?" he offers.

It strikes me that he's so polite. So genuinely modern and lax. It's all in his shoulders, the way his back moves as he walks. The way his jaw flexes from time to time.

"What's your name?"

"I don't have any of that," he quips. "I got coffee, tea, water and probably some apple juice in the back of the fridge that I opened three years ago and never threw out."

"Whatever tea you've got and your name, please."

"Show me yours and I'll show you mine." Talking to his back should annoy me. But it's just such a...a view.

"My name is Luna LeBlanc. I'm an Astro witch of The Five. I also have a wicked-good Instagram presence which doubles as my side hustle."

His phone comes out of his pocket, and he slides it across the table to me. "Open mine and follow yourself."

"I'm sorry... What?" I blink, not once, but twice.

"What?" Two cups and two coasters appear on the table just in front of me. Then a jar of honey, sugar cubes, a butter plate and a small, sweating pitcher of milk.

He scoops a small dip of butter and honey into his cup of darker liquid. I assume he's opted for coffee instead of tea.

Lifting my cup—sans any additions—to my lips, I sip slowly and, with the other hand, scroll through to his app, open it, find the magnifying glass icon and, with a single thumb, quickly type in my handle.

All dexterity and competence. I'm putting that on my résumé. It is a valuable skill.

I hit Follow, and it gives me *such* a sick thrill to do so.

The way he moves is so subdued. But it's obvious, the inherent power. It's alive and vibing like the bass in your favorite R&B song.

As soon as he has the phone back, I pull mine out and find his add, then jump into his profile. His page is private, but I follow him back immediately. The name on the top says *Night*. And that's it. No bio. No hashtags. No *Taken* with a heart and a ring emoji.

Not that I'm checking for all that.

"So…you've seen mine," I prompt him.

"Nox Texeira. Demigod. Wannabe photographer." He pauses, then, "Did you think I wasn't aware of you?"

"I'm sorry… Of me?"

He points to a jar of chicken bones—necks mostly—sitting on the counter. "That thing fell over twice. I knew the very moment you stepped foot on my mountain. The bones knew and foretold it. But I had this sick, floating feeling in my gut, too."

"Sounds like I gave you food poisoning or something," I say. What a lovely first impression.

"Not a first impression," he counters, one knee flung haphazardly over the other, bouncing to an invisible beat.

"Uh, I just met you."

"I met your Beyah once." His head falls sideways on his neck, his smile just as loose. He's adorable, and I hate it.

I shake my head but only for a moment. Nothing is impossible. When you're one of The Five, you grow up knowing to never say *never* and also to never deny the possibility of things that feel otherwise so.

"She never mentioned it. Didn't even blink when I got nosy enough and left the house to come up here."

"Yeah," he says. "There's a chance she doesn't remember it. There's also a chance that she knows that meeting was for her and kept it to herself for that reason."

"When was she here?"

"Beyah is your Angel witch, right?"

"Yeah," I say, the word dragging on itself, covered in the skepticism I'm not supposed to have.

Even though he is sitting now, he draws himself up on his spine, back broadening and lengthening. He leans in toward me, and I am nothing if not compelled to lean in to him, too. When we are close, perhaps *too* close, he whispers, "I met her in a dream."

I feel his breath on my lips and can't help but inhale deeply.

Because I'm trying to be smart, because I'm trying to stay cognizant of this experience, I lean back. *Self-preservation* would be another word for this.

"The angels allowed it?" I ask.

He nods. "They did. I asked to meet her, and the angels gained her permission before they'd ever allow it."

"But allow it they did."

"Yes."

"And you—what?—sipped brandy and exchanged war stories?"

"Don't be cute."

"*You* don't be cute. Tell me what she said."

He only stares back at me, calm and serene and quiet. Happy. Content.

"Please?" I whisper.

He runs a hand over his shaved head, closes his eyes for a long minute and then says, "Most of what we talked about is, like I said, for Beyah herself. But...we also talked about you."

"You talked to Beyah...about me?"

Nox nods. "She talked mostly. She loves you very much."

"I love her, too."

"She knows."

"She's my sister beyond more than just what The Five bond gives us."

"She knows."

I can only nod. "And the others? Have you met the others?"

"Not as such. I've been showing sigils to Keturah. The same one over and over until she picked it up. It's one she's going to need while you guys are here. And your Nilu is the one I've yet to encounter. She was supposed to come up here with you. To meet me."

Yes, and I talked her out of it. Christ. Nilu totally had that itching *Follow it* feeling.

He glances down, messes around on his phone a bit, and then I notice he's accepted my Follow request.

In that very moment, I get a text from Nilu.

Made your bed. Slacker. You OK?? How's our watered-down version of a god? Should I come up or nah?

So many questions, but that's just my girl. I switch back to IG without texting her back. She'll keep.

The first photo I see on his profile lives among a sea of nature photos. It's a selfie. Of him. He's gorgeous, all big teeth and wide-mouthed glory. He's all freckles and glasses. And below the photo is a caption.

#TransIsBeautiful.

My skin goes hot with embarrassment. "I'm so sorry. I… didn't even ask, and usually I try not to assume because I never need people to think I'm straight because I'm pansexual in, like, a *deeply* gay way, and I just don't want to be that person who assumes, and I'm really sorry I did that to you, I don't even know why—"

He sets down his coffee mug, and the sound it makes against the clay coaster is harsh. The look on his face is one of genuine confusion and maybe a little bit of concern for my mental stability. "What in the hell are you talking about?"

"I assumed your pronouns."

The way he exhales is nothing less than beautiful. I say a silent prayer to the stars. To the goddess Venus. The slant, broken thing happening to his mouth is definitely a smile. I suspect I could sleep in it all day.

"*He/him/his* is just fine. Preferred and perfect and undeniable. Thank you for…freaking out? I don't know."

He laughs.

So I do, too. "I don't know either! I'm sorry. I know I also super didn't need to be, like, *Hey! Hey, hey! Look at me, fellow queer!* just to justify myself as not-an-asshole."

"No, you did not. What did you think was going to happen? That I'd smite you or something?"

"No?"

"Good, because we stopped doing that in the ninth century."

Good to know. Good to know…

I sip a little more of my tea and dream for about two seconds. He seems content to let me. "What is your sign? Do you have a sign?"

"I wasn't born over the course of years or anything. Do you understand the *demi* part of *demigod*?"

No. Not really, no. "Uh, yes! Duh. So, like. When is it? Your birth century or whatever."

And before I can request it, he's pulling out a drawer next to his sink, removing a pen and paper from it and then handing them to me.

"*Demi. Sub. Somewhat. Half. Partial. Not fully a god.* That's dear old Dad's job. I'm just here as a representative because I'm better-looking than he is."

"Oh, I'm sure you are," I say. And though *I know* I've said it, there's some part of me that's hoping I haven't.

I write down his name, date and time of birth down to the minute, and location of his birth. São Paulo, Brazil.

Doing the math is the work of a moment, and I have literally never seen such a birth chart. I've heard the stories. The stars tell them to me, but they're not stories other people I know have talked about.

Every time I've tried to touch this kind of thing, it's been too bright, too hot, too big for me alone. It's a thing that deserves to be open, existing everywhere.

Seeing his chart spelled out like this gives me the same feelings I got the very first time I gave myself permission to be me. The revelation—the power of that—didn't come until after high school, of course. That would have been too convenient. But it came, nonetheless.

Me standing there one day, in the flowered dress and the polka-dot shoes with the striped headband. My eighteenth birthday hit, and the stars opened up their mouths and welcomed me inside.

That was the day The Five began. My Five.

The day I decided to become the pleasure-seeking missile I am now. The day they all caught my scent, gathered around and mimicked the stars, welcoming me in with their mouths.

It's a special thing for a girl to take up space. An even more special thing for a queer Black girl to do so.

His chart gives me that *exact* same fighting feeling, and I want to open up my mouth and welcome him with my words, too. To tell him my mother said I'd find a chart like this someday. The same way she found my father's.

"What...are you doing?" he says as he watches me pull a length of leather from my hair. One that's been set outside in the sun then wrapped around my locks for this very moment.

I tie it around his wrist. Touching him is...an experience, and I go warm all over.

"Leather is grounding."

"Grounding?"

"Grounding."

"The hell do I need to be grounded for?"

I shrug, then stand and rifle through his cabinets finding everything I need. Nearly.

"Grounded to Earth. They say it's good for the gods to be humbled." *Grounded to keep you here. To keep you with me.*

"Who said that?"

My head whips to him so sharply, and I catch him smiling, on the verge of a laugh so close it might as well have tipped him over a cliff edge. He knows I caught the joke.

A person who knows their memes and knows your memes is a person you do not let out of your sight for any reason.

"The stars, wiseass." In a jar full of water, I muddle a couple leaves from his devil's ivy flourishing in the corner, rose of Jericho I've never seen any person other than Nilu own and a small palmful of amethyst I find in a black jar under his sink.

I close the jar. And shake.

"How on earth do you have all these things?"

"I'm older than I look. I've lived here a while. People bring me things. Gifts. Shitty casseroles on occasion. They never let me keep the Pyrex dishware, though. They think they're appeasing the gods when really it's their own ancestors who should be getting these. I keep the gifts anyway because I'm still half-human."

"Your mother, you mean."

"Yeah. She was Afrodescendente. You know Black Brazil-ians don't throw anything away."

I didn't know this, but okay, because that all sounds very spot-on.

He joins me at the sink and says in a whisper, "Is this a spell?"

"No." I turn my head to look at him and whisper back, "Why are we whispering?"

"Because you whisper when it's about spells," he says. His coffee breath ghosts over my lips.

My head cocks at a quick angle, and I say to him at full volume, "This is just for my peace of mind. These are natural elements that have actual science-based capabilities."

There is that really good feeling again. I glance at him, not really seeing him. The beauty of his chart is laid out before my eyes, even though I'm no longer looking at the paper it was scribbled on. God, it's hard to breathe, remembering a thing so perfect.

"Then, where's my spell? I let you violate my pantries because I thought I was getting a spell."

"I *am* the spell," I say, laughing.

When he laughs, I laugh again, too.

And when he walks to a circular room full of books I know are probably all in Latin, I follow.

Seated on the couch facing the largest open window, he says, "Sit with me." And I do that, too.

"Nox," I say. Now I'm whispering. Whispers just *feel better* sometimes.

"Hmm?"

"I think... I think you're meant to be mine."

He doesn't glance up. "I know."

The sun hits my knees, my shins, and the shadow of the windowsill cuts it off just where my ankles begin. "How?"

"Demigod. Remember?" He taps his forehead.

"Oh," I say. "Right. So this is the portion of the game where the *god* perks come in. Right?"

"Yes," he says in all seriousness. So much seriousness as to render his statement undeniable.

"But your sign." I exhale hard. It feels like I've been running stairs. "The stars call it an anomaly."

"All of me is called an anomaly. None of it is true. An anomaly is just a thing or person or instance that lays outside of a group's perceived norm. The part of the story that does not exist, but only because the storytellers refuse to verbalize it."

"You know, there's a legend of the people that says I'm supposed to *change* any occurrence of this sign." *A legend of the people.* Humans. Faulty and flawed and judgy and beautiful, too, but really just so damn stupid.

He's saying, *I know* again with the way he simply swallows and exhales.

I readjust in my chair, uncross and then recross my legs to coat my melanin evenly with the sun.

"They say that Ophiuchus is *onism.* Being frustratingly stuck in just one body that inhabits only one space at a time. But you are not stuck in any one body. Your body is yours. That's been proven. I'm watching you now. And you're a demigod. Your soul is golden. Existing everywhere it wants to, all at once. But most predominantly inside this body you've chosen as rightfully yours."

He is blushing. I know he is. There's this ruddy thing happening around his cheeks. "So are you going to? Are you going to do it?" I love the smirking wit set plainly on his face, the apples of his cheeks rounding, lips full enough to bite.

"Nox," I say with a smile, then meet his eyes.

"Iron-throated hearts," he says.

Pop was right. Mom was right. "My perfect, iron-throated heart match."

* ◊ *

"Once upon a time, a starry Black girl was born beneath a white moon, and a boy named for the darkness of the night sky joined her..."

* * * * *

SAGITTARIUS

Venus in Sagittarius

* *Free-spirited, adventurous, and bold*
* *Avoids commitment*
* *Loves people who are open to growing and learning together*
* *May seem too aloof, unromantic, or blunt*
* *Values sincerity and open thinking*

Anchor Point
Lily Anderson

Freshman Year: Club Qualifying Round

I'm sure you'll be shocked to hear that archery isn't the hottest sport in town. That appears to be water polo—rugby plus drowning is hot, I agree. But my aunt wasn't a water-polo silver medalist. She was an archer.

And now so am I.

This archery club is a lot bigger than my last one. The squat brick clubhouse has an indoor shooting range, long enough for ten targets in a row, and this huge outdoor field they call *the big green*. It's the size of the playground in my old neighborhood but with a lot less cement. The coaches here must be decent: everyone lined up to shoot has picture-perfect posture. Aunt Maritza said she'd pay for my private lessons *if* I make it onto the traveling team. To prove that I'm "a serious investment" and that the coaches aren't "total fucking idiots."

Today, everyone competing to qualify for a place on the club's traveling team is a recurve-bow user. Recurves are the classic bow-and-arrow shape: a *D* with forty pounds of lethal force in the vertical stroke.

Not that *I* would ever use it for anything lethal. Judging from the array of leather shooting gloves and camo chest guards on display, I'm probably the only vegan on the field. I'm definitely the only Latina. Everyone else looks like the kids from my new school: rich white snobs, kitted out in top-of-the-line gear. I'm sure none of them are using a secondhand bow.

I already miss the privacy of Aunt Maritza's backyard and the permanent quivers she has, freestanding and made out of PVC pipe. The rattle of my arrows slung on my hip is distracting.

My hands are starting to sweat when the last competitor jogs onto the field. Since he's late, there's nowhere for him to stand but next to the weird brown new girl dressed in black.

Me.

The first thing I notice about him is how loud his clothes are. Literally and figuratively. He's wearing an all-green warm-up suit that makes a distracting swishing sound every time he moves. And he's moving a lot—pulling on a shooting glove, adjusting the sight on his bow, flipping the white-blond hair out of his eyes.

"You're new," he says, after noticing me watching him.

"You're observant," I reply. You couldn't pay me to tell this guy that before today. I've only ever shot in my aunt's yard and the teensy community center archery class I had to leave behind when I moved here. Field shooting is a brand-new experience for me.

"Are you, like, a big *Hunger Games* fan?" he asks.

I resist the urge to slap my hand over the Mockingjay pin on my quiver. A misguided but well-intentioned gift from my sister. I wish I'd left it in my bow bag.

"Are you a big Robin Hood fan?" I ask, indicating his all-green outfit. "Or do you just want to blend in with the big green?"

His whole outfit crinkles as he snorts and throws his hair back. "I don't blend in. I stand out. Usually in the winner's circle."

The first whistle sounds. Our bows go up. Robin Hood's jacket rustles louder than a pile of dead leaves as he nocks his arrow.

"Didn't anyone tell you?" I ask him. "This isn't a usual round."

I can hear him go still. "Really? How so?"

I smile, drawing my arrow back until the string kisses the corner of my mouth. "Because I'm here. And I'm definitely going to win."

And I do.

Freshman Year: Spring Club Tournament

There are no friends on competition day, but there are plenty of familiar faces. Any club member can sign up, so there are plenty of delusional newbies mixed in with all of us private-lesson jerks. Twenty-five of us stare down the big green at a row of side-by-side straw targets. I like shooting straw. It makes such a satisfying crunch and doesn't turn my stomach like the deer mannequins with marked organs they use for targets at the community-college events. I got third place at that tourney because I just couldn't bring myself to aim for the anatomically accurate heart.

Aunt Maritza and my club coaches told me I need to toughen up and learn to see the bull's-eye beyond the heart.

There are all kinds of archers here: tall, short, thin, fat, people who name their bows, people who 3-D print their arrows, people with special nocks, tactical sights, fanny-pack quivers, sports enthusiasts, people who live off the grid, kids too cool for fencing but not cool enough for polo. But for today, the most important distinction between us is bow choice—recurves, compounds, crossbows. Like bows shoot together. Compound bows have so many wheels and pulleys on them that they require almost no upper-body strength. Crossbows are for trigger-happy hunters who just want to point and shoot. There are more recurves in this tourney than anything else. We require the most coaching so we dominate the club's enrollment. There are fifty of us split into two groups.

Regardless of bow choice or gender identity, the judges refer to all of us as *Bowman*.

Down the line, arrows twitch toward the grass, waiting for the ready call. Beside me, Bowman Flukey—who trounced me a few months ago at an indoor tourney—is taking another practice aim, wasting energy. On the other side, the girl in the Wonder Woman chest guard keeps shifting her stance, open to closed, closed with a twist. Even with her guard, her boobs are in the way. My aunt always says that archery is a flat-chested gal's sport. I thought she was just being nice until my mosquito bites turned into B cups.

I tug on the sleeve of my own chest guard, squirming my shoulders against the straps of my sports bra. Out of the corner of my eye, I can see light bouncing off a blond head turning toward me. Looking at me from around Wonder Woman's Easton beginner bow is last year's county champion. He's got the braggy patch sewn to his jacket to prove it. He murdered three deer mannequins in a row for that patch on his sleeve.

He winks at me and says, "Katniss."

He knows my real name by now, and I know his. But real names are for training, not game days. Competition requires focus. Nicknames are a mutual psych-out.

"Robin Hood," I say.

The corner of his mouth lifts, but I look away before he can pin me to the spot with his eyes. They're as blue as the outer rings of the target. The losing rings.

Behind us, the countdown starts. At the ready, the swish of two dozen bows going up. Set, the groan of pulled strings. Then there's a horn, and the air is momentarily a swarm of multicolored fletch and the thwacks of arrows buried into straw.

Immediately, Wonder Woman bursts into tears, her arrow so far from the center that there's no hope of her going forward. Bowman Flukey gives a little hiss of discouragement.

Robin Hood grins at me. We're moving on.

Sophomore Year: Club Field Day

"Tic," I announce as my arrow sinks into the center square. Taking control of the bale board feels good, even though the hay bale behind the target makes my nose itch. It's still better than getting hit with a bunch of Nerf arrows. Playing arrow tag with the little kids was way harder than I thought it would be. I should have known better when none of the coaches offered to join. No sane person would volunteer to be a 3-D target for armed rugrats—even if their arrows are foam.

Beside me, Robin Hood takes his time aiming his shot. Inside a competition, he would have a fraction of this amount of time. I'm tempted to pull out my phone and hold him to the standard two minutes. But then we might have to go back to playing with the baby bowmen. I'd rather be here with the hay-bale targets.

"Tac," he says, sinking his shot in the square next to mine. The fletch is acid green. His favorite color. Next to my red feather, the board starts to look like Christmas in July. "I'm catching up to you, Katniss."

"You know we get an equal number of turns, right?" I scoff, lining up my next shot. As the drawstring hits my lips, I can feel his gaze boring a hole in my head. Lowering my bow, I cut my eyes at him. "Isn't it time for you to reapply your sunscreen?"

"Aww." He flutters his lashes at me. They're nearly colorless, almost as invisible as spider webs. "You worried about me?"

"Worried about how red your face is getting." Taking aim again, I snag the square above my last shot. "But maybe that's just the color of a sore loser."

"I'm not losing. We're already tied." He laughs and points an arrow tip at the board. "In fact, I think we've gotten too good for regular tic-tac-toe. For my next shot, I'll take that bottom square to keep you from it, then we'll have no choice but to scratch the game and start over. Then it's back to taking Nerf to the face. So maybe we should call it and try a more interesting game."

My stomach twists while I imagine all the things that would be more interesting for both of us than shooting tic-tac-toe. My eyes dart around the big green, where all of the club's current and prospective members are checking out a variety of carnival games. I lick my dry lips. "More interesting, like shooting paint balloons? My aunt would kill me if I got paint on my shoes."

"What about shooting blind?"

I roll my eyes, sure he's joking. "You won't even wear sunglasses on the field. You really think you can shoot in the dark?"

He smirks at me. "Are you scared to try?"

"Scared of you accidentally hitting someone, maybe."

"If they walk in front of a target, they get what they deserve."

"I don't have a spare blindfold on me," I say, patting my empty pockets. "Do you?"

"We'll just close our eyes."

"So you can peek and steal the win? No way!"

He heaves a sigh that blows the hair off his forehead. "Then cover my eyes yourself, Katniss. You can keep me from aiming directly at any wandering newbies."

"Fine," I grumble before I really consider what I'm agreeing to. "Close your eyes first. Lining up your shot is cheating."

I have to stand behind him, the toes of my shoes an inch from the Adidas logo on his heels. I can smell the salty sweat on the back of his neck. See the dusting of fine golden hair clipped short under the floppy bits he's always throwing around. He reaches for an arrow from his quiver, and his elbow brushes my hip.

"Watch my draw arm," he says without turning around.

"Right," I say, remembering that I'm not standing here for the view. I shuffle two steps to the left, careful not to bump into his fancy white bow as he pulls it upward. Swallowing, I reach up, setting my palm over his scrunched eyes. His skin is warm and slick, and I consider making another comment about how he really should reapply his sunscreen, but I'd rather die than tell him that his skin is hot. He'd take it wrong and tease me every day until graduation.

"Ready?" he asks, voice softening to account for our newfound proximity. "Katniss?"

I startle and clear my throat. "Just checking for newbies," I say. "You're good. I mean, clear. I mean, shoot already!"

Junior Year: Autumn Invitational

"They're calling it off!" Flukey kicks a puddle and slings his bow over his arm before storming toward the club door. "What a fucking waste of time. They should have just set up an indoor tourney."

Rain pounds against the big green. The hard gel cast that was on my hair ten minutes ago is now making sticky rivulets down my temples. My socks squelch as I curl my cold toes inside my shoes.

The field empties of people and fills with water. It sloughs down the front of the targets, making shallow pools underneath every foam 3-D deer's intricate and creepy carved guts. Ribless, each one has a green tangle of intestines worth eight points a shot. Ten-point lungs are the same lilac as my bedroom at Aunt Maritza's. The harts' hearts are red and off-center—and small enough to get you twelve points if you can hit them square.

Behind me, I hear a rustling that at first I think is a fresh downpour before I turn and see Robin Hood running toward me in his wind suit. Just under the hems of his crinkly pants, his moonlight-white ankles are showing. Soon, he'll be too tall to wear his lucky noisy outfit. I find myself hoping that his parents will shell out for another one. I'd hate to have to think of a new nickname for him.

At school, he would never be caught dead in this outfit. Just like I would never have my hair slicked back into a forehead-lifting ponytail, my curls crispy with humidity-repelling hairspray that's now a nasty river running down the back of my neck. There's no room for vanity on the field.

Even so, I pluck at the wrinkles of my soaked club polo.

"Why are you still out here?" Robin Hood calls over the rain. His pale hair sticks to the sides of his face like lightning strikes.

"Why are *you*?" I counter. I jerk my head back at the targets. If you can ignore the needless gore happening below the neck, the deer faces are so stupid cute, with big eyes and button noses aimed up like they can smell us downwind. "I came here to win."

"Not to save all the fake deer?"

I draw an arrow out of my quiver, which is rapidly filling with water. "Can't do both."

"The coaches are gonna clear the field soon," he warns.

Wind is bad for shooting. But rain? Not so much. The water will slow you down if you let it. If you take too long to shoot. Which Robin always does.

"Then, you'd better shoot fast if you want to beat me," I say. I pull my arrow back, squinting through the deluge. "I promised my aunt I'd kill three fake deer today."

Senior Year: Indoor State Tournament

Aunt Maritza braided my hair so tight at the hotel this morning that I can feel my pulse in my temples. She's somewhere in the stands, sharing a funnel cake with my sister, so I don't dare loosen it. I just keep my eyebrows up to relieve some of the pressure.

The fairgrounds vaguely smells like 4-H farm animals. Even inside the main building—which, according to the website, was a wedding expo last weekend and a gun-and-knife show before that—there's a faint whiff of sheep and straw. Bowman Flukey keeps sneezing, which does not bode well for his chances to win the big scholarship today. Fifty thousand dollars is a ton of money to lose for forgetting to pack a Benadryl.

Robin Hood walks over to me with two cups of Gatorade. He's wearing the same club polo as Flukey and me but tucked into green track pants. It's a goober look and yet still somehow better than what he showed up in. He took off the matching jacket and terry-cloth sweatband after Coach asked if he was planning on breakdancing for everyone's entertainment during breaks between rounds.

It was such a good roast, I'm ashamed I didn't think of it first.

"Are you nervous yet?" he asks me, handing me one of the Styrofoam cups.

"I'm nervous that I'm gonna lose my chance to trail shoot," I say. I take a sip of Gatorade, resisting the urge to nibble on the lip of the cup. I need to save up my excess energy for my turn. The girls I'm up against are nationally ranked and the favorites to win.

Robin Hood frowns. "I thought your aunt wanted you to get over your thing about 3-D targets?"

"Not as much as she wants me to follow in her Olympian footsteps. She's not psyched at the idea of paying two hundred bucks to enter me into another tourney. Especially one that won't guarantee a college scholarship. Or get me any closer to the World champs."

Aunt Maritza doesn't believe that I've outgrown indoor competitions, that I've really fallen in love with the less predictable field tourneys. To her, it's just cockiness until there are medals to prove my word. If I can place in the top today, she'll let me go to the hike-and-shoot competition that the traveling team has been invited to participate in.

I think back to when archery was just fun, a hobby that kept me from eating up all the data on my phone. When I was new in town, trying to prove that I belonged at the club, on the traveling team. Before I could eyeball the difference between thirty and seventy meters, before I counted time in arrows.

I bite the dead skin from my bottom lip, tasting a spot of blood. "If I place below third today, I'll be stuck chasing down scholarship competitions from now until graduation."

"Or," Robin says from behind his cup, "you could just win today, get your scholarship, and spend the rest of high school having a good time."

"You make it sound so easy," I sigh.

"Well, you make it look so easy. You never run over your time or chunk your shots, even when you're scared of the 3-D targets. You just grip and rip, every time."

My cheeks get hot. God, I hope my aunt and my sister aren't watching us from the stands. "Are you complimenting me, Robin Hood? On a competition day?"

His shoulders twitch a self-conscious shrug. "They've got us divided into gender categories. I'm not technically competing against you today. But I will be on the trail shoot, so you better get there, Katniss. If that means winning a scholarship today, then do it."

Over the loudspeaker, they announce the beginning of the young adult female division. I drain my Gatorade, hand the empty cup to Robin, and adjust the Mockingjay pin on my quiver. It's now or never, I guess.

Senior Year: Trail Shoot Tournament

I'm already flying down the trail, gravel crunching underfoot, quiver slapping against my hip. Over my shoulder the coast is clear, but I can't guarantee for how long. They staggered our entrances so all of us wouldn't get backed up at every target, but it took me forever to line up my last shot. The bull's-eye was hung between two branches, higher up than I was expecting, especially after the tiny foam turkey that was the stop before. I almost chunked it entirely, landing in the blue. Thankfully, outdoor competitions are more about points than accuracy, but still I'll need to do much better than that on the final round to keep my chances at placing.

Three hours away from home, this hiking park was built for archers, winding up and over hills with a variety of permanent bull's-eye and 3-D targets stationed along the way. So far, I've hit fake boars, turkeys, two elk, and one shocking foam velociraptor, each one behind a chain to keep our distance honest. My shoes are muddy, and my shins ache from running uphill for most of the morning. I don't know if I've ever felt more alive.

I'm on a time limit, though. The judges are following behind us, tallying up our shots. And if I don't get to the finish line within the hour, I'll end up getting docked points I can't afford to lose. Robin Hood and I have a bet on today's tourney. If he wins, I'll have to wear his old crinkly wind suit to the next club event. If I win, he has to wear tights and shoot a longbow like the actual Robin Hood.

I really, really want to win.

Leaves and branches whip past me as I search for signs of the last target. My heart leaps at the sight of descending wooden stairs set into the dirt of the hillside. I have to be nearing the end of the trail loop now. Arrows rattling together, I leap down the stairs.

At the base of the hill, the trees on either side of the unpaved path grow closer together, skinny trunks huddled together. In the distance, I can see a glimmer of light. A chain in a sunbeam.

I rush onward. The chain is strung between two posts, the

taller of which has a sign with a *12* printed on it. The final stop. The last target.

Dizzy with excitement, I have an arrow out of my quiver and drawn halfway to my mouth before I spot the deer. Just when I'm thinking about how thankful I am that it doesn't have its guts exposed like the other foam models—it *blinks*.

I lower my bow. Squeeze my eyes shut. Open them again.

It's an honest-to-God, real live deer, not a 3-D model. It's got black Bambi eyes and a fluffy white tail and a leaf in its mouth, chewing in a decidedly unbothered way. The twelfth target is a classic blue-yellow-red bull's-eye hung up on the tree over its adorable head.

"Get out of here!" I whisper-shout at it. "This is, like, the worst place you could be in right now! Don't you know there are actual hunters in this park? The kinds of people who'd call you *venison*."

It blinks at me, like it can smell how much I'd rather die than hurt it. Maybe it can? I've never been this close to an actual deer before. Its knobby brown legs remind me of my sister's.

Behind me, I hear the whoosh of a projectile. But it's not an arrow. It's a rock that clips the nearest tree, startling the deer into moving. I lower my bow and whirl around, seeing Robin Hood standing behind me.

"I saw that in the first *Hunger Games* movie," he says with a shrug. "Sorry. You didn't want to kill that doe, did you, Katniss? I heard you calling it *venison*. I didn't think you had game meats in your vocabulary. You won't even eat eggs."

"Have you ever seen an egg farm? They're filthy and disgusting." I shudder and wave my arrow at the last target. "Go ahead and shoot first. You cleared the shot, you deserve the bonus time."

"Are you kidding?" He pulls an arrow out of his quiver with his gloved hand. "I came here to compete against you. Let's go together. Then you can race me to the finish."

I scoff. I'm a much faster runner than him, even with my shorter legs. Reminding him of this now would only waste precious seconds of my scored time.

Standing beside each other in front of the chain, bows raised, arrows nocked, I inhale deeply. The trail smells like dirt and greenery and Robin Hood's eucalyptus deodorant. I cut my eyes at him, remembering the first time we shot off against each other, the day we both made the club's travel team.

He draws his arrow back to the corner of his mouth, looks over at me, and winks. "Three."

I draw. "Two."

"One."

Two arrows fly, red and green fletch blurs. We barely wait for them to land in the center circle before we both take off, sprinting toward the finish line.

In the parking lot, brake lights show where my boyfriend is waiting for me. The trunk pops as I approach. I set my bow bag and quiver inside, where they rest gently against another case and a balled-up track jacket.

The plastic gold medal they gave me bounces on my chest as I launch myself into the passenger seat.

"I won!" I announce as I buckle into my seat.

"Congrats, babe!" He leans forward, kissing me so that all of his fine blond hair tickles my cheek. He pulls back, his nose scrunched bashfully as he lifts up a medal from the cup holder. "I got silver."

Cupping his cheek, I give him a second, more comforting kiss. "Better luck next time. Now, let's go find you some tights for field day, Robin Hood."

* * * * *

CAPRICORN

Venus in Capricorn
* *Responsible and driven*
* *More low-key with showing affection*
* *Thrives on maturity and stability*
* *Traditional and practical*
* *Emotionally guarded*

Mucho, Mucho Amor
Alexandra Villasante

Mamá came home from work while I was sleeping. I can hear the TV on in the next room and smell coffee. That's my signal to get my ass out of bed. Sometime in the middle of the night, I stripped off my pajama bottoms so I'm just in a teeny tank top and undies. I snap a pic of myself lounging in bed before my frontal lobe makes me think better of it and send it to Sabina.

Then I realize why I'm wearing so little in our drafty Union City apartment. It's November second and that means the heat is *on*. In our rickety five-floor walk-up, the heat only has two settings: distant memory or melt your face. Last night had been bitterly cold, causing me to put on the porcupine fluff pajama bottoms Sab had given me; this morning it's damn near tropical.

I pad out to the living room. Mamá has already changed out of her nurse scrubs and sits in her caftan, chanclas on, a fine sheen of sweat on her darkly tanned and lined face. A cup of coffee and un pastelito, untouched, set in front of her on the wooden folding table. She looks like the poster child for Puerto Rican motherhood. Both windows are propped open, but the furnacelike heat keeps rolling off the sputtering radiators.

"Morning, Ma."

Mamá skews her eyes to me, pulling them away from the TV. The noticias on Univision are almost done. It's the celebrity-gossip segment—big smiles and lots of laughter. They'll wrap up with weather in a minute. She can spare me more than a glance, no?

"¿Por que estas en pelotas?"

I grin, because that's a Dad saying she's using. "Pelotas"—*balls*, as in butt-naked.

"I'm not, really. You know, it's a thousand degrees in here."

Another look. "The neighbors will see. Let me get you a bata like mine. They're very nice and very light."

"No, thanks. I'm good."

I go to the cabinets in the section of the living room that, by dint of being where the fridge and the plates are, qualifies as the kitchen and grab a bowl. I jimmy it under the sputtering radiator that leaks boiling hot water onto the floor.

"Can we talk?" I ask.

"No, mijita. It's almost time for los horóscopos," she says, like I don't have intimate knowledge of the horoscope—her sign, my sign, the super's sign and the sign of the girl at the Walgreens. "We'll talk later," she says, raising the volume of the TV with the remote.

"Okay. I'm going out," I say. I didn't really want to talk anyway. Sabina wants me to talk to my mom. About her.

"¿Donde vas?" Even with the impending deliverance of news from the stars, she's got to know where I'm going. At all times. It's a blessing no one ever told her about phone-tracking apps.

"With Sabina. To get your recetas from the Walgreens."

"Mija," she says, stretching out her hand with a piece of notepaper in it. "Can you stop by La Maravilla and get a few things? It's for your father, ¿sabes?"

I roll my eyes, more for old times' sake because I know she won't see it and wouldn't care if she did. Papá had been the only one of my parents who would want to cheer me out of a frustrated mood—and he's been dead three years. My gaze wanders to the side table where my father's altar is set up. His photo, fresh flowers, the cigars he had to stop smoking. Hanging above the altar is my mother's favorite photo. Mamá y Papá with smiles wreathed in joy; between them is the famous astrologer to the pueblo, Walter Mercado, legit wearing more mascara than my mom and shining like a constellation. It's hard to say who is cheesing harder in that picture.

Sabina responds to my bedroom selfie with a GIF of a dog running in circles, tongue hanging out.

"Ay dios," she texts. Not capitalizing 'Dios'. That's okay, she's learning. And I don't think religious vocabulary is featured on the Duolingo app. The sentiment is sweet; she's trying. That's the second thing, aside from her gorgeous blue eyes and the sweet indent right at the small of her back, that gives me my morning lady-boner.

Definitely do not have time to take care of that. I put on

jeans, a long-sleeved top, and socks and check the weather. It's going to sleet so I don't bother doing anything with the mop of short brown hair curling over my eyes.

I make not so much as a peep as I slip by Mom to the front door. The sleep-inducing voice of Professor Zellagro is saying he has good news for all the signos of the zodiac.

"No es Walter," Mom says, like she does every Saturday morning since Walter Mercado retired from doing the horoscopes. I don't have to answer. Mom's on autopilot. "¿Tienes mi list?" she asks.

"Yup." Even with her eyes trained on the bald old dude— who, despite wearing a blue shirt with silver foil roses, is truly no Walter Mercado—nothing gets by her. I watch the Professor for a minute, as he tells mom that "Hoy inicia el transito directo de Venus, planeta de *amor*," which, even though Spanish is my first language, I don't completely understand. Mom listens carefully as the Professor splits the zodiac into fire, earth, air and water signs, listening for Aries (me) and Capricornio (her) before, bizarrely waiting to hear Pisces (my dead dad). I finally slip out to the words, "¿Venus exultandose, donde? En el elemento *fuego*."

* ◊ *

"What does *exultandose* mean?" Sabina says, thumbing her way through the Duolingo app on her phone.

"I'm not sure. *Exalting? Glorifying?*" Sleet hits my face as I pull my hood over my beanie.

I'm pretty sure there's some disease you get by going from

scorching heat to freezing cold and back again; something Victorian and chilly sounding, but I can't remember the word.

"Fuego is *fire*, so *in fire*?" Sab asks. She does this thing that I find adorable and she hates; instead of furrowing her brows when she's thinking, she widens her eyes in surprise, which makes her look, as her dad likes to tell her, like a Muppet.

"En. Fuego," I enunciate, with bite between each word. I hope I sound like Professor Zellagro and not a dumbass.

"What does it mean?"

Besides her surprised eyes, the rest of her face is barely visible between the beanie worn low on her head and the scarf Mamá bought her for her birthday in September (Virgo). A wisp of golden, pin-straight hair floats out in the biting wind, and I reach up to tuck it behind her ear. An excuse to touch her, any excuse.

She squeezes my hand and pulls me forward, across the street to the Walgreens.

Once inside, we're blasted with hot air from the heater over the door. *Chilblains*, I remember; that's what you get when you're subjected to being alternately cooked and frozen. I bet the Brontës had chilblains.

"So, what do we need from here?" Sabina asks.

"Just Mom's prescriptions, then we go to the botanica, then we can go back to my house, if you want. Mamá will be out like a light."

"That sounds cozy. What are we watching?"

"Our choices are: fantasy with boy/girl love story; fantasy with girl/girl love story; no love story, just dragons; or we could watch *Megaparsec* again."

"You know my heart."

We're always rewatching *A Wrinkle in Time*—the Canadian TV version, though the Ava DuVernay version is cool. It's just that Katie Stuart in the Canadian version made us gay, way before middle school. The Ava DuVernay version of *A Wrinkle in Time* made Sab bi, thanks to Levi Miller playing Calvin. We spend a lot of time talking about all the fictional crushes we've had. Katara tops my list; Calvin O'Keefe and Azula top hers.

"I'll go get snacks." She gives me a quick peck on the cheek, not giving me a chance to protest that I have family in this town.

"Don't forget the Takis."

"I'm not an amateur," she calls back.

At the pharmacy counter, I wait as the tech finishes filling Mom's prescriptions—alta presion, diabetes, high cholesterol. For a nurse, my mother has a terrible habit of not taking care of herself. She'd say that's because Capricorns are hard-headed mountain goats. When I laugh, she adds that Aries are stubborn rams, so I shouldn't laugh so loud.

Back out in the cold, we walk toward Bergenline and then farther on to Park Avenue. It's so much easier in the cold to be incognito. My hood over my short hair and my general lack of ass for a Latina means that I'm often mistaken for a boy. And the biting wind means that no one's going to look too long at two bundled figures goofing, laughing and stealing kisses. At least, that's what I hope.

Because even though I'm out to my friends, I'm not out to Mamá. And that means I'm not out to my town. How could I be? My town has a constellation of immigrant families from all over Central and South America—and somehow, in the sliver of streets making up just over a square mile in area, with more than sixty-eight thousand people (my bisabuela Meji, the one from Spain that I'm named after, would have called the people gentusa—with heaps of disdain)—everyone knows me and knows my business. I can't let anything get back to Mom. The years since Dad died have been hellish. There's no way I'm adding to that.

* ◊ *

Mundo Fantasia looks like the kind of place children's dreams go to die.

"This is the botanical place?" Sabina asks, dubious at the bright colors faded almost to gray on the mural painted on the side of the building: a clown that looks like he's melting in real time.

"It's la botanica, and no, not exactly. This is the party supply place we have to walk through to get to la botanica."

"So it's like a money-laundering front?"

"You watch too much Netflix."

"With you, always with you."

We're inside and our hats are off, and I just can't reciprocate her nudge on my cheek. We're sharing one pair of gloves and holding hands inside her fleece-lined pocket. I pull away.

Like knowing she's thinking when she looks surprised, I also know that Sabina's got a face she uses when she's hurt but she doesn't want me to see how much. It's a ghost smile that arrives and realizes there's nothing to smile about. I hate that smile. She turns to look at a quinceañera display.

"Want to come look at the weird things in the glass bottles with me?" I ask.

"Um, I'm good. Gonna hang out here with Sophia the First," she says, standing near a larger-than-life cutout of the TV Disney princess.

"Yeah, she's great. Wanted to be her once."

"Same. Plus, that song was all over TikTok. Still haunts my dreams."

I wish I haunted Sabina's dreams like she haunts mine. I'm always keeping her the right distance away from me. Not too far that she'll leave, not too close that everyone will know. It's a losing proposition, I know that. I am waiting, waiting. Waiting for Mamá to feel better.

"Okay, well don't buy a crystal-encrusted quince crown while I'm in the back," I say.

"They have those? Did you have one?"

"Yes. No, and I showed you the picture of me at my quince."

"You looked beautiful," she says simply. The way she can say that to me, here in public and it's so easy for her. It's what I love about her and what makes me frustrated.

"It's easy to look beautiful in a floofy blue dress. I wanted to wear a tux."

"But your mom wouldn't let you?" she asks.

"Dad would have been disappointed."

All thoughts turn to Dad today. To the year I turned fifteen and the year he died. See, I think my mom wanted to give Dad this, this perfect version of me. A beautiful woman in a beautiful dress. Everything a girl should be so she could marry a dude and have kids one day. Well, I might have kids.

But not with a dude. Anyway, I did it. I listened to my mother and I wore the ugly thing, having to yank up the neckline every other minute so the thing didn't fall off my nonexistent boobs. I wore the blue dress, I danced with every primo—even the always slightly damp Mateo—and danced with Dad for the last time, letting him think he knew me.

The bright colors of the party-supply shop give way to wooden floors and dark wooden shelves as I cross into the back room where Botanica La Maravilla makes its home.

"¿Sí?" Marirosa asks, not looking up from the iPad that leans against a box of incense on the counter.

"Buenos dias, Señora," I say, like I have since I first started coming here with Mamá at six years old.

"Hola, baby," she says when she looks up to see me. Marirosa looks like a schoolteacher in a pink sleeveless button-up and crisp khaki shorts. Her tennis shoes are out-of-the-box white, and she's nearly the same brown as the walnut counter. She's dressed for the weather inside La Maravilla which, like my apartment, defies the November climate. I've known Marirosa so long that she seems like family. But, like family, I hardly know anything about her.

I must be in a weird-ass mood because I ask, "Señora, are you married?"

"¡Que cosa! No, I'm not married. I am married to this shop," she says with a blink of both eyes, since she can't wink.

"I just wondered. Everyone calls you 'Señora,' but I've never seen un Señor…"

"I'm too vieja to be called Señorita, don't you think?" Her tightly curled gray-and-black hair is slicked back into a ponytail. Señora Marirosa always looks cool, comfortable and moderna. How can she sell this watered-down perfume and red-dyed oil with a straight face?

"And how are you, mija?" she asks.

I look back toward the party store involuntarily.

"You have your friend with you? La rubia?" When she says *the blonde*, she makes it sound like she knows Sabina is my girl-friend and I wonder—like I always do—if Señora Marirosa is really just married to La Maravilla, or if she's like count-less other tias and tios who seem solitary—soltera, soltero, which means *single*, or *alone*—but have love lives coexisting, in worlds hidden in plain sight.

Marirosa says something, but I miss it.

"I'm sorry, what?"

"I said, if you are looking for a love potion…?" She looks back into the party store too, and Sabina's glass-clink laugh-ter spills out.

"No, no," I say, handing her my list of herbs, lotions, floor washes and candles. Marirosa puts on her glasses and swings around on the stool to reach into the dozens of tiny wooden cubby holes behind her, where fresh and packaged herbs are kept.

"Hmm. Guasatumba is almost impossible to get. I keep telling your mother. I don't have any suppliers en Uruguay anymore."

"It was the first herb Dad showed her. It's good for mos-quito bites and skin infections."

She turns back toward me and lowers her bifocals to stare at me.

"I didn't know you knew so much about botanica."

I frown. It's not my fault I've absorbed all this nonsense.

It's been years of hearing about it, buying it and using it because Mom made me. I know about TV Disney princesses too, from years of exposure. I don't believe in them, either.

"It's almost the anniversary of Papá's death, so she wanted to try to get some for his altar."

"When does she need it by?"

"December eighth."

Señora Marirosa makes a whistling sound between her teeth.

"I think there is a cousin of a friend who plans on going to Colonia this month. Maybe he'll be lucky there."

I shrug like I don't care, but actually I know that Mom would be thrilled to have guasatumba for Dad's altar.

And that sentence right there is why I'm so glad I left Sabina in the party store. Even thinking this kind of basura makes me embarrassed as hell.

The 7 Sisters Jinx Removing Floor Wash, the Palo Santo, the packets of herbs and candles go into a large shopping bag that says *MUNDO FANTASIA.*

"I'm out of my own bags, and Carmen let me have some of hers," Marirosa says, handing me the giant bag. I give her the fifty dollars. There's no change.

"Cuidate, nena, okay?"

"Yup, you too," I say.

I find Sabina flipping through the book you can order cakes from, each laminated page displaying a monstrosity of icing, lights and working minifountains.

"Look at this one with the bridge and the little figurines," she says.

"Hideous."

"I think it's kind of awesome."

"It's basically a desexualized wedding cake," I say, and it definitely comes out like I am in a crappy mood. Which I am.

Sabina turns to me, irritated.

"Does everything have to be negative? Can't something just *be*?"

I want to say *Yes* and *Sorry, I'm just not sleeping* or *I'm just worried* or *I'm just hungry*, but I can't stop myself. "Sorry, but this *just* is an example of a patriarchal ritual where the whole community comes together and says, '*This* one's ready to be subjugated by heteronormative matrimony. Come and get her, chicos!'"

She doesn't look impressed. "You don't smash the patriarchy by avoiding cake."

I do a thing I'm usually bad at. I hold my tongue.

"You told me you had fun at yours," she insists.

"I did. It was more low-key than some of my cousins' parties. Mom wanted to do it with a more Uruguayan feel than a Puerto Rican one."

"Because of your dad."

"Yeah."

She points to a cake at the back of the book that sits on a pedestal of clear plastic, four levels suspended like it's magic flying cake, and the fifth level a fountain of fiber-optic threads. The whole cake is slathered in rainbow buttercream.

"Well, I like this cake. And when our daughter turns fifteen, I will make her a cake that will rival this one."

Sabina wants to be a pastry chef. The kind that whips peaks of Chantilly and spins sugar. Her parents want her to become a pediatrician, like them. She hates blood. We both are disappointments to our parents.

"Your cake will kick that cake's ass. And then the two cakes will hug and become best friends because rivalries bring people together." I put my arm through hers, slipping my hand into her coat pocket. I hope she reads that as the apology it's supposed to be.

"All I'm saying," Sabina says, as we walk back into the shivery November sleet, "is if this were some German/Swedish custom that my parents and grandparents believed in, you wouldn't be dismissive; you'd be all into embracing your heritage."

"You're right. You're always right." I smile. "But some parts of heritage are too embarrassing to be embraced," I say, pulling out the bottle of 7 Sisters Jinx Removing Floor Wash.

"That can't be real," Sab says.

"Oh, it's real all right, and she's been using this from way before Dad died. Says it keeps the spirits of previous tenants from fouling up the space. Oh, and you can also use it as a bubble bath."

I grin at her openmouthed surprise. "Come on. Let's go get our Netflix on. I want to cuddle."

Sabina doesn't get mad often, and she almost never stays mad. I'm gonna lose her, I think. No one can stay that patient and good for that long.

* ◊ *

In the entryway to my apartment building, we shuck off our outdoor clothes because even here it's steamy. My curls are getting so tight, I have to tug at them to push them be-hind my ears. Sabina's hair doesn't move, doesn't change. Like it's never heard of humidity.

I chase her up the stairs, five levels, our laughter echoing up the stairwell. We're almost evenly matched since we met on the track team in sophomore year. She's faster than me, but I cheat by jumping over rails and skipping steps. I make it just in front of her on the fifth-floor landing and, sweaty and grinning, pull her into my arms. I should be brave, I think. I shouldn't care what other people think. I should tell Mamá. We kiss, and at first I'm not thinking of anything other than her. She took a peppermint from the bowl at Mundo Fantasia—the red-and-white swirly ones—and I can taste it on her. But the seconds extend to minutes, and I start count-ing. We should stop now, before Mom sticks her head out. Before Amparo, next door, peeks out from the peephole to see what the laughter and noise is about.

"Where'd you go, Meji?" Sabina murmurs against my lips.

"I'm here," I say, knowing that I wasn't. I was inside, think-ing about Mamá. "But we should get inside, give Mom her fraudulent-colored water and get on to the cuddling."

"Sí, por favor," she says, in a beautiful accent.

When I go to unlock the door, it pushes open. This sends a wave of unease through me. Mamá never leaves the door unlocked.

"Ma?"

The TV is blaring *Dulce Ambición*, a show she never watches.

I want Sabina to go away. I know something is wrong, and I don't want her to see whatever it is. But she steps in front of me. "Is something wrong, Señora?"

In the living room, still in her bata and chanclas, my mother sits weeping. She doesn't look up when we get close, she doesn't dry her tears with her caftan or try to pretend she's not upset, she just weeps. It is breaking my heart. I can't move.

Sabina, again, does what I should do: sits next to my mom and puts her arm around her.

I sit on her other side. It's not lost on me that I, her daughter, feel like an awkward interloper.

"What's wrong, Ma? ¿Qué paso?"

"Ay mijita," she struggles for breath. "Ha morido!" she sobs.

He died. But who? A cousin in Puerto Rico? Or one of Dad's primos in Uruguay? It has to be someone my mother loved very much. Mamá has a schedule. She loves her schedule almost as much as she loves me. She gets home from the overnight shift at the nursing home, and she changes into her bata y chanclas. She eats and has cafecito, and then she sleeps until just before dinner. But she's weeping on the couch now, and it has to be serious.

"Mamá, who died?"

She stops sobbing abruptly and turns bitter eyes to me.

"Walter Mercado, niña. Walter is dead."

* ◊ *

"Walter Mercado is—was—um, an icon," I tell Sabina as I pace.

We're in my room. Sabina sits on my bed patiently listening as I try to explain what happened. At least Mom isn't crying anymore. I convinced her to take half a sleeping pill because she has tomorrow off, and it was the only thing she wanted to do other than weep. I've checked in on her twice.

"Okay, an icon. Like Jennifer Lopez?" Sabina asks.

"I mean, sort of? Like, yeah, if Jennifer Lopez died, people who'd never met her would cry for sure. Except, Walter Mercado was just for Latinx people."

"So, he was a magician? A comedian? An actor?"

I run my hands along the back of my neck. The shaved part in the back has grown out, and it feels comforting to play with.

"He was all those things. He would read the horoscopes on TV."

"Oh," she says, clearly not understanding why some old dude who retired in 2017 and used to read the horoscopes on a Spanish-language NYC TV station would be an icon.

"He dressed in capes and wore tons of makeup. At one point in his career, I thought he looked a lot like Angela Lansbury in *Murder, She Wrote*."

"My nan made me watch those reruns."

"My abuela made me watch them, too. In Spanish."

We both make faces.

"Walter was flamboyant. The capes he wore were, like, jewel-encrusted. He was like a throwback from the 1980s."

"Is that why your mom loved him? My mom cried when Princess Diana died. Is it like that?"

"Yeah," I say, grateful that she's not just disregarding my mom's feelings. In fact, Sabina never disregards other people's feelings. That's my asshat move.

"But it's even more than that. All of Walter's horoscopes

were positive. All of them encouraged people to love other people and not to judge. Plus, he's a huge queer icon too."

"I can't believe I never heard of him," Sabina says.

I think of the snarky comment Emily Hardt made at the beginning of the year. That Sabina only knows half the queer culture memes because she's only *half a queer*. It was mean and bitchy, but it startled a laugh out of me that I'm ashamed of.

"It's probably because you're not Latinx. Anyway. It's even more than that." I take a deep breath.

"Before Dad died, about a year before we even knew he was sick, Mom and Dad went to Puerto Rico to stay with her family. They met Walter Mercado in a restaurant in San Juan. He was, Mamá said, guapo como siempre. Still good-looking, thin and a little fragile, but still, you know, *Walter*. He shook their hands, took pictures with them and then—" This part always makes me uncomfortable. Mostly because Mamá gets so emotional when she tells it. "He took both their hands in his hands and gave them una bendición. A blessing. He said that no matter what difficulties lay ahead, nothing could sever their bond of love. That Christ and all his angels would be with them both until and beyond their deaths and that their love was eterno. It would survive anything."

When Dad was diagnosed with liver failure, Walter Mercado's words helped sustain them. Throughout the disappointments of treatment and being on an organ-donor list nowhere near the top, it kept them hopeful. In the end, it didn't matter that he was dying: Walter had told them their love was eternal.

"So maybe your mom feels like Walter Mercado's death is somehow losing a little piece of your dad?"

My girl is so smart like that.

"Yeah. I guess it's just another connection gone."

"I'm so sorry," she says, taking my hand. I almost grab it back with a laugh and an *I don't care about Walter Mercado!* but I do care. I'm shocked and sad. I let Sabina pull me onto the bed, into her arms, fit me to her side, like I'm not a good four inches taller than her. I wish I could cry like Mamá.

∗ ◇ ∗

I make dinner. The one meal Papá taught me to make, lentejas con papas. When the potatoes are ready, I mix in the lentils, drizzle olive oil, lemon juice and cumin over it and take it to Mom sitting on the sofa. I set hers with a Diet Coke on her wooden folding table and put mine down with a Malta India. I'm clearly feeling the need for all the comfort foods.

"Gracias," Mom says groggily. She woke up about an hour ago on her own, even though I'd hoped she'd sleep through the night. She's been quiet, moving around like she's wading through water, but she's stopped crying.

"Where's your amigita? Did she go home?"

"Yeah, Sabina had to go have dinner with her folks."

"It's a long way on the bus to Hoboken, isn't it?"

"She drove."

"Tsk. There's nowhere good to park now."

"She found a spot, don't worry."

"She could have stayed, mijita. I wouldn't have minded."

"I know."

She tries the lentejas at the same moment that I realize I should have made something else—anything else, that wouldn't so clearly make her think of Dad. I'm an idiot. I expect her to break out into sobs again any moment. But she eats and chews and tells me it's really good.

The TV isn't even on. The one floor lamp by the window, the sputtering radiator and the street noise outside are all that's alive in the room. Now it really feels like death has visited us. Like it did when Dad died. Like we've been robbed of words because we're robbed of our loved one.

Mom pushes away her clean plate and clears her throat.

"There's something I want to ask you for, angelito," she says, using the endearment she used for me when I was little. *Angel.*

"Sí, por supuesto," I say. I don't wait to hear what it is. I'm going to do it no matter what she asks.

"Come with me to pay my respects to Walter."

I'm confused, and my face must show it.

"Come with me to Puerto Rico. The velorio is on Wednesday. I'm leaving on Monday."

"In two days? What about your job? What about the weather?"

"I have a lot of paid time off I have to use before the end of the year or I lose it. And I have savings. The weather in San Juan is nice now, see?" She shows me the weather app on her phone.

"I-I think I could miss a couple of days of school."

"Pero I don't want just you to go. I want Sabina to go too."

"What? Why?"

"Because you need a friend, and I need you."

"Ma, I mean, I love Walter Mercado, but I'm not as…as sad about him passing as you are."

"Mira," she says, swiping and stabbing on her phone until the horoscope app opens. When did she get so many apps on her phone? "It says, *Aries, the next couple of days are going to be difficult. Keep your family, your loved ones and your friends close to you. You are going to need them.* That's you. I need you and you need Sabina."

The whole thing is so bonkers I can't even entertain it.

"I don't think Sab's parents will let her miss school."

"I will talk to them," Mamá says with a finality that I know and dread.

"Where are we going to stay? Your family doesn't have room for all of us."

"I already looked up a nice little place not far from your cousin's work. She says it's very nice, not too expensive, alta calidad."

"I'm not worried about the quality, Ma. We can't all sleep in one room!"

"No, of course not. You and Sabina will get one room, and I'll get my own room. I'm too vieja to share con niñitas."

"Mom, I mean…" I sputter, like the radiator.

She levels the stare at me, the one that she's used since I first did something wrong and tried to hide la macana, to pretend I didn't do it. It's her *X-ray through your heart* look.

"If you don't want to go with me, just say that and I'll under-stand." That's exactly what she'd say if she *wouldn't* understand.

I hesitate. The thing is I *do* want to go. I just don't want to go with Sabina. Her being there will make everything more complicated. There's no way Ma won't know something is between us, and Sabina will see it as a perfect time to tell Mamá about us—and it would be the exact worst time to tell her I have a girlfriend.

"Does Sabina have to go? What if she doesn't want to go?"

"If she doesn't want to go, of course she doesn't have to go. But show her this." She waves her phone in my face, the horoscope app showing Virgo. Why did I ever tell Mamá Sabina's sign?

"It says, *Travel is in your future this week—surprises and undiscovered places. Let yourself go!* See, it's meant to be!"

The universe hates me.

"What about you? What does Capricornio say?"

Without looking at her phone, she recites, *"You must find it in your heart to say goodbye to the ones you love, even if it is painful."*

I have no response to that, so I stack our plates in the sink and start washing.

"I'm gonna miss you," Sabina says, trailing her fingers along the back of my head. I lean in to her hand like her cat, Pilot, does when I pet him. I lie on her bed on my stomach because I want to hide my face. I haven't told Sabina that she's invited to PR, that Mom wants her to come. Even though that's why I'm in Hoboken on a Sunday afternoon. I'm supposed to be telling Sabina and convincing her parents to let her come. The joke is that Sab's parents would totally let her go. They love me. They trust her. They have no illusions about our relationship and had a Pride flag flying outside their Hudson Street apartment before they ever met me.

"This might be a silly question, and I know that PR is part of the US, but do you need a passport or just a driver's license to go?"

"Just a license. I'm bringing my passport. It's the only ID I have."

"Yeah, student ID from County Prep probably wouldn't cut it. I do keep trying to teach you to drive," she says, tugging the hair at the nape of my neck.

I roll over and look into her face. It's on the tip of my tongue to tell her that Mamá wants her to go to PR with us. That we should go together. But the pressure to tell Ma about our relationship crushes me.

"You are never getting me behind the wheel with you again. I can hear you cringe whenever I hit the gas," I say.

"You cannot hear people cringe."

"Your cringing is so loud, it makes sound waves." Sab throws a Totoro pillow at me.

"Okay, can I at least help you pack? You suck at packing. Remember the away track meet in the Poconos? You forgot underwear and packed too many socks."

"Fine. Not gonna let me live down my first away trip. So, what should I pack?"

We talk about weather and clothes and what the hell do you wear to a velorio—which isn't even going to be a velorio because Mom isn't invited to the family wake: it's really just a public memorial gathering her cousins told her about. She wants to go where the grieving is happening. I get it.

My phone buzzes in my back pocket, and I fumble it out. It's Mamá. I am going to decline the call when Sabina slides her finger across the screen and hits Speaker.

"Hola, Señora Torres! How are you feeling?"

I snatch the phone away from her so quickly I scrape her hand with my nails. Sabina just stares at me in shock, surprise, and I should just play it off like it's a joke or an overreaction or just a weird spasm—Mamá is on speakerphone.

"¿Hola? Meji?"

We're both silent. The moments drag one by one as I get further away from being able to tell Sabina that everything is fine and it's all a joke.

"Hello? Sabina?" Mom says.

"Hello, Señora Torres," Sabina says, keeping her eyes on me like I'm suddenly some wild animal accidentally trapped in her room. That's how I feel. Instantaneously desperate and wanting to race back to when everything was shitty but ultimately fine, or at least in control. Not whatever wildfire this current situation is.

"Nobody's going to talk to me?" Ma says, irritated.

Sabina, steps in, her voice smooth, though her eyes, as she stares at me, are troubled.

"We were just planning Meji's clothes for Puerto Rico. She can borrow a black suit of my brother's if she wants. They're almost the same size."

Sabina couldn't have said anything worse if she tried, and she's trying so much to be kind.

"Oh. Okay, pero, Sabina, did your parents say yes?"

"Yes to what?" Sab says, confused. If I hang up the phone right now it will be weird and difficult to explain and a thousand times more awkward, but it won't be out in the open. Once the invitation to PR is out, there's no going back. I know that. I see myself, a different dimension self, punch the red *X* button on the phone, disconnect my mother's voice and deal with the consequences of being thought rude or crazy or stupid. But at least then I wouldn't have to go.

I don't remember this, but Mamá likes to tell this story about me to all my primos. When I was little, learning to use the toilet, she could tell I had to use the bathroom. I was maybe two, three years old. She'd made me wear just underwear and a T-shirt, the easier to get situated in the bathroom. She told me to go use the toilet and walked me to the bathroom. I stood by the toilet, my face set in grim determination, as she urged, then begged me to get in there and pee, carajo. But I refused. I didn't want to be told to do something, even something I wanted to do. So, I just peed on the floor. Right. Next. To. The. Toilet. Everyone thinks this is a hilarious story. But I remember what it felt like to be physically unable to do something I desperately wanted to do. That's how I feel now. I want to stop everything. Throw the phone across the room so it smashes into Sabina's mirror. And damn every consequence.

"Meji didn't tell you yet? We go to Puerto Rico! It would be so good for you and for me too, I mean for all of us. It would help so much. Do you think your parents would let you go?" Mom's hopeful voice ends in static, dropping into silence for a beat.

Sabina doesn't look at me. "Oh, sure. I mean, yes, we were just talking about that. Sorry. I was miles away." She laughs. "Let me go ask my parents while you talk to Meji." She gets up and leaves the phone on the bed without looking back.

When I come out of Sabina's room to the beautifully redone kitchen in their railroad apartment, Sabina's parents,

Mr. and Mrs. Holm (but-please-call-us-Dave-and-Cheryl),
are finishing take-out ramen.

"Hey, Meji," Mr. Holm says. "Did you have lunch yet?"
He offers up a large take-out container.

"No, thank you, Mr. Holm. I'm, uh, did Sabina leave?"

The Holms exchange looks. "She went to work. She told
us you might need a ride home. Happy to take you," Mrs.
Holm says, rising.

"No, um, that's okay. I've already got my ticket on the
Light Rail. Return ticket," I say stupidly.

"Are you sure, honey? It's so cold out." Mrs. Holm's eyes
follow me. In a minute, she's gonna offer me a winter coat
to borrow.

"No, I'm great, thanks. Want to get home to Mom. Thank
you." I feel all their unasked questions on me as I put my
beanie on and pull the hood over my head for good measure.
I wish I knew where Sabina is; she's not working at the crepe
place today. I know her schedule. But even if I knew where
she was, what would I say when I found her? I start the long
walk to the Light Rail, numb from the inside out.

* ◊ *

"¿Qué paso?"

"Nothing."

"You look terrible. And you're cold. Where is Sabina?"

"She's working."

Now that Mom has a task to do, she's back on a schedule.
The suitcase is out, and she's wearing the black dress and blazer
she wore for Dad's funeral and asking me if it looks okay.

"You look, um, good. It's good."

"Pero what about Sabina? Is she coming?"

"No."

Mom moves to her purse to pull out her phone. "I'll call her parents."

"No, Ma! It's not her parents. We're not friends anymore," I say miserably.

Ma shoves aside the piles of folded clothes on the sofa, making room for me. "Sientete, nena."

I sit.

"Why do you say you aren't friends anymore?"

"She's not answering my calls." Sabina is so slow to anger, but when she's angry, it's incendiary and at the same time cold. And how could I ever explain why I didn't tell her she was invited to PR? Saying that it was because I was ashamed of her will go down real well.

"I don't know, Mamá. She doesn't want to talk to me." I had to peel off my hoodie and beanie and even my cardigan so that I wouldn't boil to death in this apartment. Now I feel unprotected in just my T-shirt and jeans. And just to prove how unprotected I am, I start crying.

"Que, no, mijita, no llores," Mom says.

"I'm fine. It's nothing. I'm just sad about my friend."

"Are you sure there isn't anything you can do, angelito?"

That makes me cry harder.

"No, it's not a big deal."

"You know what Walter says, right?"

Oh, sweet Jesus. I'm starting to get real sick of Walter Mercado.

"Walter dice, sobre todo, amor, mucho, mucho amor. Do you know what that means?"

"Of course I know, Ma. Above all, love. Lots of love, blah blah blah."

"Ermenegilda!" She barks out my full name, invoking my great-grandmother, the ancestors on my Dad's side. It cuts through all my sad stupor. I look up.

"I'm going to say this in English so you understand, okay?" I nod.

"You love Sabina. She loves you. That is the most important thing. Amor es todo."

"Mamá, Sabina and I—"

"I know she's your girlfriend!" she says, shooting her arms up over her head, making the shoulders of her black blazer hunch up around her ears. She tugs the suit back down and takes my hands in hers.

"Meji, I've known for a while. And I've been waiting for you to tell me. I didn't want to push, I didn't want to intrude. But you can't wait, you can't hide. Life is so short, angelito, and love is the most precious thing. I thought if I made you and Sabina go to PR with me, ack!"

My brain reels in a tide of emotion and confusion soup. *I know she's your girlfriend.*

"But you wanted me to wear the floofy blue dress," I say faintly.

"What dress?" Mom says, confused.

"For mis quince. I told you I wanted to wear a tuxedo. I was telling you in my very insecure and not-too-clear way that I am different. And you made me wear that dress."

"Ese puto vestido," Mom curses. Shuts me right up. Mom never curses. "That dress!" She puts her head in her hands. I notice her toenails are painted, the big toe a perfect miniature Puerto Rican flag.

"You have to understand, angelito, I was desperate to keep your father happy. I didn't know if he'd even make it to your quince. He lost so much weight, he was so yellow. Ay. When he said he liked that light blue dress, I just wanted him to be happy. I didn't think of what you wanted or what it meant. Lo siento tanto, amor."

I know she's your girlfriend is still making the rounds through my barely functioning brain. Now this revelation that she'd only wanted me to go through with the quince-dress-from-hell to make Dad smile.

"When I was young in PR, I knew a couple of people who were... Como se dice?" she asks.

I shake my head, uncomprehending.

"L, G, T?"

"LGBTQIA," I rattle off.

"Sí, eso. I knew some people who were that. And they were nice people. But I never thought of them as something, no, some*one* that would be in our family."

I stiffen, and my mouth twists. This is why I didn't want to tell her.

"Pero, you know, this is not about me or what I thought. And Walter told me that. All those years ago."

"He told you your love was eternal, I know."

"He told me it was not about what I want. El Señor sabe mejor que yo. Dios puede juzgar, no yo."

God can judge, not I.

"And is that what you think? That God judges me, Mamá?"

She shakes her head emphatically. "No. Because you are good, and you are in love. That cannot be wrong."

She puts her arms around me, but I stay stiff. I wish I could let go and be soft. But I'm afraid.

"You know who is more stubborn than a Capricorn, right?"

"Yes."

"Yes, Aries. But I love you. And that never can change. It also is eterno, you understand?"

"Yes."

"So are you going to ask Sabina to go with us?"

I pull back from our awkward hug to look her in the eye.

"I don't know if she'll forgive me," I say.

"Ack! Of course she will forgive you! Tell her she is your moon and sun and that you are very stupid and you are very sorry."

I laugh and blow my nose with the tissue Mom hands me. She's right. Sabina only wants me to be honest. It's what she deserves.

"You really want us to be in a room alone together, Ma?"

She shrugs. "Keep one foot on the floor, and you will be okay."

I laugh. "You know that's not how that works, right?"

"How different can girls be? It's just bodies and kisses, no?"

I finally let go of my fear and let my body bend into hers, letting her hug me, all of me.

"I love you, Mamá."

"Mucho, mucho," she says.

*   *   *   *   *

AQUARIUS

Venus in Aquarius

* Unconventional and unpredictable
* Shies away from possessiveness or clinginess
* Drawn to those who are different
* Emotional bonding required
* Might seem too detached

I Come From the Water
Adrianne White

There's a time nearly every day in the fall, around five at night or so, where if I look at the right angle out the window toward the edge of the woods, I can just make out the creek, light dappling across the water as the sun deep-dives toward the horizon. It's a *crick* according to my grandmother, haunted if you let her and my aunts tell it, a bunch of superstitious bunk if Alicia has anything to say about it.

I don't tell my mother I know she says it's bunk because the alternative terrifies her. That I know she pushes what she can do, what we all can do in some form or another, way, way down so that it doesn't bubble up when she least expects it. That that water, that crick, is the source of many things good and not so good, and that I've dealt with it my whole life and I'm just fine, and she will be too, like all of us are, if she just stops being afraid. But telling someone to let fear go and actually letting fear go are two entirely different things, and it's not enough for someone to just say you need to do it.

That water, that source, has given us a lot. Crawdads satisfying Grandmama Emma's urge to boil, frogs and turtles for Gwen's tanks, a place to zone out to the water gurgling over the rocks, plenty of crickets to catch smallmouth bass downstream for fish fries during Lent. So with all that goodness, the occasional not so good is expected for the sake of balance right, so it should never be a surprise when it arrives.

And yet.

And yet.

* ◇ *

"The way I've just been calling your name for like an hour." Gwen sits on the porch steps like every bone in her body's in rebellion, buried under a black shawl big enough to wrap her at least three times. She loves its drama, loves anything over-the-top, honestly.

"I haven't even been out here an hour."

"Don't get smart with me. You ain't too big to put over my knee."

"Your knees are shot, though."

"Okay, but once I catch you—" She gestures under the fabric, some kind of chopping and flailing that fails at being intimidating but is pretty funny-looking so I laugh, knowing this is the aunt I can laugh with, who won't think I'm laughing at her.

"It's getting dark so fast now," I say. Gwen nods.

"Season's going for real. It's near winter. The way we're all stuck like this, what even is a season, anymore? What is time, really?" She kicks at a rock. "Maybe that's why everything's so riled up. It feels like everything's, like, strained, maybe? I don't know."

"I don't know."

"That's what I said." When she gets up, she looks at me, then toward the trees, clucking her tongue. "Dinner soon. Don't be late."

*   ◊   *

The way Alicia cuts her eyes at us around the table isn't unusual. The fact everyone's ignoring it is, though. She clearly wants to discuss something, and nobody's biting. Gwen's been buttering a roll for five minutes, and Dana, my oldest, prickliest aunt, keeps grunting at her phone. I'm clearly very invested in this creamy, faintly fishy soup. Some kind of chowder, maybe?

"Shelby, you don't even like soup. Eyes on me."

"You know, I thought I didn't either, but this is really good. I like—"

"Enough about the soup," Alicia says.

"But you brought it up," Gwen says.

"It *is* good." Dana doesn't look up while throwing her two cents in.

"Thanks y'all," Gwen says like she's won an award.

"Why do I even bother. Nobody takes me serious."

"Aww, Leesh, don't get all maudlin. If you'd just say you

had something to talk about instead of making pouty faces at us, that might work better."

"But that wouldn't be Alicia. It's less dramatic," Dana says. I look into my bowl before my eyes betray me with agreement.

Gwen drops the roll. "You have our attention. What is it?"

"Well. Okay. Well, let me start by saying there's nothing I value more than y'all. I'm glad we were able to keep things together after, well, you know, *after*. But it's getting harder. There's more taxes and bills keep popping up, doctors and stuff I wasn't even aware of."

"What are you saying?" Dana looks up, eyes going even darker. She's about to be seriously not happy.

"Please don't tell me Mama had another family," Gwen says, and it's hard to tell if she's playing or not.

"Well. Okay. I may have, like, inadvertently right, like, not on purpose missed a utility bill here or there, and there's the matter of a few tax returns, maybe even an…" Oh, that trailing off isn't gonna sit right.

"A what?" Dana asks. "Speak up, please."

"An audit. They said something about an audit."

"What? How do you audit a dead person?" Gwen asks.

"It's not auditing the dead. It's auditing the dead's business. Y'all, it's terrible, seriously. It's bad, like we know she's never been the best at managing things, but she must've been doing poorly much longer than we knew. By the time I got here the damage was already done, and then things started going downhill fast. Stuff just kept falling through the cracks."

"And now the piper's calling," Gwen says, shaking her head. "Damn feds."

"Probably feds *and* the state, knowing Mama," Dana says.

"Yeah. So, like, cash is needed more than anything, and the biggest assets we have are this house and the land under it. I got months of messages from developers offering, like, you wouldn't even believe what they're offering. I don't know how she ignored numbers like this, knowing how much trouble she was in."

"I don't care what they offer. Nobody's selling." Dana sounds so firm about it, like there's no point in arguing. Full-on big-sister mode.

"It's not really up to all of us, now, is it?"

"Alicia, come on now," Gwen says.

"I just mean that I'm the one left with all of this. It's falling on me, technically. If y'all wanted to walk away tomorrow you could."

"So why even ask us if you already know what you want to do?" Dana asks.

"I want your input. I'm not even sure it's the right thing *to* do."

"I know you hate doing this, but maybe try trusting your gut on this one." Gwen pats Alicia's hand twice, in a way that makes Alicia feel better, I suppose, because that about-to-cry expression just slips away.

"You know we wouldn't leave you so don't even play like that. Despite what you think about me, I'm not a monster. This house is ours, as is the land beneath it, and has been our family's forever, and there's no way in hell I'm letting some gentrifying assholes have it." Dana looks over Alicia's head, up high, smirks a bit. "And I'm not the only one who feels that way."

Oh. Ohhh. Not now. Please don't freak her out—

"Stop that," Alicia says, rubbing her arms. "I said stop."

"Girl, what's wrong with you?" Gwen asks. "Quit tripping and pass the salt."

∗ ◊ ∗

"You can't *do* that." I look them up and down. Tall Thing's taller than usual, like they're just showing off or whatever, or just want my neck to hurt because I'm beyond annoyed with them right now. I don't know what they're up to. Ghosts are fucking weird.

"I didn't. I just appeared."

"Right. Directly behind my mother, who you know's been afraid of everything her entire life, just breathing right all up in her business."

"I don't breathe."

"That's not funny."

"I'm not joking."

"I thought we agreed you'd stay away from mealtimes."

"We did. I tried. But that talk of the house going away compelled me." *Uh-huh. Like you've ever been compelled anywhere for anything.* "It was strange to me too. Concerning, even. Everything feels riled up for some reason."

"Oh god, Gwen said the same thing. Is it something, really? Like, can you tell? Or do we just gotta wait until it shows up and kicks our asses?"

They shift into something shorter, all brown and chubby-cheeked, soft pastels and gothy makeup, pink curly hair.

"Now would I look like this if something bad was coming?"

"Actually, yes. I believe you would."

They pretend to be offended for a whole ten seconds before laughing. It's always been so weird, hearing their breath and knowing there is none, sometimes even feeling it and knowing they're doing it for my benefit, so things feel more normal, I suppose, like any of this is even close to that. And they've always been my normal since I can remember, and I'm fine with them, with what they are, even if I don't fully understand it. I hope they know I don't care about them pretending to be anything, that they don't have to form themselves into anything to appeal to me. Is it even possible for them to be themselves anymore?

"Can we watch more of that show," they ask, settling near the floor, "the one about the girl and the ghost band?"

$$* \diamond *$$

"Did you get all your work done?" Alicia doesn't hover often, but it's happening more since she doesn't go out for work anymore, doesn't go out much really except to, like, the dentist or whatever. She must be so bored.

"I did. It was just some reading, nothing big."

"Oh good, because there was a message for you earlier."

"Where? On the—"

"Yes. *On the.* So please take care of that."

Before I can answer, she's gone upstairs, and I'm annoyed I don't even get the chance to ask how she knew it was for me or to complain properly. Like. Who even has an answering machine anymore? Like if you even said *answering machine* would anybody even know what the hell you were talking about? It's a big square, solid brick of a thing, sitting on a little table in the kitchen near the basement door like it's ashamed or unwanted, which is kinda true. I really wish I could talk to the boomer witch who decided this is how we should communicate.

Oh god, that beep. And then that clunky noise as you roll it back, like bricks tumbling in a bucket. I mean, *rewind* it. Dana showed me once how the symbols for all the actions haven't really changed, even as the technology did, and, like, okay, that's cool or whatever, but I'd rather get these messages any other way than this.

Oh hi, hello. This message is for Shelby Miller. You don't know me, and I'll catch hell if I say who I am, but I need to let you know that something's…that you need to—

Wait. What's this static? That can't be it. What even is this? I rewind it, hit Play, and it's just…blank. No talking. No hissing, no popping, just a whole lot of nothing, confusing silence. It's times like this when I really, really wish my life was more normal. I mean, not that I even have a clue what normal is, but I'm sure it's not getting cryptic-ass vanishing messages on an electronic fossil.

"Are you done messing with that machine? You know it only plays once!" Gwen yells from the back of the house. No, I don't know that, because this is the first one I've ever gotten, and why isn't there, like, a note or something letting people know that?

My head tingles, migraine incoming. By the time I'm at the stairs, my vision's blurry at the edges. Time for meds, bed and sleep like the dead.

* ◊ *

"It's so nice to see you. We don't get visitors lately since, well, you know." Gwen's voice is light, airy and almost breathless, like she's really excited and it's been so long since she's had something to be excited about, I'm super curious who's on the other side of the door. From the landing, I can just make out the top of a rainbow-microbraided head and wide brown eyes, thick black eyebrows, one raised just so, like they're both amused and confused by my aunt, which makes total sense. But who. And why. And is Gwen really about to let a stranger into the house?

"Stop spying." I almost pee myself. Dana laughs. "Why don't you just go down there? It's not like you don't know Yvonne."

"Know who?"

"You play too much. You can either go save them from Gwen or get this laundry going."

Those wide eyes lock on me the whole time I come down, even as I'm reaching into the side-table bowl for masks and Gwen goes, "Oh y'all don't need them. They're fine."

This person, this Yvonne, is tall, like how they describe people in romance novels—*statuesque*—hair flowing past their shoulders, and their clothes are patterned in swirls and stripes, skirt sweeping the floor. The wide eyes twinkle with recognition, and their smile is full and endearing, drawing me in.

"Hi, Shelby." *How…*

"Y'all go on the porch. I'll bring something to drink," Gwen says, shooing me with her hands.

I've been through a lot of weird stuff, experienced things

most people wouldn't believe or, even if they did, I couldn't really prove. But despite living near a likely haunted creek, having relatives with varying levels of witchiness, and having a noncorporeal bestie, I still can't explain what's happening right now. Yvonne said hi and my name, and I said hi back, and as soon as I crossed the threshold it was like we'd known each other our whole lives. Like, they're chatting about people who I swear I don't recall, but the more they speak, the more details of their lives pop into my head as clear memories. And the more they mention them, the less sure I am that I don't know who they're talking about.

It's always been hard for me to small-talk, especially with people around my age. Only child and being around adults all the time doesn't help, but if I'm being honest, most people get on my nerves bad, and talking to them usually ends in disappointment, especially at school. It's one of the few things I don't miss about being stuck home, all their assorted foolishness.

But talking to Yvonne is so dang easy, and it's not spooky or unsettling, it just feels, like, *right*. Like we're just old friends catching up, none of that weird, awkward chat that makes my soul evaporate. We just sit and drink Gwen's sweet tea and watch the sun crawl across the sky. And it's good.

"Your aunt's so nice." Yvonne's voice is melodic, deep and purposeful, like every word's carefully chosen. "And makes amazing tea."

"She puts it outside, I mean, like, out in the sun. It's sun tea."

"Oh. I've heard of that. It's neat she does that when she could, just, snap and make it happen."

"Nah, that's how you lose your Southern witch card," falls out of my mouth before I can stop it.

"This isn't the South," Yvonne says, clearly unbothered, and I'm too shocked to ask why, even though I know I should.

"You can leave Memphis, but Memphis never leaves you. At least that's what my Grandmama said."

"I don't really know exactly where my people are from. Sometimes it feels like we just... Appeared, I suppose?"

"A whole mystery, then."

"Yeah. Something like that." Yvonne smiles. "Is there more tea?"

*　◊　*

Tall Thing's frowning in the kitchen.

"What?"

"*You're* serving things?"

"Is that really so shocking?" Occasionally, I'm helpful.

"Will you be out there much longer?" They're actually pouting. Have you ever seen a spirit pout? I mean, it's not likely that many people have even seen a spirit at all, but if you've experienced a pouting one, it's something else. Tall Thing makes the air crackle with frosty energy.

I go for the pitcher without answering.

"Did you hear me?"

"Yeah and you're being weirder than usual."

"I'm not the only weird one. Who is that person on the porch?"

"Come see for yourself."

"Oh, thank you." Yvonne holds up their glass so I can refill it. It's one of Grandmama's plastic cups from an old pizza place. The logo is cracked and fading, but it still makes things cold as hell.

Even the way they sip is elegant, not like the way I usually do, chugging and gulping for air like a fish on land. Their fingers are long, wrapped almost completely around the cup, nails painted a glossy holographic color that changes in the light, almost like it's mood polish.

There's no way for me to ask if Yvonne can sense Tall Thing without coming off like a whole weirdo, but that's what I want to do more than anything right now because they're hovering super close, right above Yvonne near the fan. Every time it whips around, it makes wispy trails of their figure. It would be super spooky and intimidating to anyone who didn't know any better.

Yvonne looks around, not settling on anything in particular but like they're taking everything in all at once. It's like an inventory, I can almost hear the items being checked off a list in their head, and it seems like they find everything worthy. When they collect their braids in one hand and flip them over their shoulder, I'm hit with the smell of lavender and fresh bread and laundry soap, all my favorite things. It's so amazing and unexpected, I almost fall off the porch steps.

"So it's just y'all here, you and your aunts, right?" they ask.

"Well. Uh, yeah, it's just us for now."

"For now? Who else are you expecting?"

"I'm not really sure anymore. I mean, today was pretty ordinary, and then here *you* come."

It's quiet for what feels like both forever and no time at all.

Yvonne scans around us again, taking in every bit of the environment, every leaf and branch, every bird and flower, the bits of porch where the white paint's long flaked off. They run their hand over the rusty metal railing I swung around pretending to be a gymnast when I was little. Without thinking, I touch the scar on my forehead from slamming into a concrete step.

"Yeah," they say, "here I come. Is that a bad thing, though? I know some people don't like surprises." The wind picks up then, setting off the chimes but too chilly for summer. I look up to catch Tall Thing's undoubtedly screwed-up face, but there's nothing. "Like I said," Yvonne goes, laughing.

They finish their tea and start on the ice, crunching steadily, humming a soft lullabyish song. I have so many questions but they're tumbling around in my head so fast I can't figure out which one I want to ask first. If I had even a fraction of the confidence Yvonne seems to, I might could start with even the most basic stuff, like *What's your birthday?*, then figure out if our charts are compatible. Gwen told me once that having Aquarius in both sun and Venus made me even more special: a *heavy hitter* she called it.

"Shelby." Nobody's ever said my name this way. It's somehow firm and soft, like both teasing and scolding, and I'm really not mad about it. "You look like you're dying to ask me something."

"Well. Not dying, I mean, it's never really that deep, but—"

"Okay, so what is it then?" *Be careful* pops into my head, meaning Tall Thing's back, and I really wish they'd learn how to be a proper wingman and stop blocking.

"Um. Medium deep? Probably like super shallow, honestly." That laugh again, and my insides are vibing.

"That's not always bad. Like, I spent some time walking

around earlier, and you know that creek just past the tree line? I was so hot and just put my feet in for a bit, and it was so cool and felt so nice! That water just came to my ankles. Maybe it's the Cancer in me, but it was the best thing, super refreshing. So yeah, shallow can definitely be good."

Oh my god. Not the creek. Not *my* creek. Not my favorite place in this whole town. Now I have even more questions. Everything about today's felt fated, from the weirdness with the house to Tall Thing freaking out to Yvonne just, I don't even know, being Yvonne. The sun's just about gone now, the horizon striped with pinks and purples. With the moon nearly full, and it's supposed to be a blue one soon, I can look forward to my aunts setting intentions in the backyard and knowing most everything will come true. I try to remember what they said last time, if it had anything to do with me, if they somehow knew then that, in my heart of hearts, I wanted and needed something to break through the absolute monotony of these last several months.

Looking at Yvonne, and how Yvonne's looking at me, I suspect they did. And I'm grateful for it.

"What are you here for?" I finally ask.

"We have a kind of pact, this land and me, and there's things I'm bound to protect. I thought that was all but soon as my foot hit that water, I knew there was something else. So maybe the question's *who* am I really here for?"

I take Yvonne's hand like it's nothing, like it hasn't been forever since I touched someone I'm not related to. We fit good. It feels great. They look over my shoulder, then wink.

"Don't you worry. I got her."

*　*　*　*　*

PISCES

Venus in Pisces
* Soft, sweet, and emotional
* Hopeless romantic
* Comes across as unfocused or confusing
* Drawn to creative types
* Overly compassionate and empathetic

The Cure for Heartbreak
Emery Lee

Chimes echoed through the store as the door swung closed. Most shops on the strip had one of those annoying little bells, but of course Luis's parents had insisted on wind chimes.

"So we can hear the spirits enter," his father had said.

And sure, spirits didn't use doors so the wind chimes worked better than a regular bell, but Luis always felt uncomfortable stepping out of the back room to the sound of chimes, like he was some shady old psychic preying on the young and gullible. But really, that was what everyone at school thought he was anyway, so maybe he should just resign himself to playing the part.

Luis stepped through the beaded curtain to meet the new arrival and froze, his heart pounding in his chest, the voice in the back of his head telling him to retreat.

Alvaro Sotolongo stood by the door, eyes awkwardly flicking around as he glanced at some of the weird herbs and bottles lining the shelves on the wall.

Luis had never seen Al look so outside of his comfort zone before. He was a jock in every sense of the word—muscular phy-
sique, a smile almost as bright as his football-playing future, and
a whole pack of friends who flocked him everywhere, show-
casing just how important Al was in the high-school hierarchy.

But now he looked small. Well, not *small*, considering he
was six feet tall and ninety-nine percent muscle, but he looked
almost…fragile. Like the way Luis always felt at school, like
any misstep would have everyone throwing insults or punches
or half-eaten lunches his way.

And it was the familiarity that cut all the bite out of Luis's
tone as he said, "Can I help you with something?"

Al looked up, eyes wide, like it hadn't even occurred to
him that someone else might be in the shop. Luis waited for
Al to recognize him, to say some shit about how he was that
freak from school that everyone hated and maybe hurl some
digs at him.

But Al just shrugged and said, "I don't know. I guess I'm
not entirely sure I should be here at all."

"Everyone says that." But they wouldn't step over that
threshold if they weren't desperate. It took a desperate hopeless person to turn to the occult, especially when they didn't
even really believe in it.

Al glanced awkwardly around the shop again before sucking in a deep breath, squaring his shoulders, and stepping up
to the counter. He flashed Luis that typical jock smile, but he
still didn't seem quite as *big* as he always did at school.

"I guess—well, do you have, like…a spell or something to fix a broken heart?"

It was a common-enough request. Hell, it was probably the most common request, and Luis just kind of rolled his eyes whenever he heard it.

If there was a cure for heartbreak, well, there wouldn't be quite so many sad songs on the radio.

And frankly, Luis would be rich, but that obviously wasn't happening.

"Sorry," Luis said. "Magic can't fix a broken heart."

"Oh."

Al stared down at the counter like it was the only thing keeping him on his feet, and Luis had to wonder if maybe it just might be. Luis had never been there himself. In love, that was. It all seemed like a bad idea—pouring your heart into someone just so they could choose when to toss you away, exerting all that energy just to ultimately hurt each other. And looking at Al now, seeing all the confidence and pride drained right out of him, Luis was pretty confident he'd made the right decision.

But something about a broken heart must've been contagious because the longer Al stood hunched over in the tiny shop, the more Luis's heart began to hurt too. There was a tickle in the back of his head telling him he'd already caught the sickness, and the only way to protect himself was to find a fix for Al.

"But I might have something that can help," Luis said.

Al looked up at him, a bright smile spreading across his face. "Really?"

Luis sighed, turning toward the beaded curtain. "Just give me a second."

* ◇ *

Magic wasn't just potions and hexes. The truest of magics was about reading energy, molding and reshaping it to create a preferred outcome, but never competing with Fate itself.

That was the hardest part, of course. Nobody wanted to accept that magic wasn't meant to rewrite the world or enforce your own will. They'd seen enough *Sabrina* to know what it could really do, and they never cared about the consequences.

As Luis laid out the folding table, placing a plastic chair on either side and lighting the candle at the center of it, he couldn't help but worry Al was exactly one of those people. Of all the types of desperation Luis had dealt with from customers, romantic love was always the worst. It was the thing that always made logic go out the window.

"Sit," Luis said, taking his own seat at the table.

Al glanced at the plastic chair hesitantly before taking his seat across from Luis. He grinned wide, chuckling to himself. "Is the candle to perform a séance or something?"

Luis glared. "If you're just gonna make fun of me, you can leave."

The smile shriveled up on Al's face. "No, I—I mean, I'm sorry."

"So tell me about this girl," Luis said, turning his attention to his hands.

"How did you figure it was a girl?"

Luis rolled his eyes. "Because you're a jock?"

"I'm pansexual."

Luis raised an eyebrow. "So was it not a girl?"

Al blushed, looking down at his hands. "I— Um, yeah, I guess so."

"Look, if you're not gonna take this seriously, I have plenty of other things I could be doing," Luis snapped, even though it wasn't true. The shop was pretty slow most days, especially weekdays after school, and it wasn't like he had a booming social life to get back to.

But he hated doing this dance with people. This moment of vulnerability on both of their parts, because even if desperation had led Al there in the first place, he could get up, leave, pretend he'd never been there. He could tell his friends he'd never stopped by, and everyone would believe him without hesitation. But Luis? He'd be haunted by this encounter, by knowing he couldn't help and that all he'd done was expose this secret part of his life that he'd always been scorned for.

Al shook his head. "I'm sorry. Really. I just— It's hard to talk about. We were together for a long time."

"How long?"

"Since freshman year," Al said.

Luis paused. Almost three *years*? When Al had said "a long time," Luis had assumed he meant a few months or so. After all, there were always rumors about which girl Al was likely sleeping with now, people passing around stories about making out with him outside the locker rooms. Was he just cheating on this poor girl for three years?

Luis knitted his hands together, trying to keep his face passive. "So why did you break up?"

"She said I wasn't invested enough anymore."

"Were you?"

Al didn't answer, which should have solved the problem,

but there was obviously a reason he came to the shop. If he wasn't invested in that girl anymore, he wouldn't need Luis to fix his broken heart. So, what?

"So, what kind of magic are you going to do?" Al asked.

Luis rolled his eyes. "That's what I'm trying to figure out. There's no spell to erase your love for someone, but there are spells to seek peace or find comfort or even ease physical pain so…"

Al blinked, his eyes wide as he stared back at Luis. Not judgmental but just…curious.

"Anyway," Luis said, "the more I know about your relationship—former relationship—the better I can curate a spell to get you past it. But I can't make her fall in love with you again, so don't ask me to."

Al smiled. "Yeah, I figured. I don't think I want that, anyway. Monica… Well, I think we were really good together, especially at first, and that makes it really hard, but…this was her call, and I want her to be happy, so I think I just want to move on, you know?"

Luis *didn't* know. Not really. But he'd work out a spell for Al anyway, because that was just the way he was.

Al stayed in the shop for an hour, which was far longer than Luis had expected. It started with a few questions trying to guide Al down memory lane and then fell into an all-out therapy session with Al venting about how Monica always smelled like strawberries even though she claimed she hated fruit, how she hogged the TV but never wanted to watch anything good, about how she'd gotten him into AP classes but stopped letting him copy her homework so now he was doomed to fail. And Luis let him talk, even though all his complaints were beyond superficial, because the more he knew about Al, the better he could work his magic.

So it was only after six o'clock when Al said he needed to get home to work on some class project that Luis realized he hadn't actually *sold* him anything.

"I appreciate you helping me out," Al said as he made his way to the door. "So was the candle the magic?"

Luis rolled his eyes. "I haven't done any magic yet."

Al's eyes shot wide. "Wait, really? 'Cause I already feel like I'm getting better."

"Maybe you just need a therapist," Luis said.

Al grinned. "Can I come back tomorrow? Then you can cast whatever spell you're thinking."

"Fine. If I'm not at the counter, just ask for me. My name's Luis."

Al laughed, throwing his head back as the booming echo filled the shop. God, what an obnoxious laugh. Then he flashed Luis a smile, reaching for the door handle. "I know who you are. You're in my calculus class, aren't you?"

Luis froze. They absolutely *were* in the same calculus class, but he'd never expected *Al* of all people to notice him sitting in his corner scribbling tentative spells in the margins of his textbook.

Al laughed again. "That face you're making is priceless! Anyway, see you tomorrow."

Before Luis could speak again, Al was gone.

True to his word, Al showed up the next day, hair wet from his post-practice shower. Luis was in the back room testing out a spell when his mom pushed through the beaded curtain to say, "Hay un guapo niño esperando."

"¿Para mi?" Luis asked.

"Claro que si. ¿Quien esta?"

Luis sighed, closing his notebook. "Nobody important."

Stepping out into the shop, Luis found Al squinting awkwardly at a jar full of thyme. He met Luis's eyes as he entered. "What is this?"

"Thyme," Luis said.

"Time for what?"

Luis groaned, snatching the jar out of Al's hand. "It's an herb." He placed it back on the shelf, turning to find Al already halfway across the store looking at something else. "Are you here to fix your broken heart or what?"

Al smiled. "Yeah, I am, but I also want to know more about this place. It's interesting."

And Luis was more than familiar with the way most people used the word *interesting*. Like it meant *exotic* or *strange* or *spooky*. But Al didn't seem like he meant any of those other things, so maybe Luis was just being too hard on him.

But either way, Luis wasn't interested in giving Al the grand tour. He'd agreed to help because he couldn't stand to see those sad puppy-dog eyes, but that didn't mean he wanted to open up his whole life to the most popular kid in school. He'd tried appeasing those types of people before—offering them free spells or letting them copy his homework—and it always ended with spit in his face and a knife in his back.

"Let's just get this over with," Luis said. "I have a spell that might help you."

"Oh, really? Already?"

Luis tuned out the sound of disappointment in Al's voice. He was probably just imagining that. "It's nothing flashy, but it should help ease things a bit, if you're open to it."

"What is it?"

"A refocusing spell. It'll shift your focus away from the breakup."

"Oh? To what?"

"Anything you want, really."

Al smiled. "Okay."

Luis set the table up again, this time lighting two candles and plopping a battered notebook down on it.

"Close your eyes."

Al obliged, leaning back in his little plastic chair, eyes squeezed shut.

"First, think about the object of your desire," Luis said. "The more senses you can access, the better. Think about what she looked like, felt like, smelled like, et cetera. Now, think of something else important to you. Something you'd like to take her place."

Al chuckled. "Like all those calculus formulas I can't memorize."

Luis rolled his eyes. "Do you take anything seriously?"

Al peeked one eye open, catching sight of the scowl on Luis's face and laughing again. "I'm sorry. I use humor to cope," he said. "I'm sure you get that."

Luis's eyes narrowed. "What is *that* supposed to mean?"

Al grinned wide. "Please, I've seen the way you act. All that shit you say in class when you don't think anyone's looking. Or, oh my God, that time Jeff said that thing about creepy brujos, and you pretended to cast a spell on him at lunch? That shit was hilarious! He said he didn't sleep for like three days."

Luis's eyes fell to his fingers, his cheeks growing warm. "I didn't realize anyone noticed that stuff."

"I mean, you kind of stand out," Al said.

"Yeah, I know," Luis said. "I'm well aware that everyone is terrified of me. I don't need the reminder."

"What? No! I mean…" Al trailed off, and Luis looked up to find him staring back at him, eyes wide. "I didn't mean it like that. I mean, I know some people do, but like… You know, I'm not saying that people don't do that, 'cause I know people are shitty so they do what they want, but I just meant that not everyone's that shitty. I mean, I'm not. Or, well, I guess I could be shitty. I don't really know. But I'm not scared of you, I mean. I think you're really smart. And funny. And snarky but like…in a funny and smart kind of way."

And as much as he hated it, Luis couldn't help but laugh at the shocked look on Al's face and the harried rush of his words. Maybe he was just saying all that because he really *was* scared of Luis, and he didn't want to be caught on the receiving end of one of Luis's infamous hexes, but it didn't really feel that way. It felt like maybe Al really meant it.

"Whatever," Luis said. "Back to the spell. Close your eyes."

"Right, right," Al said, squeezing his eyes shut again.

"Focus on the thing you want to shift your focus to," Luis said. "Picture it clearly."

"Got it."

"Now repeat after me. Light my path forward."

"Light my path forward."

"Follow my heart's direction."

"Follow my heart's direction."

"Now, blow out your candle."

"Now, blow out your candle."

Luis groaned, head falling into his hands. "No, asshole, *blow out your candle.*"

"Ohhh!" Al laughed as his eyes popped open and he leaned forward to blow out the candle on the table in front of him.

Luis lifted his head and sighed. "Okay, the spell is complete."

"Wait, that's it? I don't feel any different."

Luis blew out his own candle before rising from his seat. "I don't know what you were expecting, but magic isn't quite so flashy as it is in movies."

"So this'll help me move on?"

"I don't know," Luis said. "It's different for everyone, but hopefully it'll help."

Al stared back at him a moment, and Luis waited for him to storm out of the shop in fury, but instead, he just leaned back in his seat and smiled. "Okay, I trust you."

Luis froze, his chest feeling tight. "Why would you say that?"

"Say what?"

"That you trust me. You don't even know me."

"I—"

Luis turned his face downward, quickly snatching the candles off the table before racing toward the back room. As the curtain's beaded strings swished behind him, Luis leaned against the wall, trying to slow his thoughts. How could Al *trust* him when everyone at school was firmly convinced he was a demon? What was there to trust about some kid casting occult magic for profit? Al didn't know a single thing about him, but here he was acting like they were old friends instead of two kids who didn't really know each other and had no reason to ever want to.

And as Luis leaned against the wall, the candles slipping from his fingers and hitting the floor, he realized what the ache in his chest was: desire.

No, worse. Longing.

The desperate need to hear Al say those words again. "I trust you." To say that he could see through the facade Luis put on every morning, the standoffish air he wore to keep people from realizing just how much it stung every time they called him a monster, every glare and disgusted look they threw his way.

But Luis had spent so long convincing himself that he was better off alone, that he never wanted anything more than to help people and send them on their way, that he hadn't considered what it might feel like to actually be acknowledged.

And he hated how much he didn't hate it. No, he hated how much he *needed* it and how hard it would be to pretend that he didn't, now that he'd gotten a taste.

He wiped away the dampness forming in his eyes before putting the candles away. He'd been in such a rush to get out of the room, that he'd forgotten to even give Al a bill. He could probably bring one to school tomorrow, but that would mean having to seek Al out, and Luis really didn't want to do that. Maybe he'd just cut his losses and move on.

Then he remembered he'd left the table out in the middle of the shop. With a deep sigh, Luis stepped out to retrieve it and paused.

Al was still there, this time looking at a potted plant near the window. He looked up as Luis stepped out, a deep frown on his face.

Luis sighed. "Why do you have that ridiculous look on your face?"

"I-I'm so sorry, Luis," he said, shaking his head. "I... Well, I'm not even entirely sure what I said, but I'm sorry I said it. I never meant to make you uncomfortable or—"

Luis waved him away. "Don't worry about it."

"I really didn't mean to—"

"I said forget it, okay?" Luis snapped.

Al stared back at him, wide-eyed for a moment. "Right, okay."

And a pit of guilt formed in Luis's stomach. It wasn't Al's fault that he got so touchy about some words that wouldn't have meant anything to anyone else. It wasn't Al's fault that Luis never really learned how to interact with other people or that he couldn't keep his emotions in check.

"I'm sorry," Luis said. "About snapping at you, I mean."

Al grinned, and Luis's stomach lurched. "So does that mean we're even?"

But they could never be even, not when Al was practically a school celebrity with too many friends to count and a bright future ahead of him, and Luis was just a kid who'd go back to being hopelessly alone the moment Al left the shop.

But Luis nodded anyway because his job was to help their customers find peace, even if he couldn't find any of his own. "Yeah, we're even."

Luis was used to being used and discarded, so when Al showed up in the shop again a couple days later, he couldn't process what might have brought him there.

"Need something else?" Luis asked.

Al smiled. "I don't think the spell worked."

Luis rolled his eyes. "No refunds."

"I… No, I just… Could we try another spell, maybe?" Al asked.

Luis stared back at him for a moment. It was pretty rare a customer decided the product hadn't worked and still wanted *another* product, but then, everything about Al was odd: the way he drummed on his notebook with his pencil in class, the way he always leaned a little more on his left foot than his right, and the way he'd taken to sneaking little glances at Luis when he thought Luis wasn't looking.

Though Luis had been looking a lot more than he cared to admit. Definitely more than he ever had before.

"Luis?" Al said.

Luis shook his head. "I… Yeah, we can try whatever you want, I guess."

And Al smiled his blindingly bright quarterback smile. "Thanks!"

So what Luis expected to be a one-off thing quickly turned into a daily routine. He'd head back to the shop after school to help clean things up or work on some homework until Al would show up a couple hours later for their session. And Luis wasn't even really sure what Al was hoping to get from it anymore, since none of his spells seemed to fix Al's broken heart, but he let him come because a part of him was almost grateful to have him there.

It was a Thursday afternoon as Luis wiped down the front counter waiting for Al's arrival that the usual flow of their new routine was interrupted.

The front door opened, and as the wind chimes sang, Luis looked up expecting to find Al but instead locked eyes with a girl he didn't recognize.

She had the same uncomfortable look on her face that patrons always had, but she went the extra step of clutching her purse in her lily-white hands, quickly tucking a strand of blond hair behind her ear before looking down at her shoes.

"Can I help you?" Luis asked. He'd need to get her taken care of quickly if he wanted to be free when Al arrived, but her tentative steps into the shop were interfering with his plans.

"I, um," the girl mumbled, taking another step closer to the counter before faltering. "I guess I was just hoping I could get a spell."

"What kind of spell?" Luis asked.

She shrugged, turning her face toward the far wall. He really wished people would get over their own squeamishness before entering the shop instead of always putting the burden on him.

Finally, the girl stepped over to the counter, still refusing to meet Luis's eyes. "I guess I need a love spell."

"No such thing."

She looked up, anger pulling at her eyebrows. "There must be something close, though, right? Like something to make someone fall in infatuation or fixation or—"

Luis waved a hand at her. "Even if there was, I wouldn't give it to you. Sounds like you're more interested in mind control than love."

And that was the thing that people didn't understand. Love was about finding someone you cared about enough to want them to live freely, happily, not someone you wanted to control.

The girl crossed her arms, lips pressed into a fine line. Whatever apprehension she'd had about being in a spell shop had been completely replaced by her annoyance with Luis. "So you're not going to help me?"

"I can't make someone fall in love with you," Luis said.

"I just need—"

But before she could finish her statement, the wind chimes cut through the room like an explosion, silence falling over them. Al stood in the doorway, eyes wide, as he stared toward Luis.

No, not toward Luis.

Toward the girl at the counter.

"Monica?" Al said, voice shaky. "What are you doing here?"

But Luis's mind slowed at the sound of the name.

Monica. Al's ex.

Monica whipped around, a glare on her face. "I could ask you the same question."

Al shook his head. "I'm moving on, all right?"

That's why Al looked so mortified when he saw her, and why she looked so damn pissed; neither of them wanted to be spotted in a place like this.

But Monica had been asking for a love spell, so did that mean she'd found someone else?

Or had she come here for Al?

"I... Excuse me for a minute," Luis said before retreating into the back room. He didn't really have anything he needed to do, but he desperately wanted to get out of there.

Even with the curtain and wall separating them, he could still hear the sound of Monica's voice as she said, "Moving on or *moved* on?"

Al spluttered. "I–is there a difference?"

"I just can't figure out why you'd be in a magic shop if you were really over me," she said.

"Well, I guess that makes us equal. I mean, because I don't know why you're here either, so..."

"Forget it."

The door opened, the wind chimes low and tinny, and Luis wondered if she had left or if someone else had walked in on their weird spat. Then Monica said, "I'm sorry. About before, I mean. For freaking out about everything. It's just... All these girls kept saying that they'd slept with you or you were flirting with them, and what was I supposed to think?"

"You could've started by believing me, maybe?"

"How could I, when everything seemed more important to you than me?" Monica snapped.

The room fell silent, and Luis sat frozen, listening in.

Then Monica said, "I'm sorry, okay? I–I'm willing to look past all of that. We can start over, you know?"

The room fell silent again.

Al heaved a sigh. "You know, when I said I was moving on, I meant that. I really am."

Monica's voice cracked as she said, "There's someone else."

But it didn't sound like a question. She'd certainly accepted it faster than Luis had, his head still reeling as he tried to keep up.

If Al had found someone else, that meant he was moving on. Really, concretely moving on. And that meant he didn't need Luis's help anymore.

"I'm sorry," Al said. "But after everything, I just—"

"No, forget it," Monica said. "You're right. That's probably for the best."

Luis pushed himself off the wall as the chimes filled the shop again. Was Monica gone now? Or had Al left instead?

He went to the cabinet, snatching a small green bottle off one of the shelves before racing back into the shop. He needed to catch Al before he went home.

But as he stepped back into the shop, he found Al still there, leaning against the counter with a pensive look on his face.

"Um, hi," Luis said.

Al looked up and grinned. "Hey."

He didn't look like someone who was reeling from heartbreak. Actually, it'd been a while since Al had looked half as miserable as he had that first day. Luis had been so caught up in everything that he hadn't noticed.

"So you found someone else, huh?" Luis said.

Al's eyes widened as he pushed back from the counter. "I… How did you know that? Did you cast a spell to read my mind?"

Luis rolled his eyes. "No, I heard you through the beads."

Al blinked for a moment before letting out a nervous laugh. "Oh, yeah, right. My bad."

Luis hadn't even realized he'd been holding out hope that Al was bluffing to Monica—that he'd just said he'd found someone else so she wouldn't realize that he was still spiraling—until that hope was snatched away and his stomach dropped out from under him. So this was it. If Al had found someone else, he had no reason to come back to the shop anymore.

And as much as Luis hated the idea of Al leaving forever, he knew he wouldn't stop him. He couldn't. At the end of the day, his goal was to help Al, and if he'd done that, he couldn't undo all of that by getting in his way or holding him back. It didn't matter if Luis never got anything in return. All that mattered was that Al was happy.

"Here," Luis said, extending the little green bottle to Al.

Al took it tentatively, eyeing it over before taking off the cap and sniffing it. "What is it?"

"A confidence boost," Luis said. "I'm assuming you're gonna want to ask that new girl out, so that'll give you the courage to take the plunge."

"Oh, wow, thanks!" Al said, eyeing the bottle like a child with a new toy. "Also, it's not a girl."

"Oh, okay, well, whatever," Luis said. "It'll work either way. Good luck."

Luis turned toward the back room, but before he could go, Al called out, "Hey, wait!"

Luis turned to catch sight of Al's goofy grin.

"I still have to pay you," Al said.

Luis shrugged. "Don't worry about it. Just consider it a gift."

"I—"

Al broke off, but Luis couldn't bring himself to walk away.

What was he waiting for, really? Al had made it perfectly clear that he'd moved on, found somebody to fill that gaping hole in his heart. Hell, he'd found the magical cure for heartbreak, the very thing Luis couldn't give him.

So why should Luis expect him to stay?

Luis paused, his mouth moving ahead of his brain as he said, "Can I ask who it is?"

"Who what is?"

Luis rolled his eyes. "The someone new."

"Oh, well," Al said, "I guess they're not *that* new. I mean, I guess I was always kind of curious about this person, but I didn't really realize I had feelings for them until I started spending more time with them. And it kind of made me wonder if maybe Monica had been right all along, you know? Like maybe I really wasn't that into her because a part of me knew that I would like this other person so much more."

Luis raised an eyebrow. "Someone from class?"

Al smirked. "Yeah, from calculus. I was actually kind of hoping he'd help me study for the next exam 'cause I'm totally gonna fail."

"Well, good luck asking, then," Luis said. "I hope you're happy together."

"Wait!"

"What?"

Al stared back at him for a moment. "You're fucking with me, right? I always miss it when people are fucking with me."

"I don't know what you're talking about."

Al burst into laughter, leaning onto the counter as he slammed his fist against it, laughs shaking his whole six-foot body. "And you think *I'm* clueless?"

Luis rolled his eyes. "Okay, whatever. I'm leaving."

"Wait, no!"

Al reached over the counter and latched onto Luis's wrist. Luis stared at it a moment, his heart rate pounding. God, Al could probably feel it.

Then Al heaved a sigh, using his thumb to pop the little cork top off the bottle, and chugged the green liquid inside. He spluttered for a second as he choked it down, and Luis couldn't help but laugh. He never thought he'd needed to put instructions on it, but maybe he should have.

Then Al said, "I'm talking about you."

Luis raised an eyebrow. "Talking about me *what*?"

Al blushed. "I, um, I meant. You're the someone. The new someone, I mean."

The room fell quiet, but Al's fingers never left Luis's wrist. The intensity of Al's stare made Luis want to jerk back and stumble away.

But his heart was racing, and he couldn't bring himself to speak. Had he heard Al right? That didn't make any sense. Al was a jock, the school's most beloved superstar, and he was just the local outcast.

And then there was what Al had said before. *I mean, I guess I was always kind of curious about this person, but I didn't really realize I had feelings for them until I started spending more time with them.* Sure, Al had been nicer to him than most of the other students had, but to think that Al had been thinking of him all this time... Well, there was no way that was true.

Right?

Al let go of Luis's wrist, jerking his arm back. "I-I'm sorry. I didn't mean to spring that on you. I, well, I guess I didn't really plan to bring it up at all. It just sort of happened. And it's not like I'm expecting you to return my feelings or anything. I'm totally cool hanging out like we have been and being friends. It just didn't seem right to keep it from you when you asked so…"

Luis shook his head. "Everybody loves you. You could date just about anyone at our school. None of this makes sense."

"Okay, but I'm not really interested in anyone else at school," Al said. "Or anyone else in general. It's not like I'm desperate to just date someone. It's only because it's you."

Luis leaned forward, his face just inches from Al's, but he couldn't bring himself to go any further. This was Alvaro Sotolongo, the all-around popular jock. He couldn't just kiss him, even if he kind of wanted to.

But hovering in that space, he wished he could just push himself those extra two inches, to feel the pressure of Al's lips on his.

And like he'd read his mind, Al closed the space, the two of them pressed together even as they draped over the counter to get closer to each other, the edge of it jabbing into Luis's ribs.

Al pulled back, laughter filling the air between them. "Sorry, I just took the plunge."

Luis shrugged, even though his heart was racing a mile a minute. "No, it's fine. I–I'm glad you did."

"Can I come around the counter?"

Luis nodded, and Al scooted along the side, slipping around next to Luis. With nothing separating them, Luis felt both more disarmed and more on guard than he ever had before. There was nothing in between them. There was nothing keeping them apart.

Al smirked, but instead of touching Luis, he just leaned

against the counter, his fingers twining together. "You care a lot about what people think of you, huh? You always seem so flippant, but it bothers you a lot, doesn't it?"

Luis shrugged, but he involuntarily took a step back. He wasn't one for just baring his soul to people, but Al had just been open about his own feelings, so maybe it was unfair to completely hold back now.

"I wouldn't say it bothers me a lot," Luis said, staring down at his hands, "but that doesn't mean it doesn't matter. I don't care if some people hate me or think I'm a freak, but it kind of sucks when everyone does."

"I don't hate you," Al said, his words rushing out just a little too fast. "Or think you're a freak, obviously."

Luis rolled his eyes. "Gee, thanks."

Al smiled. "I guess I just meant that I don't think everyone else does either. I mean, I'm sure some people do, and I know a lot of people have treated you like trash, but people would have to be pretty obtuse not to see how cool you are."

Luis breathed, the air rushing out of him. "You don't think people are obtuse?"

"Well, some of them are, but I try to reserve judgment until I know people better."

Which pretty much lined up perfectly with everything Luis had learned about Al thus far. He wasn't judgmental. He had a great sense of humor and a brilliant smile. And he wasn't just some beefy jock with a nice body. He was his own kind of clever and caring and kind.

And he wasn't leaving. He hadn't used Luis with the intention of throwing him away. He'd come because he was curious, and now, they were standing together in the empty store, less than a foot of space separating them, and for the first time in a long time, Luis wasn't wary of Al's motives. He wasn't carefully planning an escape route or tentatively holding him at an arm's length.

Actually, he kind of wanted to close the space separating them.

"So did you ever actually need help getting over the breakup?" Luis said.

Al smiled. "I was pretty upset about it that first day."

"And after that?"

"I think your miracle cure worked," Al said. "You're one hell of a brujo."

There was a voice in the back of his head telling Luis that he should correct Al. That wasn't how magic worked. He never gave him a miracle cure.

But Luis pushed that voice aside. And as Al leaned in to kiss him again, Luis's heart fluttered in his chest. Sometimes magic worked in mysterious ways, so whether he'd managed to brew the perfect concoction or not, what mattered was that he'd found a way to heal Al's heart.

And that somehow, in all the chaos, Al had found a way to heal Luis's heart too.

* * * * *

ACKNOWLEDGMENTS

The editors collectively wish to thank their agent, Jim Mc-
Carthy. You're an absolute rock star and we're so glad to have
you in our corner. Y'all—we cannot tell you in words, GIFs,
or mildly concerning facial expressions how wonderful it is
to be A Jim McCarthy Client.

Endless amounts of gratitude to our fearless editor, Stepha-
nie Cohen, for jumping in and really giving us their all, and
to Bess Braswell for hearing us and seeing Our Vision.

This truly extends to the entire team at Inkyard Press for
the care they've shown us and our beautiful book. To our
marketing and design teams of champions and cheerleaders.
To Alex Cabal, whose own magick is shown so beautifully
in our cover's art. To Gigi Lau for spearheading our cover's
design and giving us the opportunity to see magical love
depicted exactly as we'd hoped with our whole hearts. To

Magen McCallum for designing that magical love and rendering us speechless.

To our contributors—Emery Lee, Rosie Lim, Lily Anderson, Eric Smith, Byron Graves, Alex Villasante, Karuna Riazi, Kiki Nguyen, Tehlor Kay Mejia, and Mark Oshiro—thank you for your tireless work and endless patience, thank you for saying yes so enthusiastically when we first asked about this whole thing, and thank you for sharing your words, your gifts, your magic, and love-bombs with the world.

And now, a word from us as individuals:

CAM: The process of editing this book, seeing it from start to finish, has been a journey. And much of that journey took place during the most unimaginably horrific time of my life.

I was given a lot of grace and care from my darling coeditors, gee and Adrianne, who never failed to ply me with BTS GIFs, from the badass team at Inkyard Press, and, of course, there was so much heart and consideration and patience given to me by my dear agent and friend, Jim McCarthy.

I'm acknowledging you all not for the sake of this book—we did that above—but because you all gave me so much love when I needed it most. Thank you for the permission to fall apart and then come back swinging.

Acks are never easy to write but I'd be remiss in my duties as an author of them if I didn't mention my younger brother, Stephen, who passed away unexpectedly and on my birthday no less, right in the middle of this book's creation. It was when things were due and deadlines were hitting and the work was really movin'.

Everything I gave this book from that point on came from

all the love I have for him, from any love he'd ever shown me, and I'm going to carry that work ethic with me forever now.

Thank you, Stephen, for always being the one to stand up for me and showing me how to be strong. And for always buying a copy of my books for each of your girlfriends. I love you, kid, and I miss you something fierce.

ADRIANNE: A list of everyone who's helped me along this writing path would likely wrap around the earth several times. I was going to keep it short for brevity's sake but this is my first book and it's been a long time coming so strap yourselves in.

My parents: Frank White, Jr., Gladys White Taylor. Children of Mississippi and Tennessee respectively, who let me read just about anything and everything, never discouraged me creatively, and gave me an upbringing full of adventure and discovery. I hope you both realize how amazing you are in your own right, and never give up on your dreams like you taught us. You've been through so much and yet you're still kicking, even if it's not always high. Thank you for my humor, work ethic, education, and love of Black and Southern culture. It's overwhelming how much I love and appreciate you. Look, I did it!

My siblings: Frank White, III, Terrance White, Courtney Prugh. My first and oldest friends, y'all were a blast to grow up with and influence me in the best ways. I'm blessed by your presence and awed by your achievements. I can't wait until we can all get together again. From learning basslines by osmosis to epic video game battles to laughing about terrible art, there's been very little greater than being your sister. Life sometimes gets in the way, but I will move heaven and earth and slash every tire whenever you need me. I'm so proud of you. Love you forever and a day.

My in-laws: Shelly White, Meg Russell, Thad Prugh, Norris Taylor. Like, seriously, I can't imagine what our family would be like if you weren't part of it. I'm so glad to know I have your love and support and it's definitely mutual. Your advice and guidance means the world and it's so cool how we pick up where we left off, no matter how much time has passed. Thank you for being supportive and caring partners to the people I hold dear. Your talents are so vast, it's amazing. I definitely want to be y'all when I grow up.

My niblings and godkids: Kaiya White, Micah White, Reghan White, Leah White, Brenna Russell, Evan Russell, Cleoh Russell, Autumn Hughey, Lily Hughey, CJ Hughey. You inspire me to embrace joy, play, and laughter whenever possible. Y'all taught me the biggest lessons about being brave and expressing myself fully. My memories of you as you've grown are some of my most cherished and I look forward to making many, many more. If I can be even a fraction as cool as you, I've really done something! Please remember I'm always here for you, cheering you on and sending so many good wishes with an infinite amount of love. I feel like you're my kids as if I birthed you myself. Thank you for letting me share your lives.

My It's Complicated: Timothy Russell. We may end differently than we started but I'm grateful for the love and care you gave without reservation, no matter its tenure. You read my writing, gave great notes, encouraged me endlessly, and most times had more confidence in my talent than I did. Many laughs, much memories. Thank you for it all.

My dearly departeds: Louella Bradley, Stevie White, Daisie White, Frank White, Sr., Othella Luster, Brenda Anderson, PawPaw, Emma Jean Miller, Bonnie Russell, Jim Russell, Travis Russell. Beloved forever, from this life to the next, I continually feel your presence and guidance. For real, though, Travis can you stop moving my things or at least put them in more conspicuous places? It's cool you're still a trickster but come on, man. Oh, and if any of y'all can punch through the veil with some lotto numbers or stock tips it would be appreciated. Your girl is struggling out here! Until we meet again.

My ride-or-dies: Kreshaun McKinney, Aleia Brown, Suzi Steffen. There's no way I'd be where I am without your friendship, love, and willingness to break kneecaps on my behalf. If there's anything you need, I got you. Excited to see where this life takes us as we grow into our purpose. I'm pretty good at this writing thing but still fail to find the words to encapsulate how much you mean to me. I'll keep trying, though!

My Pantheon: Nik Traxler, Renée Reynolds, g. haron davis. My favorite trope come to life, found family! Legit the missing pieces to my puzzle and some of the most talented writers I've ever met. I'm so glad we're in this together. The day we take publishing by storm is fast approaching so y'all need to get ready because I'm singing your praises loudly and without apology. Thank you especially for helping me through this past year, one of the hardest I've known.

My Wakandans: Angie Thomas, L.L. McKinney, Camryn Garrett, g. haron davis. Every day y'all tell the publishing industry to move or be moved. *Inspiring* seems inadequate to describe your impact but best believe it's massive. Reparations are due! Thanks for kicking in doors so I don't have to.

My Twitter Writing Pals: Emily Timbol, Rebekah Faubion, Stitch, Bethany C. Morrow, Amy Suiter Clarke, Tee Franklin, Shawn Pryor, Jen Ferguson, Brandy Colbert, Nova Ren Suma, Megan Rivers, Jay Coles, Dahlia Adler, Mike Jung. Your talents are both awe- and envy-inducing and it's been my great joy to witness your growth and experience your friendship and comradery. You're killing the game and the world is infinitely better for it.

My Creative Inspirations: BTS, whose music saved my life, Norma Klein and Virginia Hamilton, whose books transformed me from reader to aspiring writer, and Kerry James Marshall, whose art reminds me that Black is beautiful, always.

My Digital Village: Everyone who's donated to or boosted my fundraisers, left tips, sent self-care funds, and championed my business endeavors. You've literally saved me and my loved ones, many times over. I'll work hard to pay your generosity forward. Support mutual aid!

My Cocreators-in-Crime: g. haron davis and Candice Montgomery, who generously invited me into their cocreation circle. If "do no harm but take no shit" was a person, they'd be y'all's child. I'm forever indebted and love you madly.

If I forgot anyone, please charge it to my head and not my heart. But listen, encourage enough people to buy this book and/or request it from libraries and I might get a chance to put you in my next acknowledgements.

gee: As this is my first book, I want to thank people more generally rather than specific to this book. Obviously I have to thank my mother first. You were always my biggest supporter and I feel grateful every day that I grew up in a Black household that embraced weirdness and valued creativity. Hey, look, Ma, I made it. I only wish you were here to see it.

The rest of my blood family, in particular my aunts—Mandy, Lisa, and Wanda Gailliard, and Janae Thompson. You've always been awesome examples of the wide ranges of Black womanhood, and despite not being (fully) a woman myself, I've learned so much from y'all. Miss ya, love ya, see ya soon as the world stops being full of cooties.

My found family, starting with my beautiful sister Jessica Etheridge: we've had some bumps and bruises but you've been my person since tenth grade. You're a badass and you inspire me to be a better writer daily. Can't wait to read what you have to say to me in your own acknowledgments because I know that day is coming. Michael Etheridge, my awesome brother-in-law: I miss hanging out with you and talking to you. I'm proud of everything you've accomplished, and I appreciate how happy you make Jess. My wee nieces, Jimi, Mischa, and MJ Etheridge: I love y'all so much and you probably don't even know it. Looking forward to the day you're old enough to read my words so I can force you to be my personal focus group. Sharon and John Antoine: thank you both for being an extra set of parents and another place to call home. James Antoine: my favorite little brother, I miss you regularly. Proud of you for surviving.

My Pantheon, my Edgar Allan Hoes, my butt monkeys—Renée Reynolds (Jimin), Nik Traxler (Jungkook), and Adrianne White: literally my family. So so SO glad to have met you all. Y'all are the smartest, funniest, baddest bitches in the game and I am so excited to run publishing with y'all one day soon. Beyond being awed by your talents, I'm convinced we're somehow one soul split into four pieces. Grateful we've been put back together.

Sonora Reyes and Emery Lee: I can't even properly explain how important y'all are. So much encouragement, so much venting, so much love. I'm ready for both of you to blow up. I'm infinitely grateful to know y'all.

My middle school creative writing teacher, Mrs. Chris Allen, a very odd, very cool woman: you gave us wild personal stories and wacky prompts and taught us that words have immeasurable value. (And you swore and gave us snacks and let us listen to music for inspiration and honestly were the coolest teacher I'd had.)

My high school creative writing teacher, Mrs. Kimberly Eneks-Plunk: you motivated me to push myself and my writing to limits I never would have gone to on my own. If I weren't terrible and awkward you'd have certainly been one of those teachers I'd be in contact with years after graduation. Maybe we'll go camping again one day. I promise not to fall off a horse this time.

My oldest friends—Keri Riddle, Lauren Trubic, Sara Gaudard, and Massiel Gutierrez: I barely remember life before y'all. Thanks for everything. Y'all mean a lot to me.

Alex Brown: where to even begin. I love you so freaking much. I'm in awe of your talent and your drive and I can't wait to do more together. I miss you! August and Cory McCarthy Rose: infinitely envious of your love, truly relationship goals. August, I'm so glad to call you a friend. We gotta meet up again soon. Love you! Jonathan Lenore Kastin: we're so awkward but I love talking to you and getting to know you and I just know we'll grow closer over the years. October demands it. Ezrael Maher: from the moment we showed up for the day in the same Sesame Street shirt, I've wanted to be besties. Someday! CL McCollum: thank you for being such a vocal supporter. We're gonna write a thing one of these days! The rest of the crusty dragon muppets of Rainbow Weekend: you're gonna blow the world away.

My publishing friends on Twitter—Amparo Ortiz, Bethany C. Morrow, Amy Suiter Clarke (Alistair!), Nina Varela, Mason Deaver, Lily Meade, Joelle Abejar, Carly Heath, Julie Block, Adam Sass, Diana Gunn, Chace Verity, Shenwei, Stitch, May, Jenniah, Rebekah Faubion, Emily Timbol, Kosoko Jackson, Saundra Mitchell, Alex Villasante, Rosie Lim, Eric Smith: I look up to all of you. You're smart and witty and talented and I just wanna be besties with all of you. Thanks for all the encouragement, laughs, tears, pep talks, crowdfunding, call-outs, call-ins, everything. You all deserve the world.

My publishing friends in my head on Twitter—Kwame Mbalia, Dhonielle Clayton, Zoraida Córdova, Olivia A. Cole, Jason Reynolds, Tochi Onyebuchi, Laurie Halse Anderson, Malinda Lo, Hafsah Faisal, Leah Johnson, Grady Hendrix: y'all are the gold standard and I'm constantly striving to get to that level. So much admiration from afar. Thanks for the inspiration and motivation.

ARMY friends who are just everyday friends at this point— Ain, Isa, Nini: I adore y'all.

Angie Thomas, L.L. McKinney, Camryn Garrett: Wakanda forever.

CW and Skye: so so many hearts to y'all.

Lauren Lake: thank you for my sons.

My coeditors: we're on each other's team. (Please sing that to yourself à la Lorde.)

People who will never read this, starting with (of course) BTS: there's a zero percent chance I would still be pushing through without your music, your encouraging words, your support from afar. Doing my best to step harder. 보라해. The Try Guys: y'all gave me so much to look forward to even in moments where everything seemed hopeless. And particularly Zach Kornfeld: thank you for allowing us space to talk about marginsbox, and we hope to be able to gift you a box one day. Rhett and Link and the whole Mythical Crew (especially Emily, Vi, Josh, and David Hill): I'm trying hard to be my mythical best every day. Kelsey Impicciche: from even before the 100 Baby Challenge, it's been a joy to watch your career blossom. Your videos always make me smile even when I don't feel like smiling. Halsey: I love you. Your songs make up a decent percentage of my writing playlists. Thanks for being not a woman, but a god.

I'm certain I've forgotten people. So everyone I've forgotten: thank you, too. Chalk it up to my brain forgetting I even know any humans at all upon being tasked to write this. It's not you; it's the ADHD. I'll probably remember you as soon as it's too late, so see you in the next book.

ABOUT THE EDITORS

G. HARON DAVIS (they/them) is a New York–born, Tennessee-raised young adult author. Currently residing in the outskirts of Kansas City, Missouri, they specialize in horror and several shades of fantasy. They cofounded marginsbox, a diversity-celebrating book subscription box, with Adrianne White in 2019. They can be found online at ghdis.me, on Twitter, @burnonblackhome, and on Instagram, @sopescum.

CAM MONTGOMERY (nonbinary she/her) spends her time teaching dance to queer kids, bingeing anime, tending bar, and writing romancey novels. Two of her YA novels—*Home and Away* and *By Any Means Necessary*—are available now. Having ditched LA, the transplant now lives in Seattle and has made a habit of complaining about the weather even though she secretly loves it.

ADRIANNE WHITE (she/her) is a born-and-raised Midwest-erner living in the suburbs of Kansas City, Missouri. When she's not writing or editing young adult content, she's usually napping, watching movies, listening to K-pop, and uplifting marginalized voices in children's literature. In 2019, she cofounded marginsbox, a diversity-boosting book subscription box, with g. haron davis. Creating the stories she needed growing up is her joy.

ABOUT THE AUTHORS

LILY ANDERSON is the author of several novels including *The Only Thing Worse Than Me Is You*, *Undead Girl Gang*, and *Scout's Honor*. A former school librarian, she is deeply devoted to Shakespeare, fairy tales, and podcasts. Somewhere in Northern California, she is having strong opinions on musical theater.

ROSELLE LIM is the critically acclaimed author of *Natalie Tan's Book of Luck and Fortune*, *Vanessa Yu's Magical Paris Tea Shop*, and the upcoming *Sophie Go's Lonely Hearts Club*. She lives on the north shore of Lake Erie and always has an artistic project on the go.

ERIC SMITH is a literary agent and young adult author from Elizabeth, New Jersey. His recent books include *Don't Read the Comments*, *You Can Go Your Own Way*, and the anthology *Battle of the Bands*, coedited with Lauren Gibaldi. He lives in Philadelphia with his wife and son and enjoys pop-punk, video games, and crying over every movie.

BYRON GRAVES is an Ojibwe author from the Red Lake Indian Reservation in northern Minnesota.

Byron is represented by AKA Literary Management and recently signed a two-book deal with Heartdrum, an imprint of HarperCollins that highlights the voices of Native creators.

Byron's writing is a fictionalized reinterpretation of his lived experiences growing up and being from the Red Lake Indian Reservation, and as of now has been written as young adult. His writing portrays an honest balance between the trials and tribulations that his people face, the hope that so many hold in their hearts, and is laced with plenty of "Indian Humor" as well as life lessons.

Byron currently resides in the Denver, Colorado, area. When not glued to a book or his laptop, he can be found skateboarding or at a retro video game arcade.

EMERY LEE is an author and artist whose love for chaotic and morally gray characters started at a young age. After graduating with a degree in creative writing, e's gone on to author novels, short stories, and webcomics across a variety of genres and demographics, though YA fiction has always held a special place in eir heart. Drawing inspiration from Eastern media, pop punk music, and personal life experience, eir work seeks to explore the intersections of life and identity in fun, heartfelt, and inventive ways. In eir downtime, you'll most likely find em marathoning anime or snuggling cute dogs.

ALEXANDRA VILLASANTE has always loved telling stories—though not always with words. She has a BFA in painting and an MA in combined media. Born in New Jersey to immigrant parents, Alex has the privilegio of dreaming in both English and Spanish.

When she's not writing or painting, Alex is the online program manager for the Highlights Foundation. Her debut young adult novel, *The Grief Keeper*, was an Indie Next, Indies Introduce, and Fall 2019 Junior Library Guild Selection. *The Grief Keeper* is on ALA's Rainbow Book List 2020 and is the winner of the 2020 Lambda Literary Award for LGBTQ Children's Literature/Young Adult Fiction. Alex is a cofounder of the Latinx Kidlit Book Festival and a member of Las Musas. She lives with her family in the semi-wilds of Pennsylvania.

MARK OSHIRO is the award-winning author of the young adult books *Anger is a Gift* (2019 Schneider Family Book Award) and *Each of Us a Desert*, both with Tor Teen, as well as their middle grade debut, *The Insiders*, out in 2021 with HarperCollins. When not writing, they are trying to pet every dog in the world.

Mark is based in Atlanta, Georgia.

They are represented by DongWon Song of the Howard Morhaim Literary Agency.

KIANA (KIKI) NGUYEN is a novelist, screenwriter, and literary agent whose love for storytelling leads her to creating her own worlds centering queer girls and women who experience complex emotional lives from wanting things they fear they'll ruin. She is currently based in Los Angeles while missing Brooklyn, New York.

KARUNA RIAZI is a born and raised New Yorker, with a loving, large extended family and the rather trying experience of being the eldest sibling in her particular clan. She holds a BA in English literature from Hofstra University, and is an online diversity advocate, blogger, and educator. She is a 2017 honoree on the NBC Asian America Presents: A to Z list, featuring up-and-coming talent within the Asian-American and Pacific Islander community, and her work has been featured in *Entertainment Weekly*, Amy Poehler's Smart Girls, Book Riot and *Teen Vogue*, among others.

TEHLOR KAY MEJIA is the author of the critically acclaimed young adult fantasy duology *We Set the Dark on Fire* and *We Unleash the Merciless Storm*. Her middle grade debut, *Paola Santiago and The River of Tears*, released from Rick Riordan Presents in 2020 with its sequel *Paola Santiago and the Forest of Nightmares* having landed in 2021.

Tehlor lives in Oregon, where she grows heirloom corn and continues her quest to perfect the vegan tamale.